PRAISE FOR "THE DAY I GOT TRAPPED IN MY BRAIN"

"An imagination explosion: funny, silly, sweet and sad...
and then funny all over again... Ridiculously funny"

– Derek Landy, author of *Skulduggery Pleasant*

"A truly special story, told with Huberman's characteristic
humour, empathy and charm. I thoroughly enjoyed it"

– Catherine Doyle, author of *The Storm Keeper Trilogy*

"I WISH I had this brilliant, funny, hopeful and meaningful book when I
was 9... Kids big and small will love this book" – Aisling Bea, Comedian

"A beautiful & funny book with real heart" – Roisin Conaty, Comedian

"A world–skipping, seven–star snail hotel, giant–eyed dog kind
of a book. FABULOUSLY FUN AND INVENTIVE!"

– Steven Butler, author of *The Nothing To See Here Hotel*

"I read it over and over. Lovely stuff"

– Chris O'Dowd, actor and author of *Moone Boy*

Published in the UK by Scholastic, 2022
1 London Bridge, London, SE1 9BA
Scholastic Ireland, 89E Lagan Road, Dublin Industrial Estate,
Glasnevin, Dublin, D11 HP5F

Text © Amy Huberman, 2022
Illustrations by Katie Kear © Scholastic, 2022

The right of Amy Huberman to be identified as the
author of this work has been asserted by her under the
Copyright, Designs and Patents Act 1988.

ISBN 978 0702 31464 3

A CIP catalogue record for this book
is available from the British Library.

Printed by CPI Group (UK) Ltd, Croydon, CR0 4YY
Paper made from wood grown in sustainable forests
and other controlled sources.

3 5 7 9 10 8 6 4

www.scholastic.co.uk

THE DAY I GOT TRAPPED IN MY BRAIN

ILLUSTRATED BY
KATIE KEAR

AMY HUBERMAN

■SCHOLASTIC

*For my children Sadie, Billy and Ted and
for all your adventures that lie ahead.*

*And for my own siblings Mark and Paul,
for being my very first best friends.*

CHAPTER ONE

GIANT EYEBALLS

Hi. My name is Frankie Finkleton.

I am eleven and one twelfth years old, and I think I'd like to be a detective when I turn into one of those adulty types. It may very well be the only consolation, as there seems to be little else that appeals about being an adult. I feel sorry for them; really, they have so many boring things they need to do. And so many of them eat mushrooms. *Mushrooms.* Like I said, I just feel sorry for them.

FRANKIE FINKLETON

aka -ME!-

SECRET DETECTIVE

SCAR FROM <u>WALL</u> RELATED INCIDENT

PETITION TO MAKE THEM ILLEGAL ONGOING

MAGNIFYING GLASS = EXTRA MYSTERIOUS

AVERAGE HEIGHT FOR AN 11 ½th YEAR OLD

<u>NO</u> MUSHROOMS OR ONIONS ALLOWED IN THIS BELLY!

LEGS FOR "QUADRUPLE" CARTWHEELS

I got a magnifying glass for my birthday and I carry it around with me to look extra mysterious. It helps me in my investigations and even in solving local crimes. Many of these crimes occur in our own kitchen when Dad tries to add MUSHROOMS AND ONIONS to the dinner. But I can spot a finely chopped onion from the opposite side of the road with this thing.

And when I slink along walls and peer around corners with it right up to my eyeball, I look extra doubly mysterious.

Speaking of eyeballs, I have a dog named Blue who has GIANT eyeballs and tiny nostrils.

I can do four cartwheels in a row before feeling dizzy. I've only accidentally whacked someone in the face with my foot once during one of these quadruple cartwheels. And that person was prone to nosebleeds anyway so it *might* not necessarily have been my fault.

I have a scar on my eyebrow from when I was playing a game of chase with my brother Fred and didn't realize there was an entire wall in the way.

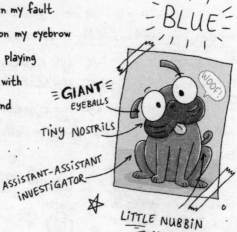

BLUE

WOOF!

GIANT EYEBALLS

TINY NOSTRILS

ASSISTANT-ASSISTANT INVESTIGATOR

LITTLE NUBBIN TAIL

He won that game. Fred, not the wall. Well, actually, possibly the wall too.

I am average height for an eleven-and-one-month-old, although not much research has been done for this specific age bracket, and I have average-length hair (that can almost reach my bum if I bend backwards into a crab).

I am really good at investigating, and I recently discovered an entire ancient civilization near our house using nothing but my magnifying glass and my above-average investigating skills. Mum says it is in fact a community of "elderly people" who live close together for company, but she has a lot on her mind right now so I don't want to burst her bubble.

If she is right, however, I might suggest we send Granny Doris to live with them because she often wants to hang out with me, and I'm afraid Granny Doris and I just don't seem to get one another. Her only hobbies appear to include wondering when to hang her knickers on the line in case of rain, and eating potatoes. She has no interest in cartwheels or building snail hotels or adding mints to fizzy drinks to make science explosions.

Again, she is an adult so she probably can't help it, the poor thing.

I love hedgehogs, snails, building snail hotels, blowing dandelion fluff, riding my bike and writing lists.

I like writing lists because:

a) They are fun if you have multicoloured pens.
b) It helps me to organize my thoughts. I have a lot of thoughts.
c) I have quite cool handwriting.
d) Please see points a to c.

ASSISTANT INVESTIGATOR
FRED
VERY CUTE CURLS
TEETH GAPS
LAUGH IS LIKE
SECRET GIGGLE MEDICINE
BEST INVENTION EVER MADE

I have a little brother called Fred, who is my assistant investigator, and a baby sister called Flo, who is my arch-nemesis. Villain music plays in my head whenever she's around. She has all the traits of a typical movie baddie, except she is miniature. She doesn't carry a loaded weapon as such, but she once threw a wet nappy at me, which is

ARCH NEMESIS

FLO

EVIL
BUT CHARMING

THINKS SHE'S CUTE
WITH HER TWO TEETH
AND FLUFFY CURL

i MEAN, SHE IS,
BUT **PLEASE**
DON'T TELL
HER

DEFINITELY PLANNING
— WORLD DOMINATION! —

almost worse. Especially because it landed right on my head. Fred is a goodie and so is nice to her, but I know what she's *really* like. As the eldest, I have unfortunately been born with the responsibilities of the household. Sometimes I feel like the eldest sibling in a monarchy but without any of the carriages and palaces and things. I mean, technically it's my mum and dad who go out to work and clean the house and cook the dinners. But it's me who shoulders the invisible emotional burden of everything, which I try to do with as much grace as I can. I guess I know how the Queen feels, is all I can say. Although, when I insisted on wearing a crown for cartoon time, Fred did let me know he thought it was "a tad too much drama".

So now I only wear it on the loo.

Then Flo tried to wedge a raisin up my nostril, and honestly, I should have sent her to the gallows. It's a constant battle to keep

5

justice and order out there in the badlands of 34 Cottage Orchard Road. That's where we all live with my mum and dad.

Dad has big green eyes that almost disappear when he smiles. I told him he could join a travelling circus with that trick, but he said he wasn't sure when he'd fit it in with work and all the bits he has to do for us kids. Mum's eyes remain the same size most of the time, and I often think they hold a similar wonder and curiosity for life as Fred's do. Mum and Dad both have jobs that involve "adulty things", probably very boring, but I feel like too much time has passed to ask them for any detail now. I should have asked them when I was about six or seven, but I forgot. Mum has a brown-coloured bob that goes curly when she washes it. She smooths it dry with a large barrel brush and a hairdryer, only to curl it again with a curling tong as soon as it's straight. I've never understood this process, and she's a smart woman so I'm not sure why she hasn't figured it out. Look, her life is so full of boring adult things, who am I to judge where she gets her kicks from?

The only good thing about the curly–straight–curly bafflement is that I know how long it takes. A full forty minutes. And in that forty minutes, I can just sit on the bed and be with her; we don't have to be anywhere else, do anything else, or discuss anything else. And she's happily distracted enough not to ask, "Are you OK there, Frankie?"

Dad's hair is far less complicated in general. He has had the same haircut since he was in senior infants apparently. I didn't know him then. I first met him the day I was born in the hospital and he seems like a solid bloke.

Only joking. I *love* my mum and dad so much. Even though they make me eat FIVE fruit and vegetables a day, which HAS to be some kind of human rights violation — still, they are kind and fun and give the best hugs, so I don't want to lodge a formal complaint against them at the moment. But I am going to keep a magnified eye on matters.

They also seem to really like Flo. Everyone has fallen for Flo's evil charms. Except for me.

Villains *can* look adorable with two little bottom teeth and one fluffy curl on the top of their head too, you know; it's all a part of their evil genius plan.

So, again, I will be keeping one magnified eyeball on her at all times.

I also have some grandparents. We lost one a few years ago. Not like when I got lost in the supermarket and a lady with a high bun and large glasses had to ask over the intercom system if my mum or dad could please collect me from next to the knickers stand. (I was so mortified I considered leaving the country for a while.)

We lost Grampa Pinky because he got very, very old indeed, the way old people have a habit of doing. He was called Grampa Pinky because he had a pinky finger that wasn't able to bend after he broke it as a child running away from some war guys. He always stuck it up in the air and said it was his special radio antenna that was able to pick up feeling frequencies. He was actually quite good at it. He always knew when I felt hungry for chocolate pancakes. Or worried we might run out of sprinkles.

Granny Doris was married to Grampa Pinky for three hundred and fifty-six years or something. She lives on her own now, but I think she's OK because she has her potatoes. She is more obsessed with potatoes than I am with blowing bubblegum bubbles the size of my head before they burst. Which is A LOT.

But I guess I could try to communicate with the ancient civilization I discovered and see if they might take her?

My other two grandparents are called Granny and Granddad, and I'm sure they have real names too, but much like Mum and Dad's jobs, it's probably too late to ask them at this stage. They are averagely old and Granny can still touch her toes, so we are probably a good way off losing them too. Which is nice because I like going to their house and playing with their dog. Their dog isn't as fabulous as Blue, but she does have long fur that I can gather into a tuft and tie with a bow between her ears. And, as they say, life is all about compromise.

Other things to know about me are:

1) I don't love:
    a) potatoes
    b) giant squids in dark waters
    c) adults being nosy
    d) spelling tests on Fridays

2) I am allergic to:
    a) potatoes
    b) love songs on the radio
    c) spelling tests on Fridays

(All three make me want to be sick so I *must* be allergic.)

3) I am a big fan of:
    a) lists within lists (particularly when you're having a good
        handwriting day, or are having some pretty excellent
        thoughts and observations)

But the most important thing you should know about me?

I am carrying around the BIGGEST secret IN THE WHOLE
ENTIRE WORLD.

CHAPTER TWO

SPAGHETTI BRAINS, "PUFFARTS", DIFFERENT TYPES OF SECRETS ... AND CUCUMBERS

And I am *actually* carrying the secret around with me!

Not in a backpack or stuffed in a pocket, though. Or the way Blue has a microchip in his neck with his owner's name and address on it in case he gets lost. Why kids don't have these I'll never know: it would save unfortunate incidents on tannoy systems in supermarkets next to knickers stands, is all I can say.

Hmmmm.

How to explain it? It's quite complicated.

The thing is, I have quite a few secrets. As in, a lot. But one is BIGGER than all the rest!

Sometimes I imagine my secrets in a big pile, as if they are different stones or rocks.

Some secrets can be cool and mysterious. Or super fun. Like small pebbles that you can bop and bounce off the surface of a pond before they eventually disappear.

Other secrets are more like heavy, solid, weighty boulders. They're too massive to lug around. Or hide. Or carry. Or push to the top of the pile by yourself. They involve the sort of huffing and puffing that might lead to a shameful and rather unfortunate "puff fart", known in certain parts of the world (my school) as a "puffart". Sounds cuter than it is. The puffart is a certain breed of fart that emerges under extreme exertion and can lead to a medical condition called "mortification". I suffered both that time I got lost in the knickers aisle at the supermarket. Not nearly as humiliating as a "snart", mind you: a surprise fart that comes with a sneeze.

I had my own personal experience of the snart once. It was a Thursday. The incident took place right in the middle of the very sad, reeeeeaaallly quiet bit in the school play when all the parents were staring at the stage, holding their breaths, and wondering if they would ever see the likes of such raw talent ever again ... EVEN in a professional Christmas panto where the actors earn millions of euro. I would love to get paid a million euro to be told, "It's behind you!" loads of times while wearing a really cool golden costume with wings. I might put it down for my next career day.

Anyway, it was a big dramatic moment in the production when ... *Sffffffffffiiiiiiiiiip!!!*

Actually, I don't think I'm ready to talk about it yet. It's one of my biggest regrets in life that this is *not* one of my secrets. I wish it was, but everyone in Ireland probably knows about it. Maybe even everyone in Wales and a few people up as far as Scotland.

I would like to be known for other things, like discovering cool science stuff, creating the world's first seven star snail hotel, and being a legendary private investigator. But so far this snart is my legacy.

I aim to change this, though. And I'm pretty sure this GIANT SECRET I'm carrying around will help me. And the best thing about being a private investigator? They deal in secrets! If you were a regular investigator, you might have to tell everyone, but by being private, you get to keep secrets. It is literally part of the job description. And part of the reason I believe private investigators should get an extra five per cent salary bonus or more holiday time or free crisps or something because I'm telling you, some secrets are very, very large. And very, very important. And very, very INCREDIBLE.

It definitely feels like there are extra responsibilities attached.

A list of *all* my secrets is written down in my Secret Book of Secrets notebook that is hidden safely under my bed.

12

Thinking about it now, it probably isn't the best title for a book of secrets that I really hope no one ever finds out about.

Hmmmm.

I'd be way better off renaming it: Boring Things That You Will Definitely Fall Asleep Reading If You Ever Decide To Look Inside. So You Absolutely, Positively Shouldn't. Yes, that would do it — the perfect, deceptive ploy.

I really should be a detective, you know. I would be, if I weren't so busy being an eleven-year-old. Being eleven is practically a full-time job.

Especially an eleven-year-old with a pile of cumbersome secrets. But I am going to put it down on my college application when I'm old enough.

My Granny With The Dog With The Longer Fur That I Can Gather In A Tuft Between The Ears, or just "Granny" for short (like I said, I'm busy. I don't have time for full titles.), gave me a book called *A New Word a Day*, which I read on the loo as there's not much else to do on the loo. *Cumbersome* was last Thursday's new word. Turns out it has nothing to do with cucumbers. Unless you had a really massive cucumber. In that case, I guess it would be a cumbersome cucumber. And I try not to have anything to do with cucumbers. They aren't as odious as mushrooms or onions, but I still don't trust them.

"Hey, Frankie," Fred said one day as I was studying my dinner with my magnifying glass for evidence of concealed vegetables.

"Yes, Fred," I answered, thinking that even if you dressed a piece of onion in tomato sauce, it still was – and always would be – an onion underneath it all.

"If you do one of your investigations around vegetables in the dinner, do you get a celery increase?"

Fred has a natural ability for being funny. Just like Rena Mongton four doors down has a natural talent for Irish dancing and has won a billion medals. Or Flo has a natural flair for being annoying. Medals pending.

Another important thing you should know about being me, Frankie Finkleton, aged eleven and one twelfth from Dublin, Ireland,

MY SPAGHETTi BRAIN

ME

the World, the Universe, the Galaxy, is that I have what the adults refer to as a "spaghetti brain".

That is no secret.

I really wish it was, but unfortunately the adults are all obsessed with talking about it. Again, who am I to judge how they get their kicks? It's just that this particular one is rather inconvenient for me.

"The adults" is the collective term I use for all of the main

14

adulty types in my life. It makes life simpler when I have a complaint that spans multiple adulty-type groups because there are A LOT of them. Adults are literally *everywhere*. So far, this term includes:

- Mum and Dad
- Granny Doris
- My dad's mum and dad, Granny and Granddad With The Less Interesting Dog Who Does To Be Fair Have Better Hair That You Can Do More With.
- My teacher, Ms Hammerhead, who I'm pretty sure is a direct descendant of an actual shark. I know technically humans are descendants of apes, but maybe Ms Hammerhead's family could be fourth cousins twice removed from a shark or something. More on this later. I have many investigations on the go at once. It comes with the territory of being the only private investigator in my village.
- My school principal, Mr McNogg, who is the most boring person I know. Fred and I looked him up in the *Guinness Book of World Records*, but he is not there. YET. Fred has a theory that they might have accidentally taken the fun part of his personality out too when they removed his tonsils as a kid. All the adults I know have had their

tonsils removed — it was very fashionable in the olden days apparently. I've decided I'm keeping mine. I don't know what they are for, but I'm not one for trends.

- Mum's friend, Margery Lonergan, who tries to be a private investigator but just doesn't have the personality. I honestly think she should give it up and maybe take up golf if she's looking for something to do?

- Dr Hilda Stitch. We have differing opinions when it comes to medical science. I know she studied for *weeks* or something in college, but I've done my own research. How can you explain the fact that if an earthworm gets chopped in two it can still survive? Sometimes things don't have to be too broken to ever be fixed. She doesn't get it and I'm exhausted trying to explain it to him. Perhaps she should take up golf too. If I wasn't so busy I'd actually set up a charity for adults because I just feel so sorry for them.

The adults are *constantly* saying, "Frankie has a spaghetti brain." *All* of them. Surely they have other things to talk about, like:

- The news
- What to make for dinner

- Getting an early night
- The shocking price of a punnet of raspberries
- Not getting crumbs in their car
- Golf?
- The most efficient way to slice onions

But sometimes it's like the only thing they talk about is my "spaghetti brain". Why are they so obsessed with it?

Fred says I might get into the *Guinness Book of World Records* one day, and I don't want to say it because he entered his "extra-bendy elbows" two years ago now and hasn't heard back, but I think he might be right about my spaghetti brain.

To my knowledge, a "spaghetti brain" is neither an official medical term, nor is it a dinner option from a specials menu in a fancy-schmancy restaurant that serves seventeen different varieties of pasta. How many can you name? I have a list here which sort of explains a few:

1. Fusilli if you refuse-ily to eat flat pasta

2. Tagliatelle like fuzzy reception on your telly

3. Orzo like measles on your torso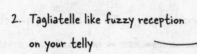

4. Farfalle for the fella at a black-tie ball

5. Ravioli the most comfortable pillow of all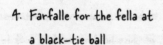

6. And tortellini like a tortoise in a Lamborghini

"A penne for your thoughts," Mum says when she hands me one of my favourite dinners of plain pasta and butter.

That's one of Fred's jokes! He could sue for copyright! I know he won't, though. He likes her too much.

"Spaghetti: it's always messy," Fred says too.

He's right. Apparently there's a prize you can win for eating spaghetti and not getting any pasta sauce on your face or your clothes. I'm pretty sure this is scientifically impossible, much like being able to breathe underwater or enjoy the taste of a mushroom. I'm not sure who is in charge of giving out this prize but I might look into it for my own records.

Either way, spaghetti is messy. It's loopy and twisty and turny and upside downy and inside outy.

In fact, "spaghetti brain" is the adults' term for me being a bit all over the place, and for getting lost in my own head sometimes. Like a bowl of spaghetti. I guess I love the sound of getting lost in a bowl of spaghetti!

Wait! What were we talking about?

Ah, yes, my spaghetti brain.

But they never say "spaghetti brain" like it's a good thing. I don't know why not. Spaghetti is yum. When they talk about it, their faces go all worried like they're saying EEEK inside.

Well, they really should go back to worrying about raspberries or the the news instead, because there is absolutely nothing wrong with my brain.

If anything, my brain is one of the best things about me. (And that's something coming from someone who can flare their nostrils in and out like a rabbit and has a freckle the shape of Ireland on their toe.)

The adults say things like:

"Oh! There's Frankie off in her own world again."

"Earth to Frankie, are you in there?"

"Frankie, are you going to join us? Please get your head out of the clouds."

Little do they know what's *really* going on inside my head. Because there's more to it than just a distracted spaghetti brain. A LOT more to it.

And that it is my biggest secret of all.

(Sometimes I do an *EEEEK* face when I think about it, but not in a worried way, in an excited way, and there is a difference if you look really closely with a magnifying glass.)

Shhhhhhhhh.

They really should be called shhhhhhhhhhhhhhhhhhecrets, but I'm not sure who to contact about this. The dictionary people? My mum once rang the park people to come and fix the bench beside the playground and it took them four years, so I probably shouldn't hold my breath.

Shhhhhhhhh, the shhhhhhhhhhhecret!

I need to be very shushy and secretive in case there are any spies about, listening.

Adults don't normally sneak around and hide in wardrobes to listen to other peoples' conversations like Fred and I do. Or make themselves into really stiff flat logs and hide under the cushions on the couch for some silent loggy eavesdropping.

But I guess it's not my fault if adults don't know how to be cool spies.

20

Adults have too much time on their hands. What do they do all day when we are at school learning and working really hard? They should take up real hobbies like rollerblading backwards and seeing how long they can do a handstand against a wall before they fall over.

I'm pretty sure Mum and Dad aren't listening right now. Flo, on the other hand, is small enough to crawl into a drawer or hide behind a cupboard so I really need to watch out for her. I know she can't speak, but she throws her dinner at the ceiling and that *has* to be code for something otherwise WHY on earth would someone do that?!"*

NO ONE CAN FIND OUT ABOUT MY SECRET.

That is FINAL.

It would ruin everything!

But now that I've explained that last bit about it ruining everything, I should probably end with THAT IS FINAL BECAUSE IT FEELS MORE FINAL, so...

THAT IS FINAL!!!

*Unless it contained an undercover munion (mushroom—onion hybrid)... The ABSOLUTE worst!

21

CHAPTER THREE

LIFE AS AN UNOFFICIAL PRIVATE INVESTIGATOR

PLUS OTHER THINGS ABOUT MY LIFE

That afternoon sitting in my bedroom, I decide to get out my book of secrets. I know everyone else is downstairs because Mum has just made snacks and it is a well-known fact that kids look for snacks approximately every twenty minutes, so they will all be congregating down there.

Except maybe for Flo, who with any luck is giving everyone a break and having a nap. Being annoying must be utterly exhausting because she always seems to fall asleep at some point during the afternoon.

I have been up in my room for some time, staring at the lilac walls with the funny cartoon decals Fred and I stuck up last summer. Mum and Dad weren't thrilled because the Stick-It Forever superglue turned out to be rather permanent, and even though they tried to peel them off, the wallpaper had decided that if the decals were going, it was going as well! It doesn't bother me that I have small chunks of wallpaper missing – Fred and I had so much fun putting up the decals that we unlocked two top-tier laugh modes that day: the "snort laugh" (laughing and snorting at the same time) and the elusive "nostril spritz laugh" (when you laugh so hard indeterminable fluid starts flying out of your nose)! Right beside the decorated wall, in the corner, is a small teepee tent with fairy lights adorning the entrance. This was also known as Finkleton Headquarters where Fred and I have business meetings to discuss things such as:

a) Ways to get out of eating mushrooms
b) Ways to get out of doing homework
c) Ways to get out of having our toenails cut
d) Ways to solve mysteries

Blue always keeps watch outside. One meeting we tried to get him to take minutes, but he ended up eating one of my fancy pens that smells of strawberries and Mum had to take him to the vet. He was so embarrassed, but I assured him it was a common mistake. My friend Tess once ate an eraser that smelt of cola, but her parents didn't take her to the vet thankfully. Either way, Blue's not allowed to take minutes any more.

But he's still our bouncer at the door. And I've told him under no circumstances can Flo be allowed in. She is BARRED!

Everything else in my room is pretty standard for an eleven-year-old who is also sometimes a private investigator:

- Curtains for hiding behind.
- A lamp with a swivel head which can be used for both looking at things really closely and interrogating suspects. (I haven't done this yet, but it is only a matter of time before I get Flo on her own!)
- A swivel chair, for turning around really suddenly when I've figured out a clue. It makes me look so dramatic, honestly, Fred gasps and claps every time. Fred used to use it to spin around in circles really fast, but once he puked a bit on my carpet, so now he's only allowed do it on special occasions like his birthday or Christmas. And maybe Easter.
- A bed. Even detectives have to sleep.
- Books, clothes, toys, a hula hoop.
- A secret bin for when I sneak snacks from the kitchen when Mum and Dad aren't watching. It gets kind of gross when Mum uses it as an actual bin and piles my snotty tissues in there too. But I guess that's what "rinsing stuff in the sink" while no one is looking is for.

Before going to my hiding place to get out my book of secrets, I pick up my magnifying glass and draw it close to my left eye, squinching the other tightly shut, and do one final check for potential spies.

Nothing.

I sniff the air. No dirty nappies from enemy lines.

My magnifying glass settles on two giant black eyeballs staring at me. They don't blink once. And then an accompanying high-pitched squeaky noise gives the game away.

My dog Blue.

Phew.

I am very fond of Blue, but he isn't the best assistant for a private investigator on account of his very loud breathing. It's difficult to sneak around the place with a small furball squeaking and wheezing behind you. It blows your cover a bit. But no one is perfect and Blue has a lot of great qualities as well. Such as:

a) He is kind.
b) He has very short hair so you don't have to brush it. Unlike mine. A design flaw for someone as busy as me.
c) He has a little nubbin of a tail. He has to work extra hard to wag it, so I know he isn't afraid of hard work.

d) He doesn't poo in slippers any more. Much.

e) If you are sad, he tucks himself right in
   beside you and puts his paw on your hand and won't leave
   your side until you're feeling better.

Blue's eyes take up ninety-five per cent of his face, and in contrast
his nostrils are the size of an ant's baby toe. Come to think of
it, I'm not sure ants have toes — I'll investigate that in the garden
later.

Blue's nostrils are so tiny I have no idea how he can breathe. In
fact, our vet once asked if he could enter Blue into the *Guinness
Book of World Records* as Pug With The Smallest Nostrils On The
Entire Planet Ever. I said, "Sure." Perhaps Blue will be the first of
us to end up in there!

I once read about a dog who could do aqua aerobics and became
so famous online he has his own celebrity clothing line. Imagine if
Blue got famous? I guess I'd have to become his agent — I could do
with the twenty per cent commission plus VAT to buy more private
investigator gear. It could be cool to have a famous dog. Although I
really hope it wouldn't make Blue incredibly vain and self-obsessed.
I wouldn't want him to get a nose job. I love his impossibly small
nostrils. They make him HIM. In the end, though, it turned out that
all pugs have minute nostrils — and Blue lost out to a chihuahua called

Jose from Brazil who was born WITH NO NOSE AT ALL! He now has a YouTube channel called "Jose Nose Best" so I guess that's that.

Anyway, more on Blue's career prospects later.

I have mentioned already, quite a few times, that I have a little brother called Fred Finkleton. But what I haven't told you is that Fred Finkleton is hands down one of the best inventions ever invented. Even better than extra-large bubblegum balls, trampolines, zip-up onesie pyjamas, squirrels, dogs, some goats, all guinea pigs, rabbits without red eyes, two wheel scooters AND popping fizzing candy.

I know little brothers are *meant* to be horrible. They are supposed to be smelly and mean and bubbling over with endless burps and farts. They are meant to flick snot at you from across the room and leave slugs on your pillow and spiders on your toothbrush. They are genetically designed to tell your parents on you, and wrestle remote controls out of your hands when you're watching your favourite TV programme. Essentially, little brothers are supposed to be utterly awful. And you're meant to just put up with them until they eventually grow up and head off to work in a bank or something.

Little brothers are *not* supposed to be like Fred.

Fred is FABULOUS. If fun could be made and packaged and sold as a boy, then Fred Flynn Floyd Finkleton is it — aged eight and four twelfths with two missing front teeth, humungous cartoony green eyes, a squinchy button nose, curly blond hair, bouncy balloon cheeks with a hundred and fifty-six freckles (I've counted) dotted across them and along the bridge of his nose. I reckon he'll be at a hundred and fifty-seven freckles the next really sunny day we get. He is clever and smart and funny and kind. He once kept a blob of chewing gum in his belly button for a week in between chews and Mum and Dad never found out. I thought it was so ingenious I hired him on the spot to be my private investigator assistant. He didn't even have to interview.

Sometimes in school, I have to pretend he's annoying because that's what everyone else expects when it comes to siblings. So I sigh and say, "Ugh, I know, I wish my parents would sell him out the front of the house the next time we are clearing out old books and toys we don't want. Even though we probably wouldn't get much for him!" Everyone giggles, but then I wink at him when we pass in the corridors and I can hear his laugh ricocheting off the grey school walls behind me like a giant springy ball.

Fred's laugh is like secret giggle medicine that makes everything better.

Fred is human sunshine.

Fred knows all of my secrets, and he keeps them safe with him at all times. And I know all of his secrets, and I keep them safe with me, for ever.

I am the luckiest big sister in the whole school. This is one of my super top best secrets.

School is tough enough with everyone pointing and laughing at me lately. They say things like, "Ha ha! You can say what you like about Frankie Finkleton because she won't even hear you! She doesn't even live in the real world! She lives in her *own* world, hahahaha!"

Veronica, Monica and Nell are the worst for this. Nell laughs the longest and loudest. I think she does that to make up for the fact her name doesn't rhyme with Veronica and Monica. She's known as *Death Nell*, because it's a play on the words "death knell", a noise from olden times when people wore tablecloths around their waists, and always carried spears. It marked when someone was about to die and it would actually be quite a funny and clever play on words if it wasn't so horrendous.

When they're laughing at you, Veronica and Monica and Nell's *HAHAHAS* go on for as long as maths tests or eating a pile of mushrooms or tidying your bedroom. Time slows down and you are convinced it will never end.

Sometimes they like to mix things up and the *HAHAHAHAHAS* are interspersed with whispery *PSHHHHWWWWSHHHHHWSHHHHS* and sometimes I would really like to Google Translate the *PSHHHHHSWSHHHHHHHSSSS* to know what they are saying.

And, other times, I'm glad I can't understand them.

29

I used to have a best friend, who I could roll my eyes with when Veronica and Monica and Nell started. Tess. But she's been distant with me for ages and I don't know why.

It often feels like the kids in my class don't know how to talk to me, which is weird because we all speak the same language. Or used to. And I've learnt so many more words from all my time on the loo.

But it's like so many ways I used to communicate with the kids in my class don't work for me any more. Sometimes, it's like I'm on my holidays in my classroom and don't know the language. Except I don't even have an ice cream to make up for it.

It can feel pretty lonely.

But I still have Fred, and Blue, and my secret.

CHAPTER FOUR

THE SECRET BOOK OF SECRETS AND ... THE BIGGEST SECRET OF ALL...

I poke my hand under the bed and into the swell of darkness, feeling around carefully – I don't want to disturb any spiders. They always seem to be in the middle of a game of hide and seek, that lot! How are they always so quiet even though they have EIGHT feet? I have to sometimes concentrate on tiptoeing around the place and I only have two!

Where *is* my Badly Named Secret Book of Secrets?

My fingers continue to patter cautiously through the dark until they reach Mr B – who is not a person lurking under my bed but a teddy I used to love as a kid. I still do, in fact, but I can't admit that. It would get me a LOT of hassle. I took him to a sleepover once and the kids said, "Do you need a nappy and a soother and a bottle of milk as well, Frankie Finkleton?"

There are kids my age who would be egged in the street for less.

Phil Phleeples carried a secret "blankie" with him until he was twelve and when everyone found out, his entire family had to relocate to Galway.

This could just be a rumour; maybe his Mum got a new job, but it has kept me on guard ever since.

Fred has a teddy too. She's called Ms P and we are pretty sure they are also brother and sister like us. We won them when we were kids at a fairground Mum and Dad took us to. I mean, sure, we are still kids. But back when we were just starting out and knew nothing.

My hand continues patting along the carpet under the bed until it lands on something cold and hard.

It could be an apple Fred promised Mum he'd eat later — those never age well, sort of like grandparents, actually. I pull it out.

BLUE, STANDING GUARD

No. Definitely a book.

More specifically...

My Secret Book Of Secrets. (Soon to be cleverly renamed with cool swirly writing with even cooler glittery rainbow gel pens.)

I take a breath and open it gingerly. My heart is racing for a gold medal in my chest and my breath is coming in for silver in my throat.

I *know* all my secrets, but sometimes seeing them written down makes them seem even more REAL.

I stare down at the page.

Secrets So Far, aged eleven and one month.

1. It was me who ate the vanilla sponge cake four years ago and not the neighbour's golden retriever Rufus Rotherford. Who likes sponge cake anyway? I thought I was doing everyone a favour! (I have apologized separately to Rufus, who did not deserve the bad reputation he's been lumbered with for eating other peoples' vanilla sponge cakes. Rufus has droopy eyes and a distant stare and I'm not sure if this is down to genetics or the fact he has not forgiven me. He has since cut Blue

out of his life and I feel awful.)

2. I have farted in every bath I have ever had. I just find them so relaxing! Once a teeny tiny poo escaped and I blamed it on Fred because he was too young to disagree. He has since been nicknamed the Dublin Bath Destroyer by my dad and I know I should feel bad about this, but I'm just relieved it's not my nickname.

3. I have a two-year-old piece of bubblegum stuck on the back of my headboard in my room which I chew on special occasions. I'm normally only allowed bubblegum on holidays so this makes me somewhat of a rebel. It tastes of nothing and takes a full ten minutes to work a chew back into it, so being a rule breaker is not always as glamorous as it seems. I just can't do the bellybutton thing like Fred. There's too much fluff.

4. Fred is my favourite person in the world ever.

5. My baby sister Flo is my least favourite person in the world ever. I think she's worse than all the horrible tyrants we learnt about in history class. Probably one day people will be learning about her atrocities. Watch this space.

6. Even though I will hopefully become a singing scientist

detective veterinarian artist, who is fluent in French and Japanese and who does trapeze in my spare time, and I will probably be far too busy to even consider it, I might, maybe, possibly MAYBE marry Ross P. Rossdale one day.

(I blush as I read this back.)

7. Sometimes I hug Mr B when no one is looking. Even though I am very grown up and wouldn't dare to ever do this in public.

8. I once saw my teacher Ms Hammerhead's knickers when she bent down to pick up chalk on the ground, and they were grey. This piece of information may seem like nothing, but I'm pretty sure it's a big clue about a secret investigation I'm conducting on Ms Hammerhead. (The title is "Ms Hammerhead: Shark or Woman?")

9. I saw Mum crying at a sad movie one time and she told me that it was because she'd been chopping onions even though I know for a FACT no onions were harmed in the making of beans and waffles for tea that night.

10. I once saw Dad cry too and he said that it is important for men to cry and this isn't a secret but I wrote it down anyway as I didn't want to leave Mum hanging as the only person I had caught crying. He muttered something about

onions too and both of them should consider wearing goggles when cooking these non-existent onions.

I should state that they can eat all the onions they wish themselves, I just don't like to get involved or be associated with them.

11. Sometimes (a lot) I sneak into Fred's room at night and watch him sleep because it makes my heart feel safe.

This is not cool and word of it *must not* get out. The only reason to sneak into your little brother's room should be to put slime in his socks.

12. All those posters that appeared in the neighbourhood saying: *Baby Girl For Sale. Good price on account of being annoying. However, looks cute when freshly washed and in a clean onesie. Open to offers.* Those were me.

(I did feel bad and went and took them down after.)

And then finally; my eyes hover over the last secret. Secret Number 13. Scribbled in my very best handwriting. The one that none of the adults can ever find out about because they won't understand and they will surely think I'm lying and send me away to a Correctional

Boarding School for Girls Who Tell Lies in the middle of a dark forest in the country somewhere with itchy woollen uniforms and porridge for breakfast, lunch and dinner.

I hear a noise and shriek. It's only Blue, staring at me with his giant eyeballs and breathing at me with his teeny nostrils. He is such a fascinating dog, and it's interesting that some pets just have much more to offer than just cuddles and pooing in your garden.

I pat Blue's head.

"Don't breathe a word of this to anyone, Blue." I instantly feel bad for even mentioning breathing. It's a sensitive subject for poor Blue with his microscopic nostrils. I'll try not to squeak of it, I mean speak of it, again. Blue can't read.

But he knows all my secrets anyway. As does Fred.

Even this one.

The biggest secret of all the secret secrets.

I look down and read out the final one ... secret number 13. They say the number thirteen is unlucky.

Not for me.

13. I am ... *MAGIC*.

Gulp.

CHAPTER FIVE

BRAIN MAGIC

OK, so exactly *how* am I magic? Well, that is a very interesting question indeed.

I am not magic in the way people may think when they think of magic. I can't make bunnies appear out of hats; I can't make lemonade flow from taps; I can't make homework disappear. I can't even make Monica, Veronica and Nell stop laughing or making *pshwwishishhy* whispery noises. I cannot fly or turn invisible, and I have no superpower abilities to fight off villains. (If I did I would definitely use these on Flo.)

My magic involves travelling to a place where no one else can go.

Well, actually, Fred and Blue can come too. But it sounds cooler and way more mysterious when I introduce it like that, especially if I say it like the deep voice in the movie trailers:

"A PLACE WHERE NO ONE ELSE CAN GO."

It's true, though. Fred and Blue and I all travel to a magic secret place together — which is handy because I like them both and they are part of my investigating squad. It would have been unfortunate if I had discovered that the only person I could bring with me was my school principal Mr McNogg who, as I mentioned earlier, is officially the most boring person ever to have been born. He doesn't believe in jokes and apparently only smiles twice a year — once on Christmas Day and once again on his birthday, and then that's it for the year.

This *might* be an urban myth.

But Fred and Blue can obviously magic to this secret magical place because they are my *anam caras*. My Grampa Pinky told me what an *anam cara* is one day when Fred and I were eating ice cream on a wall looking out at some boats bobbing on the sea.

"Frankie?" Fred asked.

"Yes, Fred?" I answered, wondering if it was possible to eat a flake in one bite. (It's not. And you sort of end up looking like a gerbil with giant puffed-out cheeks, like a stick has been wedged right in there.)

"If you could go anywhere in that boat where would you go?"

"I'd sail to Australia and bring home a koala bear and it could live in the tepee tent in your room. You?"

"I was about to say the same thing!"

"I know," I smiled. Fred is obsessed with koalas, even though they are really grumpy, sleep all day and stay awake at night. Sounds like a certain Flo Finkleton, if I'm honest. Except, to be fair to Fred, the koalas are way cuter.

"You two," Grampa Pinky chuckled. "You are *anam caras*, to be sure."

"What's that, Grampa?" Fred asked, chasing a rivulet of melting ice cream as it ran down his cone.

"Well," he said. "In Gaelic, *anam* means soul, and *cara* means friend. An *anam cara* is a soul friend; it's someone who just gets you in a very unique and special way. And makes your heart happy. And your soul shine."

That sounds about right.

A soul friend. There's an extra-special ingredient to it over and above a regular friend.

"Can you be a friend to your brother?" I asked Grampa.

"You can be a friend to anyone, Frankie. But you can only be a *soul* friend to a special few."

I wondered if you could be a soul friend to a dog, but I forgot to ask. And now it's too late because Grampa Pinky isn't here any more.

I destroyed Blue's only other friendship with Rufus Rutherford around the cake-eating scandal. And I must say, Blue gets me too. And so often without me even having to say anything at all.

Perhaps Blue is my canine *anam cara*.

I need to explain why Fred and Blue are the only two who can travel with me to the secret magic place.

This place I can magic to is ... well, it's pretty INCREDIBLE! More incredible than the time I found a fiver in a packet of crisps. It's been happening for a while now and NO ONE ELSE knows — although I think some of the adults are getting suspicious. They think that "Something is up with Frankie." Which is why I need to be extra-double-triple-sniffle careful.

I began going to this magical place around the time Flo showed up, which is pretty much the ONLY good thing about Flo.

Apart from the fact that that kid knows how to wear a onesie. I will give her that.

Little do the adults know that when they say things like, "There's Frankie, off in her own little world," that it's actually true!

I am in a magical, remarkable, mysterious, phenomenal and fantastical world that exists...

IN MY OWN HEAD!

Another world IN MY OWN BRAIN.

And not in any way like what happens when you daydream or imagine things. No, no.

It is an actual place.

With trees and houses and trains and cars and shops and villages and a palace and playgrounds and forests and lakes and beaches and all sorts of strange and wonderful animals. And ice cream. So much ice cream; three hundred and forty-two flavours to be exact! And electricity wires made from red liquorice ropes! And rainbow popping fizzing candy that plays your favourite pop song as it pops.

Everything in this magical place is, well, magic. In the secret, curious, enchanted world of THOUGHTOPOLIS.

And when I do go to Thoughtopolis, ALL the adults in my life look at me with one eyebrow higher than the other and their eyes narrowed like they are trying to work out how to add six hundred and seventy-eight to four hundred and sixty-two and then divide the answer by twelve. But they can't see what's going on in here. No matter how hard they try to figure it all out.

Where do I go?

Thoughtopolis!

And that is just for Fred, Blue and I.

CHAPTER SIX

THOUGHTOPOLIS, OTHER STUFF ABOUT MAGIC AND THE UNFORTUNATE CONDITION OF ADULTHOOD

The first time I ended up in Thoughtopolis, I was so confused that when I got back to the Real World, I almost blurted everything out to Mum and Dad right on the spot.

That would have been a HUGE mistake.

Mum and Dad are the **LAST** people I can tell. **NONE OF THE ADULTS CAN EVER KNOW. I AM SPEAKING IN CAPITALS TO CONVEY HOW SERIOUS I AM ABOUT THAT.**

They can never find out because:

A) They would think it was "daft" and go back to being obsessed with wondering how long the hot water switch has been on.

B) They would try to stop my magic. This is because...

C) They do not believe in magic.

D) And if they *did* believe in magic, they would just use it to magic away boring hot water bills, but they can't so they won't ever believe in magic. Which brings us back to **A)**. It's a vicious cycle.

There's one more reason I don't want them to know. I don't want them worrying about me even more than they already seem to.

They will take me to see Doctor Hilda Stitch again and she will try and fix things by offering me a lollipop and a sticker. There are a lot of things lollipops can fix, like using a licked one to glue a poster up on the wall, or put a plaster back on that had lost its stick. But this? This really can't be fixed by a lollipop.

The very first time we went to Thoughtopolis was

around the time Mum and Dad brought Flo home from the hospital. She looked like a plucked chicken in a fluffy blanket and when Dad asked me if I wanted to hold her, I was absolutely appalled! I had never particularly wanted to hold a plucked chicken in a blanket before, so why start now?!

Things went from bad to worse: Mum was tired all the time. Flo only slept when Mum was awake and started wailing when Mum was ready to go to sleep. Honestly babies are so self-centred and immature. I was utterly convinced she was doing it on purpose.

Fred and I started to feel **FED UP**. We call it **FRED UP** and Fred folds his arms and scowls in a huff. But then he smiles his big grinny smile because he doesn't like to scowl for too long.

We felt like Mum and Dad didn't care about us as much any more because they thought Flo was cuter. Even though I had started to put my hair in pigtails and was trying out a new giggle and Fred still pronounced umbrella as "umbrerra". All pretty adorable, if you ask me.

But not quite cute enough for them, it seemed. They just stared at Flo all day.

They really needed to get some sleep if they thought

chickens in blankets were that delightful.

Fred and I wanted to get away from *everything*. Flo's crying, Mum and Dad being distant and exhausted and all cooey-eyed over this new intruder.

We wanted to escape.

So that's what we did.

I remember the first time so clearly. I was standing in my bedroom, squeezing my eyes tightly shut, unsure if I was going to cry or not. I could hear Flo wailing in another room; I could hear Mum's tired grumbles, Dad's worried murmurs.

I could sense Blue somewhere beside me before he placed a supportive paw on my foot. I closed my eyes and called for Fred. He was the *only* one who understood.

Like he always did. Because it was Fred.

"FRED!!! FRED, LET'S GO!!!"

"Go where?"

Not even I knew at that stage. But I just knew we had to go!

My head was fizzing with a hundred and one feelings; **NONE** of them good. All of these strange emotions I couldn't understand bubbling up, bubbling over, ballooning and growing bigger and bigger; expanding, mashing and mixing together; increasing with an unyielding pressure until I thought my head was going to explode and shoot right off my shoulders!

And then all of a sudden…

It happened!

POP!!!

An instantaneous giant humungous massive *explosion*!!!

Was it gone?

My head?

Like a champagne cork shooting off into the night sky?

I reached up and patted around with my hands to find my head was in fact still there, but when I finally opened my eyes … I wasn't in my bedroom any more.

I was somewhere else entirely. Standing in a narrow tubular corridor that stretched all the way down to a little gold door at the far end. I moved my feet and patted the walls; everything was pink and squishy, like we were standing in a long cocoon of marshmallows.

After all the noise, there was a very still silence.

Just Fred, Blue and I facing a very mysterious golden door.

"Hello?" I called out, my voice bouncing along the corridor before chasing back in a fleet of echoes.

"Where are we, Frankie?" Fred asked. I could hear the confusion in his voice as I took his hand and inched forward, Blue at our heels.

I had absolutely no idea, even though it kind of felt like I had wished us here.

The door in front of us was golden and glittering with a large shiny brass knob to the right and a spyhole set into the centre panel.

I leant forward and pressed my eye to the spyglass, only to be met with an eyeball pressed against the other side looking right back at me.

ARRRGGGHHH!!!!

I jumped backwards.

"What is it, Frankie?" Fred whispered. "What's in there?"

I could feel a giddy energy coming from Fred as he reached up on his tippy toes to take a look too.

"What's in there?" he repeated in a whisper.

Blue scratched at the door impatiently as I took a breath and reached for the doorknob. I was the oldest. I was the one who had to be brave.

"Let's see," I answered steadily, trying to fool my own nerves.

Somehow, even though I didn't know exactly where we were going, I knew this was leading into a whole other world. A million miles away from crying babies and jeering kids. From former best friends.

Away from Mum and Dad and their new favourite child.

And beside me, I had my favourite four-legged friend, Blue, and my favourite two-legged human, Fred.

I turned the doorknob.

Nothing.

I tried again. It was locked.

"Oh," Fred murmured. "Well, I guess that's that,

then." He half-turned to walk away.

It couldn't be, though. It just couldn't be.

"Wait!" I called.

Somehow I knew I was responsible for getting us here… I wasn't a part-time unpaid unofficial private investigator – that wasn't really one but really wanted to be one – for nothing!

And also, plain and simple: I didn't *want* to go back!

"Fred, we need to try again. We aren't giving up now."

Fred craned up on his tippie toes once more.

"I can't … quite … see … Frankie," he said. "I ate three peas last week and went to bed early at least once, and I haven't grown a millimetre since. I think the adults are lying to us…"

As Fred slumped back down and Blue momentarily stopped scratching, a piece of paper shot out from under the door and landed at our feet.

It was a note scribbled with some messy handwriting. I picked it up, taking out my magnifying glass to study it closer.

"You need a password to get in."

Oh. What was the password?

Fred looked at the note and then at the door.

I tried the doorknob again. Harder this time. Nothing.

We didn't have the password!

Another piece of paper flew out.

"Oh, sorry, you need the password, don't you?" it read. This was very curious.

I tried knocking this time – I even knocked out a little tune to be polite. Still nothing.

Yet another piece of paper flew out to us from under the door...

"Oh, gosh! Sorry! The password is *Fibbleswizzle1234*. Do NOT tell anyone!"

Fred and I read the note together aloud.

"Fibble—" we started before we were interrupted by another note flying out from under the door. "Seriously, you really **CANNOT TELL ANYONE!**"

"OK!" we called back before glancing at each other, looking back at the door and shouting **"FIBBLESWIZZLE 1234**!" in unison.

The door suddenly flew open. It was too bright to see anything at all beyond it, so I picked up Blue and tucked him tightly under my arm. Then I grabbed Fred's hand,

and together we stepped through the doorway ... into a whole new world.

As soon as we broke through the brilliant light and into the other side, my senses were amplified by everything around me. I could smell the sweetest flowers, hear the most melodious birdsong, see rainbows of a billion colours arch across the sky, feel the warmth in the air as if it were a giant hug – just like the ones Mum used to give before Flo came along.

This place was buzzing with so much colour, so much sound, so much cheer and marvel and wonder: birds chirping, sun shining, rolls of green fields stretching as far as the eye could see, and a bustling village ahead in the distance with shops and houses and movement and life. It was perfect. Exactly how I would design a world if I could design a world.

Full of wonderment and magic, and a million, zillion miles from the real world. It was like the very best dream ever.

Fred, Blue and I looked at each other; each of us bubbling with curiosity.

"Where are we, Frankie?" Fred asked in dazed amazement.

"Where are you?" we heard a voice saying. "Why, you are in Thoughtopolis! We've been waiting for you, you know!"

And as we all turned to face the mysterious voice, the door slammed shut to everyone and everything else behind us.

SLAM!!!!!

CHAPTER SEVEN

GEOGRAPHY LESSON OF THOUGHTOPOLIS (LESS BORING THAN IT SOUNDS, I PROMISE)

So this incredible world beyond the door is Thoughtopolis, and that was my first trip. There were just so many questions...

- **WHAT HAPPENED NEXT?**
- **WHERE WAS THE VOICE COMING FROM?**
- **WHO WAS THE OWNER OF THE MYSTERIOUS EYEBALL THAT WAS STARING AT US FROM BEHIND THE DOOR?**
- **HOW?**
- **WHAT?**
- **WHERE??**
- **REALLY??**
- **HMMMMMM?**

- **EVEN MORE QUESTIONS THAT ARE JUST TOO DIFFICULT TO EVEN ARTICULATE.**
- **ETC., ETC.**

When we returned home to the Real World after the first visit, I wasn't sure we'd be able to get back there again. What if it had just been an accident? A brilliant, curious, fabulous accident.

And when we did get back, no one was any the wiser that we had even been gone! I put this down to a few things:

A) Mum and Dad were too busy doting over how cute Flo's toes were. They said they wanted to "eat" them? I have never heard of anything more revolting in my life! And I thought mushrooms were bad.

B) Apart from me, Blue is the best for noticing things around the house. And when he does notice something of interest, he points his ears up as high as they can go, scratches at the floor and does a very high-pitched bark until someone pays attention. It's normally if he's found a piece of food stuffed down the back of the sofa or needs a poo. But still. As Blue was in

Thoughtopolis as well, he couldn't alert Mum and Dad to our strange adventure.

C) Tess was too occupied trying to find a new best friend, so she definitely didn't notice I was gone. She doesn't notice anything about me lately.

But it wasn't all a brilliant, curious, fabulous accident. I figured out the way to get back, and now I can come and go pretty much as I please. There's no booking tickets or making reservations, which is handy as I am too busy for life admin like that.

I can visit any time I want! And that's usually when Flo cries, or the other kids are mean, or when Mum and Dad – or any of the other adults – say any of the following:

"Frankie, are you OK? What's going on inside that head of yours?"

"Frankie, I think it's time we dealt with this."

"Earth to Frankie? Are you going to join us in the Real World?"

Nope! No, thank you very much! I just scrunch my eyes and ball my fists, call on Fred and … *POP!* There we are. Back in front of the golden door waiting for the password to slide under the door. Sometimes they reset the password for security purposes, but it's *Fibbleswizzle1234* for now.

As to the *exact* location of Thoughtopolis? Well, it's in my brain. I can give you some directions if you like. I mean, it doesn't come up on a sat-nav, I've checked. That's because secret magical worlds are not officially recognized by the geography map people, and that is because those people are adults. Adults do not believe in magic. Remember the park people? Exactly. I'm not going to sit around waiting! But also, I don't want them to know.

But it's basically: go through the eyeball, turn right at the skull, down to the left past the mushy brain stuff and then it's the second door on the right. Gold, with a shiny doorknob. Knock twice, do three burps (their two-step verification process). Wait for the password, say it aloud and...

WHOMP! You're in!

Fred, Blue and I have been coming back a lot more recently. Things are heating up in the Real World at the moment with Flo slowly implementing her World Domination Plan. How can someone so tiny be so ferocious?

So here we are again, standing at the golden door, ready to cross the threshold. Some days it takes a little longer to get all three burps out because some days are just like that, I guess.

But usually the giddiness and anticipation helps us along with it.

BURP. BURP. BUUUUUURP.

Fred is able to do the loudest burps. They are almost like works of art. I think he could make a living out of it — there must be some way to monetize it — but he says he wants to be an astronaut and run a llama farm so there might not be much time for anything else. I tell him it's all about time management and he says he'll work on it. But, despite the volume, Fred can only ever do two burps at a time.

Blue punctuates each burp with a nasal whistle, and sometimes the golden door doesn't accept whistles, which leaves the burps down to me. Ms Hammerhead says burping isn't ladylike, but I think if that was the case then girls wouldn't be programmed to burp. But we are — just like boys. I'd like to see a lot more equality when it comes to things like this. There's a counsellor in our area who looks after promoting equality and I'm going to write to her to see if they can put burps on the agenda. When I'm not so busy travelling to secret worlds in my own brain. I'll pop it on a to-do list.

"Frankie?"

"Yes, Fred."

"Do you think snails can burp?"

"I can't imagine why not," I reply.

"They always seem so polite."

"That's true. They really do. But I'd imagine their burps are *tiny*."

"Yeah, me too. I'm going to listen really closely next time. There's often so much going on that can be missed when you just assume things are a certain way."

"You're right, Fred." I marvel at how smart my little brother is. Even though he accidentally drank washing-up liquid once, he really is very clever.

We stand at the door, waiting.

"They make a mess. But it's not their fault," Fred says after another moment

"No, they can't help it. Life is just messier for some."

"True."

"You know, I think snails are ... misunderstood. It's easy to like butterflies. It's easy to think ladybirds are lovely. Just because they're shinier and have cuter outfits."

"Do you know they can live for ten to fifteen years?" Fred says.

"Really?"

"Really! Imagine if there were snails in our garden older than us! Mum could pay them to babysit!"

We both chuckle at the thought of a tiny snail telling us to go to bed and reading a bedtime story.

"Can we have a pet snail and call him Alan?"

"Of course we can, Fred. He can be the manager of the seven star snail hotel and he can live with us when he's not working his shift."

"That's good. We'll start interviewing a few for the job soon."

Fred and I have always loved snails. We've made friends with many of them over the years. He says they remind him of me, which I was majorly offended by at first, but then he explained it was because when I got embarrassed I also went into my shell. Which was sort of true. I also sometimes have pigtails which are a bit like antennae, so there's that.

I had been going to suggest that Tess and I make a snail hotel in her garden, because Tess is really good at constructing things. We once made a bunkbed for two woodlice out of bubblegum containers, with a slide down one end of it, and Tess was chief operating engineer. I was in charge of bedding and toiletries. And I have so many ideas for this snail hotel – the Lettuce Dance Ballroom, the Shellac Nail Salon – but then she started ignoring me, so I never asked her.

Sometimes I used to wish I had an actual shell on my back to disappear into, but now I have Thoughtopolis. And even though I don't want to insult any snails we meet by saying it, it's definitely better than a shell. Unless they disappear somewhere magical in there too.

Either way, we are back here again and I muster up my final burp, take a deep breath and say: "*Fibbleswizzle1234!*"

As the door opens, a flood of sunlight spills out, drenching Fred, Blue and I in beautiful golden luminescence. This place is more and more glorious every time we come!

Once our eyes adjust, we can see Bundlenugg standing there, arms outstretched, eyes bright and smile even brighter. Just like always.

And to answer some of the billions of whos, whys, hows around Thoughtopolis, it is *Bundlenugg* who is the owner of the spyglass eyeball, the possessor of the *we-have-been-expecting-you* voice and the keeper of the password. He has been looking out for us since we first arrived in Thoughtopolis.

He is teeny tiny: the height of two small raisin boxes stacked on top of one other. He dresses quite like my dad does for work: a shirt and tie with a jacket and trousers. Except on casual Fridays when he wears shorts and flip-flops. I would describe Bundlenugg as fumbly. He's always saying, "Whoops!" and, "Deary me!" and, "Wimble bottoms!" which I'm pretty sure is polite bad language in Thoughtopolis. Sort of like when Granny With The Not As Cute As Blue Dog But Still Cute Enough says, "Oh, swan poo! I forgot to get milk!" She says "swan poo" is not too bad a profanity, seeing as swans are very graceful, and it makes saying something unpleasant a little nicer.

But much like onions, or snails or butterflies, no matter how you dress them up … they are so often just what they are underneath it all.

Bundlenugg says, "Wimble bottoms!" *a lot*! And yes he is clumsy and flumbly and bumbly, but he is also very wise. He can make sense of things and explain them in a way that's easier to understand. And that is a huge relief, seeing as me and everyone else back at the Real World do not seem to be on the same page lately.

I often think that the adults at home skirt around telling me *everything*, guess at *something* and I often end up understanding **NOTHING**.

"Oh, these things are difficult to understand, Frankie."

"Well, that's the way it often goes, as they say."

"It will all make sense another time; you don't have to worry about it now, you see?"

No.

I don't see.

But here in Thoughtopolis, I can make sense of things a little easier. And Bundlenugg is always here to help me figure it out.

He is sort of like a small man teddy person who is neither a person nor a teddy. He can walk and talk and cry and sing, and do all of the things we can. Although he can't whistle, unfortunately. He does have a beautiful singing voice and has brought us to tears with his renditions of some well-known power ballads. He can speak seven languages and is fluent in Ancient Thoughtopolineese. He says not many people or creatures here speak it any more, but he has taught us the basics and it's nice to make an effort when you're a tourist in a magical land inside your own brain.

BIMBORNOG – Good morning

FANSWIPPOL – I think I need more ice cream

SWARNARDIN – Where to next?

YORG! – Look at that strange and interesting creature!

YAMYAM – I don't want to go home

SNOPPLEBOBBLE – Are you feeling OK?

SNUPPLEBUBBLE – I am feeling OK

SNAPPLEBABBLE – Actually, I am not feeling OK

NORBBLEFOGSNOUT – We are ready for our next adventure!

FAMBAMBLEDOBBLE — Can I try the one-million-flavours-in-one popping candy, please?

TANSYPANDLEFORBISWARFINANDLEPOPBIBBLEEIDASYLLIBDET — Hi (I'm not sure why this has to be so long, but I don't make the rules here)

Fred and I think that Bundlenugg is our mentor, because he is always here waiting for us. He offers us advice, shows us around and knows everything there is to know about Thoughtopolis.

We haven't ever asked Bundlenugg what exactly his job is. I think I got distracted by what was going on inside my own head and forgot. It feels like too much time has passed now and it might be a bit rude. This seems to have happened to me quite a lot but, then again, I do have a lot on. It's like how I've known Tess too long now to ask her if *she* thinks snails are cute or not. I know she had one as a pet once, until it disappeared and was discovered a year later in her sock drawer, not exactly alive.

This still doesn't give any definitive answers really.

But I'm guessing she does quite like snails.

I'm just not so sure she likes me any more.

I wonder if I disappeared and hid in her sock drawer, would she even notice? I don't think I'd manage to stay in there for a year, though. I would miss Fred and Blue and marshmallow twists too much. And Mum and Dad. But I'm not sure they'd notice either.

Either way, private investigators have their limits, and I can often get cramps from sitting in the one spot too long.

Thinking about it now, Tess probably prefers butterflies. Mindy Morgan in our class is like a butterfly and Tess seems to be hanging out with her a lot lately. She's shiny with cute outfits and funny and knows all the right things to say.

Anyway, I'm getting distracted again. Maybe Bundlenugg is our tour guide. He certainly does his best to show us around the vast and varied world of Thoughtopolis. But not in a boring way, like tours where they stop at certain landmarks and blather on about two kings a zillion years ago who didn't like each other and ran at one another with pointy sticks shouting, **"RAAAAAAAAAAAAAAR!"** until one king finally said, "OK, fine, you take this land, I'm done with all this arguing," and went away to enjoy his crowns and jewels and purple velvet robes in peace.

No. Bundlenugg makes **EVERYTHING** fun.

I look at him and feel … relief. Or comfort. Or both.

"Welcome back to Thoughtopolis, Frankie! We've been expecting you," Buddlenugg says, beaming.

I love it when he says this. It lets me know I'm where I'm meant to be right now. And that there are adventures awaiting us. Many, many adventures.

He looks behind me cautiously, peering from left to right before grabbing my shoelace (which is all he can reach).

"Frankie! Frankie, are you doing your homework?" I can hear my mum call out behind me

And then Bundlenugg pulls me further into the magical world. Blue and Fred follow and we slam the door once more behind us. Slam.

SLAM.

SLAM!

I enjoy that slam behind us to the Real World every time!

CHAPTER EIGHT

BUNDLENUGGET AND OTHER INTERESTING THINGS

"How was your day, Bundlenuggie?" Fred asks politely. "Any news?"

Our Granny Who Is Married To Our Granddad Who Is Still Alive says we need to remember to ask other people about their day rather than just talking about your own. EVEN if you know for sure that your day has been more interesting because you discovered a line of ants carrying a segment of a mandarin on their backs along the garden wall (or tangerine or clementine or satsuma. **IS THERE A DIFFERENCE?** People say yes there is but they haven't presented me with any concrete evidence.)

"Oh, always lots of news, Fred," Bundlenugg replies, keeping pace beside me. Even though his legs are only the length of an average pencil sharpener, he can somehow still keep up with our longer strides.

"How are you both?" he asks.

"We are **FINE!**" we shout.

He always asks how we are and never in a way that tells you he's worried about us or just being nosy! Like the adults at home. When they look at you, one eyebrow always goes up and it's like they are saying, "Hmmmmmmmmmm," in their heads.

Bundlenugg doesn't do that. It's nice and uncomplicated.

Bundlenugg's full name is Bundlenugget. Well, actually, it's Bundlenugget Ian Liam Lorcan Yeates, but he says no one ever calls him that other than his mum when she's cross. Fred calls him Bundlenuggie because he says it makes him even cuter than he already is, if that's even scientifically possible.

Buddlenugg is like a walking, talking, larger-than-life teeny tiny human – but not human – teddy. A "heddy". Which is cool because I can't hang out with *my* teddy Mr B in the Real World. Like I said, other kids would make fun of me and point and shout, "Frankie Finkleton is a baby wayby and has a teddy weddy and probably still wears a nappy wappie." And I find it nicer when people just say, "Hey, Frankie," and don't shout stuff like that at me. But, hey, maybe I'm old-fashioned.

It's OK because I have Bundlenugg in Thoughtopolis and he's **EVEN** better than Mr B because I can carry him around with me whenever and wherever I like!

I'm not sure how he feels about it necessarily – he prefers to walk around on his own two legs – but he knows it's because he's adorable. He's always open to hugs and gives some pretty good advice (unlike Mr B, who isn't much of a talker), and he still has both his eyes (Mr B lost an eye in a tragic accident involving an aggressive sixty-degree hot wash spin cycle. I blame Dad. He was trying to get grass stains out of socks and poor Mr B got caught in the fracas and ended up an unfortunate victim in the whole operation.

Bundlenugg is the best. And I haven't even told you the best thing about him yet. I know what you're thinking. What could be better than having a teeny walking teddy-human who assures you everything is going to be OK, talks in riddles you can make sense of, tells great jokes, has magical powers, can sing like a choir angel in a Christmas concert, gives super hugs and can speak seven foreign languages?

Well, I'll tell you. Bundlenugg also has a tiny dog called Pickle.

Pickle is the size of a snail, but has a heart as big as a T-rex.

"Hey," Pickle says now, stepping out from behind a pebble.

Pickle has the deepest barrel-booming voice I've ever heard. It's an interesting combo, because she's just so very, very tiny.

Oddly, Pickle reminds me of Fred's teddy, Ms P. She is the same faun colour and has one raggedy ear almost rubbed away from over snuggling the same spot. Bundlenugg must cuddle Pickle the exact same way Fred does with Ms P in the Real World.

But here we are, free to enjoy them!

"Yo," Pickle says and I can feel the earth beneath my feet reverberate slightly.

"Hey, Pickle," Blue replies in a high shrill voice. "How are things?"

Oh, yeah, and there's that. Blue can talk in Thoughtopolis. Which is no biggie.

(I'm joking … it's **AMAZING!**)

His Thoughtopolis voice is incredibly high-pitched and nasal, like someone playing the top notes on a tin whistle, badly.

"How is everyone today?" he squeaks.

I had so many questions for Blue once I found out he could talk:

A) What is so fascinating about trucks? Why does he feel he needs to bark at them and chase them? (He says it's just instinct, the way humans say, **"I WANT ONE!"** and chase after ice cream vans.)

B) Why does he hate going to the groomers? Mum loves going to the hairdressers! (He says dogs and hairdryers don't mix).

C) Does he mind eating his dinner from a bowl on the floor or would he prefer to eat at the table with the rest of us? (He says mostly he's OK with it, but actually he wouldn't mind sitting in Flo's highchair once in a while.)

D) What does he mean when he puts his paw on my hand? (It can mean "Please let me outside, I'm bursting for the toilet", but mostly it means "Frankie, I hope you're OK. And if you're not, I'm here.")

Oh, and I would like to say, for the record, that dogs don't like it when we age them up by seven years every birthday. (They are trying to stay young like everyone else.) He also wonders why humans are so bad at Fetch – dogs return the ball and then the owners lose it again. But, as he says himself, "You can't teach an old owner new tricks." He also says he's aware that sniffing other dogs' bums in public is absolutely mortifying, but humans fart in the bath so they can't exactly point fingers.

All in all, we are a really great team. Fred, Blue, Bundlenugg, Pickle and I.

And it is in Thoughtopolis where we have the best escapades.

"What adventures lie ahead today, Bundlenugg?" I ask, jittery with excitement.

"Well, you are the Chief Monarch Overlord Keeper of The Secret of Thoughtopolis," Bundlenugg replies.

"Yes, but you know I prefer when you call me Frankie."

"As you wish, Chief Monarch Overlord Keeper of The Secret of Thoughtopolis."

I raise an eyebrow; Blue bulges his eyeballs **EVEN BULGIER.**

"Sorry! Habit!" Bundlenugg says. "So for today we were thinking some general frivolity and frolickery in the fields and meadows, followed by a lot of fun, plenty of giggling, tonnes of playing, a little ice cream sampling, a lot of bubblegum blowing, some exploring and finally, you know, the usual two hundred barrels of laughs!"

Just then, two hundred barrels of laughs come rolling over the hillside, tumbling and laughing as they gather momentum.

It is never usual in Thoughtopolis. Ever.

"YAAHOOOOOOOOOOOOOO!!!" I scream, running into the sunshine. A warm breeze makes my hair dance.

I am chasing after Fred. Chasing with the barrel of laughs.

WE *LOVE* BEING HERE!

Thoughtopolis stretches out before us in rolling hills and fields, mountains and endless blue skies.

We run faster here; we jump higher here; we laugh louder here. There are no adults and certainly no Flo, and everything is just … better!

We are both free from all our worries. And all the mundane boring things that everyone in the Real World decides are very important, like picking your socks off the floor or being able to multiply fractions. A million miles from crying babies, tired parents, boring teachers, vegetables, chores, mean kids and nosy adults.

Fred and I run, letting our laughs bounce right up to the tip of the sky and back down again.

"**FRANKIEEEEEEEEEE!!! CHASE ME!!!**" Fred cries as he hunkers down on the ground, tucking his arms in by his sides and launching himself down the side of the hill. He hurtles faster and faster, gathering pace and speed like a little hot dog rolling down a mountain.

Fred is always too quick for me. I can never quite catch him. It's as though he has secret engines in his knees.

This is true in the Real World as well. Fred won the four-hundred-metre sprint on sports day. He hadn't been quite sure exactly how far four hundred metres was, however, so he kept running past the finish line, out of the school gate, down Conker Hill all the way to the village, and eventually came back with a pint of milk and two orange swizzles from the newsagents.

One for me and one for him. The milk was for Mum because she is always saying we need more milk in the fridge. She said once that she'd consider having a cow in the garden if it wasn't already a big job cleaning up after

Blue. Fred said he'd help by walking the cow and I asked if we'd need to use the wheelie bin liners as poo bags and she said it wouldn't work so we all just sort of forgot about it.

Anyway, you can get milk from oats and nuts now too, and they are far easier to keep in your garden. Although Fred and I haven't quite figured out how to milk an almond yet.

I hurl myself off the hill behind him.

"Wait for us, Fred!" I call. Blue tries to do the same, but I guess it's harder when you have four legs and huge eyeballs. He's not exactly aerodynamically designed. But let's not forget he can waltz with me on his hind legs and we can't all be good at everything.

I watch the blue of the sky and the green of the grass and Blue my dog – who isn't blue, but Brown just wasn't as nice a name – blur together until they become a smudge of glittering aqua as I roll.

This is *bliss*!

"Fred! **WAAAAAAAAAAAAAAAATCH OUUUUUUUUT!**" I yell as I crash into him at the bottom. We lie there, laughing breathlessly. A few barrels of laughs barrel past, howling in hysterics.

A tiny chorus of cheers starts up beside us. I peer at the grass. I see a crop of … are they dandelions? There's something strange about them.

"What are they?" Fred asks.

I take out my magnifying glass for a closer look. From a distance they look like dandelion clocks: a long stalk topped with a fluffy mane. On closer inspection, however, they are faces of *actual lions*!

"Oh, heyaaaaaaa!" they call, swaying in the breeze. "We are a pride of dandy lions, and we are proud of you, GUUUUUUUUURL!"

From Granny Who Eats Things Other Than Potatoes' word of the day book I know that *dandy* means "someone who is about being cool and fashionable". I can confirm that these dandy lions are absolutely definitely dandy!

I am used to this sort of thing here. I've already seen a giraffe on a scooter, a mouse on a motorbike and a Daddy Long Legs playing basketball in the Bugs Sporting Emporium in the Teeny Tiny Woods. If ever there was a bug for that sport, well, Daddy Long Legs and all of their eight long legs are it!

I stare at the dandy lions, thinking about my own Daddy Regular Legs. Dad always says that dandelions are weeds. At least I think that's what he says – whenever he gets me to help with the garden, I usually just cartwheel on the grass while he digs the flower beds.

"Come on, Fred and Frankie!" calls one of the dandy lions. "Make a wish!"

We've plucked dandelion clocks so many times in the Real World, making wishes and scattering their fluff, hoping we might get that pet frog, or a few extra hours before bed to watch cartoons, or own a llama one day, or be able to do a double back-flip on the trampoline.

"I wish—"

"WAAAAAAAAAAAAAIIIIIIIITTTTT!" one of the dandy lions roars and Fred stops.

"A wish isn't a wish unless it's kept under a dish," Bundlenugg advises. "Meaning: you must keep it a secret if it is to come true!"

Yikes, those wishes for llamas in the Real World might not work out.

I look at Fred, wondering what his wish is going to be. Maybe something to do with bubble gum and belly buttons?

I think and think. Then I make a wish.

I don't tell anyone. Another secret. Another one to

add to my list. Fred knows all of my secrets. I'm not sure I can tell him this one, though.

I look at him guiltily and he smiles back at me.

"Come on, Frankie," he encourages.

We inhale deeply, right to the bottom of our lungs, then blow.

One of the dandy lions shrieks in excitement as the fluff tufts lift and disperse around us.

We stare in wonder as the dandy lion fluff floats like tiny rainbow-coloured glitter parachutes under the sun. The pride of dandy lions instantly grow new manes.

Everyone applauds. And I think how lovely a simple thing like a cheer instead of a jeer is for your heart.

We chase the fluff tufts up the next hill and watch them scatter over the towns and villages below.

Then we sit and I hold Fred's hand as we look out over the plains of Thoughtopolis.

So many adventures we have already had here.

So many more to come.

We never want to go home. Why would we *want* to go home when we have so much right here?

"Fred, we are so lucky that we get to come here and have these adventures."

Fred is quiet for a moment.

"Some people don't get this," he says softly.

"No one else gets this... Fred, we are *magic*."

He is silent and I wonder if we are talking about the same thing.

"You see the joy in everything, Fred." I grin. "Everything is an adventure with you. You invent fun with your curiosity and your imagination. Topped with a little bit of bravery."

"I am only brave because you allow me to be brave, Frankie. That's what big sisters do so well, you know."

I smile, feeling as proud as a dandy lion.

"Sometimes," I say, "I only feel brave ... here ... with you."

We look down at the glistening green fields, blades of bright green grass dancing in the sunshine.

We have spent endless days here building dens and tree houses lit with twinkling fairy lights, ones with slides that looped from the very top branch right down to the forest floor. We have built rockets that light up and buzz into life like our own personal robots.

"I hope we go to space one day, Frankie."

"Roger that, Captain Fred."

Here we can sit on the top of a hill in the moonlight when the sun has gone down and watch a breathtaking firework display burst into a million shapes and colours.

And be away, together.

Everything here, with Fred, is just simply *better*.

"Where to next, Fred?" I ask, pulling myself to my feet once more.

"The Wizzleworld Playground? What about the Merry-Go-Round That Leaves the Ground, Frankie? It soars right up into the sky, whisks the clouds into meringues you can eat, and then twists around and lands right back down again!"

Yum. I like the sound of that.

"LET'S GO!"

CHAPTER NINE

BUBBLEGUM FLIGHTS AND MORE INSIGHTS

In the months we've been coming here, we've still only scratched the surface of what Thoughtopolis has to offer. It's teeming with all sorts of interesting characters and creatures.

Tall creatures, small creatures, different-coloured creatures, mythical beings who live in trees and houses and surrounding woodlands. Animals with three eyes and seven legs and supernatural powers.

We have come to discover more facts about this amazing land. For instance, the indigenous animal of Thoughtopolis is a squidgenflidge which has rainbow-coloured hair and looks like a gerbil, and sort of like a squid, but barks like a dog. It is a peaceful, funny creature that lives on bran flakes and bubblegum and is on the central emblem of Thoughtopolis's national flag. (I learnt the word indigenous when I had an upset stomach one day and spent a good portion of it on the loo. Indigenous is different to indigestion and means when something is from a certain place. But actually I reckon you would get indigestion from an indigenous squidgenflidge. But I would never test it out.)

There's a King and Queen who live in Proud Palace beyond the mountains – they look a bit like Mum and Dad, except she has pink hair and he never wears grey. They are never sad or tired or distracted and they love building dens out of sofa cushions. That's what Proud Palace is made of: towers of cushions and beanbags like one giant den! They always tell Fred and I that we should be proud of our achievements: like fitting seven bubblegums in our mouths, or burping the letter "F" in the alphabet.

Things the adults in the Real World don't hold enough stock in, if you ask me. Everyone knows that "F" is the single hardest letter in the alphabet to burp ... along with the number "four". Everything here is just sparklier and interestinger and funner.

I know Mum and Dad at home are proud of me, but lately I'm just not doing things the right way. Or at least not the way they want me to.

Not that that matters any more; they have Flo now. And they'll probably have the Flo Finkleton-Is-The-Best-Child-Well-Done-Flo-You-Are-So-Much-More-Fabulous-Than-Your-Older-Sister-Frankie certificate up on the wall soon.

But who cares when we have Thoughtopolis? Where there are hover boards and mystery streams and lakes that turn into frozen rollerskate rinks. Where the streets are lined with cobblestones that light up in different colours as you run across them. And instead of parking meters? Bubblegum machines! They only cost two sense. In Thoughtopolis, the currency is in sense, not pence or cents (which I guess **DOES** make sense, given that it's a magic world somewhere in my own brain). Only two Thoughtopolis sense for twelve bubblegums! Better than a parking ticket any day of the week.

"Look! Look, Frankie!" Fred is blowing one of the biggest bubbles I have ever seen him blow.

And then, like always, the bubble takes flight and Fred's feet begin to lift right off the ground.

"Wait for me, Fred!" I shout, clinking two sense in the meter, stuffing seven bubblegums in my mouth and chewing them furiously in a bid to catch up with him.

I throw a spare bubblegum to Blue and he swallows it whole. Ordinarily this would not be great for a dog. Once Blue ate an entire slipper and it cost so much at the vet to get him right again, Mum said she could have gone on holiday to French Polynesia for a month for the same price. And that didn't include the extras of luggage or getting Dad new slippers or buying those really expensive sandwiches in the airport!

But of course, in Thoughtopolis, it's safe for dogs. Blue hasn't quite figured out how to blow bubblegum yet, though, so his only way of joining in is to swallow it in one gulp and then … well … fart.

A bubblegum parachute appears as Blue's bubblebum rises into the air, floating after Fred.

And I'm not too far behind. Blue is sort of embarrassed, but he thinks it's worth it.

"Look at me, Frankie!" Blue squeaks. "If Rufus Rutherford could see me now!"

Bubblegum parachutes aren't advised for long-haul travel here, but they are a handy mode of Thoughtopolis transport if you're not going too far and all the hover boards are occupied.

Blue starts laughing, and then Fred starts laughing and

then I start laughing. It's hard to keep hold of a bubble from your mouth *and* laugh *and* fly, but **WE ARE DOING IT!**

They think I am daydreaming back in the Real World. They think I'm lost in my own world. They are wrong.

Well, they are right.

It *is* another world. A whole other world entirely. All tucked away in my own brain.

HAAHAHAHAHAHAHAHAHAHA right back at the *Haaahahhaahhahahah*-ers!

"Right, Frankie," Fred says once he's landed two feet back on the ground. "We've been gone for ages. We need to get back."

"I guess," I sigh. "We don't want them getting suspicious."

"Yup, it's back to the Real World for dinner and homework and baths."

"Remember when Mum found a wad of bubblegum in your ear and made you soak in there for an hour!"

"Yep, my stockpile for 'bubblegum emergencies'. Couldn't hear a thing, but it was well worth it."

Yikes, I'm probably going to get a good scrub too. I wrote "Ross P. Rossdale" on my arm with marker today and I'm not even sure why because it's not like I'm ever going to marry him. I know I said I might one day, but there is also a very strong chance I might not! He is so loud and annoying! But what if it's permanent marker, and it just makes life easier if I do marry him? I don't want Mum to see either.

Mum and Dad still laugh about how I once wanted to marry some kid called Paddy Nolan in Montessori. Everyone found it hilarious because we held hands **ONCE**. But I could never marry a man who ate crayons. End of.

"Do we have to go back already?" I plead. "Can't we just stay a little bit longer?"

Fred looks at me, his eyes scrunched. Fred has always been more sensible than me, even from a very young age.

Who am I kidding? He once stapled his fingernail to a wall! But he is next in line to the throne of being the eldest sibling and he is good at decision making when he believes in himself. And it lets me off the hook with all of my burdensome eldest sibling responsibilities from time to time.

"Right! Come on, guys," Fred says.

Bundlenugg and Pickle eventually catch up with us, out of breath now. Bundlenugg doesn't like to fly by bubblegum, as he has to fly gluten free, and with bubblegum you never can be too sure about the ingredients. As for Pickle, she is afraid she'd float all the way to Pluto ... which I have to say, there is every chance.

"Last bit of fun before homework and bath time!" Fred says.

"You either do it or you don't, but you'll regret it if you won't!" Bundlenugg cheers.

"It's the same dinner for me as last night and the night before and the night before ... actually all the nights of my life, so I'm in no real rush back," Blue reasons.

"I'm ready," Pickle bellows.

"Well, then," Fred exclaims, "Off we *GOOOOOOOOOOOOOOOO!*"

And then he hunkers down on his side again and barrels off down the hill like a squealing sausage as the rest of us chase after him.

I stand up at the bottom of the hill, out of breath from laughing again, and think:

A) I love Thoughtopolis.
B) I'm not as wild about baths when you've written something in marker that you didn't really mean to probably because you were distracted

again. Spaghetti brains, eh? We don't need any
repeats of the Paddy Nolan from Montessori
matchmaking proposals.

C) How come humans are waterproof? Don't we
have tiny holes in our skin called pores? How
come the water doesn't leak in and turn us all
into sponges. Should we be wearing raincoats in
the bath?

D) How much bubblegum can someone actually fit
behind their ear for it to be a stockpile?

E) What actually qualifies as a bubblegum-related
emergency?

F) Maybe I should help Dad with the gardening
properly, instead of doing cartwheels and letting
him do all the work. Maybe flowers are more
interesting than I'd thought – those dandy lions
certainly were! Maybe really regular things
have special qualities to them if you make an
effort to look at them a different way. Of course
it's easier to be impressed by flowers. They
have the advantage of looking more interesting
on the surface. But what about the things that
people disregard as ordinary? The ones that

have to work a little harder to get noticed?
Just like the dandelion clocks considered to
be weeds but holding a hundred "wish puffs".
There must be more things like that, that might
just have magic within... Things like me?

G) I may investigate f) further

H) I hope my wish comes true.

I) I LOVE THOUGHTOPOLIS.

CHAPTER TEN

THE BLUES (SOMETHING ALTOGETHER DIFFERENT TO THE DOG)

"Frankie? Did you hear what I was saying?"

"Hmmmm," I reply.

"Oh, good," Mum says with a little chuckle. "I thought you were miles away."

It wasn't that far. Just through the eyeball, turn right at the skull, down to the left past some brain matter, and second door on the right.

I still don't know what's in the first door. I'm thinking a storage cupboard and a mop. Or maybe it's a place where all the useless bits of information in my head are kept. Random facts like a human strand of hair being as comparable in strength to steel. Or that sometimes birds can sleep while they are flying.

Although, actually, both of those facts are quite interesting and probably don't live in that cupboard.

"Frankie," Mum says gently. She's holding a hairbrush, hovering over some of my knots. We're sitting on the sofa in the living room and I can hear the clock on the wall tick-tock away, filling the silences for us.

Tick tock.

Tick tock.

"You know, Frankie," Grampa Pinky used to say, "the big hand looks like it's doing all the work, but that little hand is busy in there too. And, sometimes, the smallest little things can <u>really</u> make a big difference."

Mum rests her hand on mine, and I let her keep it there for longer than I normally do. It's nice to sit here with her. Sometimes we understand each others' silences better than our conversations lately.

Sometimes it's the little things.

"Are you missing him, Frankie?" Mum asks gently.

I nod softly. I always miss Grampa Pinky when Mum mentions him.

She hugs me and I make an imaginary wish on an imaginary dandelion that she won't say anything else about it for now.

Miraculously, Flo is nowhere to be seen. She is probably in bed, exhausted from trying to figure out how to take over the world: I think her plan is to round up all the older siblings and send them to a dungeon on an island somewhere in the middle of the Atlantic Ocean.

94

We rarely sit together, just the two of us any more, me and Mum. There is always a small, bald human with no teeth shouting nonsense at us. Long gone are the days when she, Dad, Fred and I built forts out of sofa cushions or sat on the wall outside the bakery in the village and ate warm buns fresh out of the oven.

"Like I was saying, Frankie, I think we need to talk about your report card."

Uh oh.

She pauses and I know she's trying to pick the best words so as not to worry me. Because even though Mum is tired and prefers my baby sister, she is still mostly really kind.

"The school think you might be slipping back a little on your studies, and they were wondering if a support teacher after school might be a help. Just until you catch up a bit? Do you think that might be a good thing?"

Extra classes after school??

That is absolutely NOT a good thing!!

For one, school is long enough already! And they expect me to put in an *extra* shift? And I'm not even getting paid?

While everyone is heading home to watch cartoons or go to the park to hang upside down off the monkey bars, I would have to try to divide 567 by 12 (which is impossible, unless you want one of those truly messy numbers with a decimal place slap-bang in the centre).

Those numbers really need to pull themselves together! I have enough to be dealing with with all the other numbers out there!

This is the worst thing to happen to me since Dad told me that the watermelon ice-pops I love had been discontinued in the local supermarket. Or that Fimplewoggle from The Woggles is actually a grown man in a costume.

Everyone will laugh at me. Everyone will be whispering and pointing at me even more than they already do!

The only two kids I know who are doing extra classes after school are:

- Hector Hensbottom in the class below. He has to go because he only ever seems to shoot rolled-up bits of paper from his nostrils at other kids during school time, which if you ask me is not a display of good time management skills. And I know for certain it's not on the curriculum.
- Audrey Blenerhassett, and I think she's only really there as a form of detention. Last week she tried to set fire to a banana. I'M NOT SAFE AROUND AUDREY BLENERHASSETT! AND NEITHER ARE BANANAS!

Monica, Veronica and Nell's laughs will turn from *HAHAHAHAHAAs* to *HAHAHAHAHAAAAAAAAS!!!!!* and the whispering will go on for eveeeeeeeeeer.

And if I'm never again available for best–friend duty to go to the park after school instead of extra support classes, Tess really will forget all about me. For good.

Maybe she'd be happier hanging upside down off the monkey bars making new friends. New friends like Mindy Morgan, who I bet can hang upside down like a bat for days.

I heard she went back to Mindy's house after school the other day, and hearing that hurt even worse than a really bad paper cut. Mindy has a dog, two cats, five gerbils and a tortoise called Karen who pokes her head out of her shell whenever anyone shouts, "LETTUCE!" I just can't compete with that.

Sure, I have Blue, and he's getting better at his hind–leg dance, but he has his limits. He just doesn't like lettuce, and I can't force him.

We like what we like, I suppose.

I sit fiddling with my shoelaces as Mum brushes my hair. A play date is OK. A play date shouting, "LETTUCE!" at a tortoise I can handle. But what if they go on to have sleepovers like we used to? Building duvet forts and having midnight feasts and telling ghost stories about haunted houses until we eventually fall asleep.

I used to like doing that with Tess and Fred.

But I can't really find the words to tell Tess I miss hanging out with her. I know the words are, "Do you want to come over to my house and play?" but every time I try, they just come out in a tangle of silence instead.

Everyone in my class is going forward. They are getting better at everything – spelling, times tables, verbs. I can't keep up. The further and faster they get ahead, the more I slip behind.

Sometimes I just want everything to stay where it was. For everything to stay the same.

For time to slow down like I am a snail.

Tick tock.

Tick tock.

But it's OK, I figure, because if I let them all go on ahead, I can hang back here and slink off to Thoughtopolis with Fred whenever I want.

At that moment Flo crawls around the corner.

DUN

DUN

DUUUUUUUN!!!!

She's been hiding nearby the entire time! I knew it!

Well, I didn't know it!

But now that I know it, it makes perfect sense!

She looks at me for a moment, our eyes locked on one another, and then shouts something incomprehensible along the lines of "BLADABABPOOPBLADDAH."

I'm not sure what a BLADABABPOOPBLADDAH is, but knowing

Flo, it isn't positive. She reminds me of that cantankerous old man who shouts at the kids in the park when they go too fast on their scooters.

Cantankerous – that's a good word. Most trips to the loo make very little impact on your life, but the day I learnt the word *cantankerous* was a wee I'll never forget. Sure, my grades are slipping, apparently I'm going to have to DO EXTRA CLASSES AFTER SCHOOL with a child who likes to set fire to bananas, but I have learnt a very fancy alternative word for "cross". Life is all about balance.

Mum continues to brush my hair and Flo crawls across the rug in front of us, doing a new trick where she lifts her bum in the air and laughs. Mum gives another little chuckle. Not me. I know not to encourage her. Flo has a habit of running with the same gag over and over again when she gets a laugh, and I don't buy into that

sort of lazy humour where you just repeat the same joke. She should really think about expanding her material. No one can hope to have a successful career in comedy with just high-fives and bums in the air.

I close my eyes and feel the brush running through my hair as Mum sighs, almost to herself.

"What shall we have for dinner tonight, Frankie? Lasagne? One of your favourites?" Mum says.

I shrug in answer and she continues:

"I feel like lasagne is a good dinner for a Monday night, don't you?"

Is it? I wonder. Poor Mum having to figure out what day a lasagne should be eaten on. Gosh, being an adult really must be so time-consuming and uneventful.

"Hmmmmm," I answer. I've eaten lasagne on Thursdays before and been just fine with it.

Just like when I sit with Mum as she does her own hair, I like when she sits like this and does mine. It's sort of become our thing. Mum brushes my hair and we talk. Or she talks and I say, "Hmmm." We can sit close to each other without having to look each other in the eye too much.

Sometimes when people stare at me for too long, I get really uncomfortable. It's like they are searching for an answer I don't have. Blue and I lock eyes for yonks upon yonks during our staring competitions, but that's different. He accepts that I don't always have the answers. Some things I just don't know. Like how a walrus can possibly swim two hundred and eighty miles from the Arctic to the west coast of Ireland without several protein bars and a snooze. Or why you feel things you can't understand or why other feelings take you by surprise, like someone hiding in the dark who jumps out and shouts, "BOO!"

Like something from a ghost story.

Either way, Blue normally wins the staring competition, and I am happy for him and all, but I do think he has an unfair advantage because of his bulgy, starey eyes. And I am not entirely confident he has eyelids all the time. Sure, he has them when he goes to sleep, but where do they go for the rest of the day?

The brush snags harshly on my knots, but it's nice to feel Mum close by so I brave it out.

"Granny is coming for dinner which will be nice," she says, changing the subject.

"Which Granny?" I ask nervously, wondering if Mum will have to make a lasagne out of potatoes alone.

"Gr-Annie."

"Yes, but which one?" I ask again.

"Gr-Annie. Granny Annie."

It suddenly occurs to me that Granny With The Husband Who Is Alive is called Annie! Gr-Annie! My mum has lots of clever and interesting ideas when she isn't thinking about boring adult things like what day different dinners should be eaten on.

Like I've said, I do like Gr-Annie. She lets me sit on her lap without saying anything, and holds my hand in hers without it being weird. Because the world sometimes gives you the impression that at eleven years and one month you are too old to sit on your granny's lap and let them hold your hand.

That you are too old for Mr B.

That you are too old and big to feel so young and small when life is simple and full of fun. Does anyone else feel this way, or are they all too busy moving forward?

Surely it can't just be me?

Although sometimes it feels like it is.

And then out of nowhere I think how weird it is to miss someone who is sitting in the same room as you.

Like Mum. She's beside me, brushing my hair. We are sitting close by one another, but somehow really far apart.

And Tess who sits just two rows from me in class. I stare at the back of her head and think how many secrets we once shared, how many fun things we've done together, how we taught each other to French plait our hair and do the "Sailor Went to Sea Sea Sea" hand-clapping routine flawlessly in under eight seconds. Honestly, we were a marvel in the playground.

Now, although she's sitting in seat B5 and I'm in D4, she might as well be all the way at the North Pole.

But it's OK, I have Thoughtopolis.

And I was happy to be there, away from here, with Fred.

CHAPTER ELEVEN

LASAGNE AND GRANNY FOR DINNER (AS IN HAVING HER OVER FOR DINNER, NOT ACTUALLY HAVING GRANNY FOR DINNER. I AM NOT A CANNIBAL)

One of the great things about getting older is that your eyesight gets really bad and you can develop cataracts, which is what happens when the lens of your eyeball clouds over and you can't really see anything.

To be honest, I don't want this to ever happen to me, but I am happy it has happened to Gr-Annie. Well, not happy as such, because it's not a great thing, but it does mean that she doesn't look at me as intensely as some of the other adults because she can't see me very clearly.

One of the other great (not-great) things is that you can go rather deaf and your hips stiffen up so you can't move much.

Again, I know this doesn't sound very glamorous, but it does have its benefits too.

It means that Gr-Annie doesn't really wait with bated breath to hear every word or answer I might give to certain questions. Which is good, because as I have said before, I often don't have any answers. And it means that we can just sit and watch the world go by to avoid her hips crumbling away and falling off or something.

GROSS!

Gr-Annie never judges me too harshly either. And I think it's because she keeps her false teeth in a glass of water beside her bed at night, and if you are someone who does something as savage as that, you probably go a bit easier on other peoples' "quirks".

Mum is making The Monday Lasagne. She keeps looking over her shoulder at Granny and I as she makes it. I'm not sure why because we aren't doing much. Just playing a game of gin rummy, which incidentally I always win as Gr-Annie can't really differentiate

CHEESY

MUM'S LASAGNE

POSSIBLE 'UFO's
↑
UNIDENTIFIED
FRIED ONIONS

a nine of spades from a six of clubs.

Afterwards we go to the park together. Fred has homework and it's Pamper Evening for Flo. This is as ridiculous as it sounds. Firstly Dad runs a lovely bath and they put a thermometer in there just to make sure it's acceptable to her. Who does she think she is? Cleopatra?!

Then they file and buff her nails, massage lotion all over her body; even on her bum. And then they brush her hair with one of those soft bristle brushes while she falls asleep drinking warm milk from a bottle.

I've never heard of anything more lazy or indulgent in my life.

It takes Gr–Annie quite a while to get to the park with me, and I figure that if Fred is the fastest at the five-hundred-metre sprint Gr–Annie could possibly be the *slowest*. Could she get into the *Guinness Book of World Records* and is there a medal for winning at being the slowest? It has to count for something, surely, and her commitment to the cause is undeniable. I'm just glad it's downhill. I am already wondering when we might make it back home up the hill afterwards! July? August?

We sit on the bench in the park and look over at the playground in a comfortable silence. It feels very exotic being in the park on a Monday evening after dinner on a school night. I'm beginning to think maybe my Gr–Annie might very well be *wild!* I bet she drove motorbikes and had arm wrestles with other local grannies before they all became grannies too.

Has she had a life full of adventure? It's hard to imagine it now as old people don't seem to have that much energy. They all need a snooze after the simple task of eating a scone. How would they ever have managed playing Pirates and Lizards? (Pirates and Lizards is one of mine and Fred's favourite games. It's a remake of the original Pirates and Other Pirates. We figured it was more fun if one of us is a lizard, and it turns out we figured right).

I stare at the playground and I feel something crawl up the back of my throat out of nowhere and almost make me cry. I have no idea what it is. Probably a lasagne burp. Mum obviously hid an onion in there! The deceit! I had been too distracted to take my magnifying glass out for a full inspection.

"It's OK to feel sad, Frankie," Gr–Annie says softly.

Mum must have told her about Tess and that she has a new best friend called Mindy Morgan who has more pets than I could even imagine. Even though Fred and I are going to get a pet snail and call him Alan, that would still only add up to Blue and Alan. I can't compete.

I turn my head away so she can't see the big fat tear that bellyflops out of my eye and tumbles down my cheek.

"So many fun times you had here. I know it's hard, Frankie," Gr–Annie says softly, letting my hand sit in hers.

I miss swinging upside down on the monkey bars with Tess. I can't ask Gr–Annie to do it as I just know her hips couldn't hold up.

"I don't mean to dazzle you with my science, Frankie," Gr–Annie chuckles. "But have you ever heard of the phrase: *every action has an equal and opposite reaction?*"

I shake my head, afraid that if I speak, the only thing that will come out is more tears. Sometimes I imagine my silence as a dam, holding all the floods inside as best it can.

"It means that if there are a pair of forces interacting, the force on the first object will equal the size of the force on the second object. So if you see the first object as loving someone, the other side of a force that great is the loss you feel without it."

I furrow my eyebrows. Another "adult riddle". I need Bundlenugg to help me right about now.

"Frankie," Gr—Annie says just as I scrunch my eyes tight together, ready to head off to Thoughtopolis. (It's perfect, she'll think we are sitting in silence together while I disappear into my own brain. She won't suspect a thing!) "The thing about great loss is you only feel it once you have loved with all your heart. One cannot exist without the other. To know great loss is to have known great love. And that is a rare and beautiful gift."

In that moment I really miss Grampa Pinky. I miss Tess. I miss feeling like I understand my feelings.

And I know the exact place to go to whenever this sort of thing is happening.

CHAPTER TWELVE

THE SQUIDGENFLIDGE RINGS A BELL

"Frankie and Fred! Welcome back!" Bundlenugg exclaims, his small furry arms open wide.

Pickle stands beside him. **"HEY,"** she greets us, and it's as though a nine foot brown bear has spoken.

"What's on the itinerary this time?" Fred queries, already climbing a tree. The most wonderful thing happens when you climb trees in Thoughtopolis: you somehow have the expert climbing ability of a gibbon! You can climb right to the very tops of trees that almost touch the sky and you can swing from branch to branch just like a monkey too!

"Frankie!" Fred calls. "What type of underwear do moneys wear?"

"I dunno, Fred," I call back.

"Chimpantsies!"

"OH, DEARY ME, OH MY!" Bundlenugg chuckles in a fumbly way. He covers his eyes with his fluffy paw hands. "Good one, Fred!"

Blue trots over to the tree and makes an attempt to climb it.

He turns back to us. "Nope. Dogs can't climb here either."

"The itinerary this trip, Frankie, is, I must tell you, chockablock right to the brim with fun. Does that work?"

I nod enthusiastically.

Bundlenugg checks his notes. "Yes, a gift indeed..." he mumbles, almost to himself.

One of the indigenous squidgenflidges of Thoughtopolis appears suddenly, scurrying up a flagpole, and ringing a bell right at the top of it.

"What is he doing?" I ask.

"Oh! That's when something rings a bell in your mind, Frankie. This is what actually happens in here. Everyone thinks the squidgenflidge is merely adorable, but it does also have a job, and one that it takes very seriously indeed."

Hmmmmm. Bundlenugg had mentioned a "gift". And Gr-Annie had been talking about gifts too. Not that I had any notion what she had been trying to say.

"What is the gift, Bundlenugg?" I ask excitedly,

thinking of the myriad possibilities within Thoughtopolis. "Is it a puppy that never grows into a dog? A dog that never grows into a frog?"

"Hey!" Blue interjects.

"A bicycle that cycles on rooftops? An underwater scooter? A doll's house filled with teeny tiny creatures in cute outfits that run baths and sit on sofas and use the adorably tiny stove in the kitchen to heat up teeny weany beans?"

Bundlenugg thinks for a moment. "The teeny weany beanies?"

I nod my head.

"Perhaps!" he says. "But underneath it all is the gift … of a wonderful adventurous time with your brother."

To know great loss is to have known great love. And that is a very rare and beautiful gift.

The squidgenflidge rings the bell at the top of the flagpole once more.

I had a lot of great adventures with Grampa Pinky. We had so many great thumb war championships before he got arthritis. And we even went to Cork once on the train! Gr-Annie hadn't even been married to Grampa Pinky; she had her own ancient husband, but that didn't mean she didn't miss him too, I guess. And I bet she's lost lots of her own friends by now too. That's just what happens to ancient civilizations like Grandparents.

I smile. That's the very best thing about Thoughtopolis. That I get to have all my adventures with Fred.

Bundlenugg is right, it really is a gift.

"Oh, wimble bottoms! We'd better get going, Frankie. There is a full-to-the-brim itinerary of fun to be had because, as that very not-well-known expression goes: *a tumble of fun is worth more than a rumble of none.*"

I know what he means!

"Off we go, you lot! To wherever your wildest imagination can take you first!"

Fred climbs back down the tree and we ready ourselves to set off deeper into the wonderful world of Thoughtopolis.

Bundlenugg pauses, before looking at me and suddenly becoming more serious than I've ever seen him before.

"Frankie, I want you to have fun today, for I think you need it, you really do. But then, my dear, I think, perhaps" – he fumbles with his paws – "it's time that you and I had a talk about … something."

And for the first time, I'm not quite sure what he means.

CHAPTER THIRTEEN

THE VERY BEST OF TIMES

Stella Sourcou sits in the Thoughtopolis Viddledwee Village, stirring her giant silver pot of spells and waving at us as we pass. Her long violet curls dance in the breeze and her hazel eyes smile warmly. I try to shrug off what Bundlenugg just said and enjoy whatever adventure lies ahead. Stella's cat Miguel Meowerson sits beside her in silent contemplation of the world.

Cats always look like they have the answers to everything and are just waiting for the rest of us to catch up. They never point this out, which is decent of them. They seem happy enough for you to get there in your own time.

"WAAAAAAZZZUP!" Pickle and Blue high-five Miguel Meowerson as we walk by.

Animals seem to get on better than humans. "Don't stir the pot," Ms Hammerhead always warns Monica,

Veronica and Nell back in our Real World classroom. Whatever that means. They don't carry pots; they carry lunchboxes and fire grapes out of them at my head.

Here, stirring the pot means spells and sorcery. Stella Sourcou can make clouds rain lemonade, turn your hair blue just for fun, or put an invisible force field around you that would make any sniggery **HAHAHAAHAHAHAAAS** and **PPSSHHHHHHHHHHWISHHYYYY** whispers bounce right off you.

Not that anyone here is mean, just in the Real World. Like when Mindy said I looked like a gerbil when I had my mouth stuffed full of gobstoppers. But fitting eleven gobstoppers in my mouth was a personal best record, so nothing can be all gain.

It is time for a SPELLing test – and a spelling test in Thoughtopolis is *way* more fun than the ones at school. We get to test Stella's spells. Invisibility spells or spells to make us shoot popping candy out of our ears for no reason other than it looks really cool.

Fred tries the invisibility spell first. "Fred!" I shriek. "You are invisible – except for your bum!"

He walks around giggling, a tiny bottom floating in mid-air.

"Needs more otter snot," Stella muses, taking her spell book out and jotting down a note. "There!" she marvels as the concoction sparks and hisses. "More ... snotter..."

Fred's invisibility spell has worn off and now it's his turn to laugh at me. "Frankie!" he cries, pointing. "There are liquorice strings growing out of your ears!"

Blue and Pickle grab either end and begin looping round and round like I'm one big skipping rope.

"Hmmmmm," Stella ponders. "Needs more giraffe toenails."

She reaches into her long green velvet coat and pulls out a ziplocked bag of giraffe toenails and I gasp at the sight of it.

"Ethically sourced, Frankie, don't worry," Stella reassures me. "I buy them from the You Have Some Neck Giraffe Nail Salon around the corner; five sense per kilo!"

Fred reaches over and snaffles two giraffe toenail clippings and holds them up to his face.

"Frankie! What did the giraffe say to the walrus?"

"I dunno, what did he say?"

"Give me back my toenails!"

I blink back at him as he holds the toenails to his mouth like two long tusks.

He shrugs. "Sorry, Frankie, I can't think of any specific giraffes–toenails–walrus jokes right now."

And I figure that's fair enough. It's a particularly niche corner of the comedy market.

Talk of giraffes and walruses makes us want to visit the ConfooZ Zoo next, which isn't your average zoo. Then again, nothing here is average.

The ConfooZ Zoo (a mixture of the word *confuse* and *zoo* spelt backwards) was founded when a rare breed of animal called a piglican (half-pig, half-pelican) was discovered roaming the plains of Thoughtopolis, looking lost and separated from the rest of its herd. The local zookeeper, Edwina Elderbright, rescued it and treated it with some "oinkment" which seemed to do the trick nicely. Edwina is always dressed in wellington boots and dungarees with scraps of food in the front pocket, oats and grain for the animals, and a large cheese and coleslaw roll for herself. She then went on to create the most fantastic zoo that allowed all the animals to roam free without lots of observers. Because, like humans, there are times animals don't want people staring at them and wondering what's going on inside their heads.

Edwina says she often finds it easier to communicate

with animals than humans and I think of Blue. And a few random snails in my garden.

"Frankie, this is a place for creatures that neither feel they are one thing or another, that they are neither this nor that and are a little bit of a muddle of both," Edwina explains to me. "Sometimes they are not entirely sure where they fit in."

I feel like that at times, not knowing where my herd is. It's not the Monica, Veronica and Nell pack. It definitely isn't the Ross P. Rossdale lone wolf pack (although wolves are supposed to be quiet. He doesn't have the qualifications). Or the Tess and Mindy magpie gathering. Two for joy, no room for the third magpie wheel.

"Frankie?" Fred says now. "What do you get if you cross a weasel and a donkey? A wonky!"

"Or a litre of diesel," Pickle retorts, and I marvel again at how a big personality can fit into something so impossibly tiny.

"Always underestimate your estimations," Bundlenugg says looking out at the animals in the zoo, and I know that he means there is often so much more to things than we figure there to be.

I wonder what we'll see today as Edwina takes

my hand in her right one and Fred's in her left and walks us through the zoo. The ConfooZ Zoo has so many jumbled-up creatures – sometimes you can't tell a rhino's ear from a crocodile's bottom. And I like that! (Not that I like crocodiles' bottoms. Or crocodiles, really – I'm sure some crocodiles have nice qualities, but I do think they need to work on their mindfulness so they aren't as quick to **SNAP**.)

"Let's check out the shiraffes!" cries Fred. He loves animals. He once spent two whole hours trying to get an exhausted limp bee to drink some sugar water. It

eventually did, slowly building up its strength before eventually flying off into the blue sky.

I wish everything could be that easy.

The shiraffes (half-sheep, half-giraffe) extend their necks right up to the sky to munch on clouds instead of grass.

There are teeny tiny pairs of pants everywhere, half-panda, half-ant, that march up and down long green bamboo shoots. I stare at them under my magnifying glass, marvelling at their little black and white furry bodies.

There are moodles that are half-moth, half-poodle and only ever eat noodles. Zoats, a hybrid of zebra and goats that only eat oats. What is utterly remarkable are the gats who were half-gnat, half-cat: teeny tiny and only the size of a full stop. If you look very carefully at them under the magnifying glass you can see them swishing their teenchy tails and meowing. And if you listen closely, more closely than you would normally think to do, you can hear them too.

Blue chases after them and Fred gives a delighted laugh.

"Even when a cat is a gat, the instinct remains to do just that!" Bundlenugg smiles.

Some things remain the same when things get muddled up. And other times, I think, looking at a moopard (half-snow leopard, half-moose) sitting on its own in quiet contemplation, it's difficult to imagine how things could ever return to how they originally were at all.

Finally we reach our favourite animal in the ConfooZ Zoo:

"The lemurdillos!" Fred shrieks excitedly. The lemurdillos are half-lemur, half-armadillo – I like them because they have a tough armour that protects them from their enemies, and Fred loves them because they are fluffy underneath and laugh when you tickle them.

"Would you like to feed them, Fred?" Edwina asks, handing him a bag of oats.

"Oh yes, please!" Fred replies, taking the oats and offering them to the lemurdillos. I sit on the ground and watch him; freckles scatter his nose in the sunshine.

In the middle of all the fun and bustle of Thoughtopolis, I really love doing this with Fred. A few moments of calm as we stand next to each other. So different to being near someone and feeling far away like I have recently with Mum and Dad, and Tess.

As Fred feeds the lemurdillos, I look around for the fails. I think I find these the most interesting because to me they aren't *fails* at all, they're *wins*! Half-snail, half-firefly, it would be easy to disregard the common fail. They look like your average snail on the outside, but just at the right moment, just as everything gets dark, and you can't see a thing, they fly! Up into the black sky like a spill of stars, lit from the inside out with a magic of their own!

CHAPTER FOURTEEN

THE GIFT THAT KEEPS ON GIVING

After all the animals are fed, we stop off at The Thoughtbulb Emporium, a huge balloon-shaped tent glowing with golden amber luminescence. A place where no idea is ever a bad idea – but *great* ideas are rewarded with a particularly zealous lightbulb switching on. (I once thought that "zealous" was a jealous zebra. I had been spending too much time at the ConfooZ Zoo. What it really means is doing something with enthusiasm.)

"If you feel a particular zeal, it is impossible not to squeal! But if you are feeling jealous, remember to do nothing zealous," Bundlenugg proclaims, lifting a fluffy arm into the air as a lightbulb pings.

"Frankie!" Fred cries. "Let's get your rollerblades and stick them to my skateboard – that way we can travel faster. Like a caterpillar on wheels!"

Fantastic idea! **PING!!**

"Fred! Let's paint Blue blue!"

Blue isn't so much a fan of that idea, but the lightbulb goes off so we run to get the paint anyway. It's blueberry flavour so he's OK with it in the end.

"Let's go to the Think Tank!"

Another light bulb pings: another marvellous idea! **PING!**

The Think Tank is Thoughtopolis's vast aquarium where we can snorkel with the most beautiful brightly coloured fish and all sorts of fascinating sea creatures.

"Ah, Fred and Frankie!" the manager says, greeting us in a full scuba suit and clipboard. "I see you have been booked in for an appointment with the brain sturgeon."

The brain sturgeon pokes its head out of the tank, resplendent in a shimmering aqua-blue surgery scrub outfit and a fibre-optic surgical headlight on its fish head. "Afternoon. I am here for all your aquatic brain sturgery needs. I can whip a worry right out of your head for the bargain price of five sense if you have decent insurance. And I promise you won't feel a thing."

Hmmm, even though it seems a little more medically

sound than Dr Hilda Stitch and her lollipop prescriptions, I'm still not sure I'm up for that! But I might ask her if my health insurance covers worries such as living with a baby tyrant, being signed up for extra classes after school with a kid who dabbles in pyrotechnics, my former best friend Tess having a new best friend, not knowing what to say to who when the **HAHAHAHAHAAAS** and the **PSHHHWHWHHWHWWWWSHHS** start, and having every adult staring at me with lasery eyes and wondering what's going on inside my head.

Hmmmm, I honestly don't think my insurance would cover it all.

"Another time, Brain Sturgeon!" I say, climbing into one of the scuba suits the manager has brought us. I zip Fred into his and adjust Blue's goggles and snorkel.

"Hurray!" cries Fred. "We're in time for the show!" He climbs the ladder on the side of the tank and dives right in.

We swim through beautiful coral reefs as shoals of rainbow coloured fish swim by us. A hundred eyes swarm by and it doesn't feel the same as it does at home with everyone's eyes on me.

"Hello, hello, hello, hello," they say as they zip along.

A hundred hellos as we swim. Blue makes his way over to a patch of aquatic grass, lifts his leg, and does a little wee.

"Sorry," he squeaks through his snorkel. "This feels weird, but Fred did a wee in the paddling pool once!"

"I did! You're right, Blue! And Frankie called it the piddling pool after that. Happens to the best of us."

"Tickets, please! Get your tickets for the show!"

A little telescope fish with giant bulgy eyes, (sort of like a regular goldfish who's just been told some shocking news) is swimming at the entrance to a conch shell stadium where the show is taking place. Blue and the fish stare at each other, recognizing a similarity in their ginormous eyes.

"Hello," the fish says to Blue.

"Hello," he replies in wonderment.

We swim into the stadium and take our seats, which really involves floating about and trying not to drift too far.

The clownfish shows are always the best – the white and orange striped little clownfish does a brilliant stand-up comedy routine. He makes us "snorkel" in the front row (a snorkel is a cross between a snort and a chortle, and is the only proper way to laugh underwater.)

"OK, OK, quiet down, everyone," the clownfish

orders, standing on his back fins. He is speaking into a microphone. "What did one seaweed say to another seaweed when he was asking for advice?"

"I dunno!" Fred shouts.

"Hey, I'm just asking for a frond."

"A frond!" Fred laughs enthusiastically. "Frankie, do you get it? A frond is the long bit on the seaweed!"

"Sorry, sorry," the clownfish interrupts. "I couldn't *kelp* myself!"

Fred erupts into another fit of laughter, which in turn makes me laugh. Laughs really can be infectious, I've discovered. And it's much better catching a laugh than a cold or a flu or even a yawn.

"Careful, careful," the clownfish says, as we roll around on the sea bed. "You know what happened when they laughed too much? Well, the sea *weed*!"

That sets Fred off again.

And we laugh.

And I laugh at him laughing. And he laughs at me laughing. And Blue laughs AND wags his nubbin tail which has to be a double laugh.

And I feel giddy in my head and full in my heart. And I think of what Bundlenugg said about me needing this.

This truly was a gift.

And I wonder if Dr Hilda Stitch or the Think Tank brain sturgeon have ever prescribed laughter as the very best medicine of all. And then I think about the other thing that Bundlenugg said about needing to talk to me about "something", and the way his teddy paws fumbled together in an extra fumbly way. And it looms there in the shadows of my thoughts, like something playing hide and seek amongst the good times.

CHAPTER FIFTEEN

THE WHISTLESTOP TOUR OF THOUGHTOPOLIS AND THE MYSTERY OF THE MYSTERIOUS SIXTHWISP

Fred and I run out of the Think Tank feeling lighter and freer, and chase down Viddledwee Village main street, the cobbles underfoot lighting up in different colours as we run. I'm not going to think about the "something" that Bundlenugg wants to talk to me about for now. That's the great thing about Thoughtopolis: there are so many other things to distract yourself with!

These are all the shop fronts, stacked beside each other one by one like dominoes all the way along the roadside:

- The Biscuit Banquet Bakery, where you're paid

three Thoughtopolis sense to be an Official Biscuit Banquet Bakery Taste Tester. The melting marshmallow doughnuts are the best. We left a five-star review.

- The shop at the corner of Runnerbean Lane that has the coolest trainers in the world – ones that can help you jump over fences, walk upside down on ceilings, freewheel down hills or skate on ice.

- The Curiosity Shop, which doesn't sell items but is full of answers for things you're curious about, like do snails burp or do cats really have nine lives? (Thoughtopolis doesn't test on animals thankfully, so this is still very much an unsolved curiosity.) Being a part-time private investigator, this is one of my very favourite shops. The sign on the door says "Dogs and magnifying glasses welcome".

- The Hoinky Toinky Dinky Winky Twenty-Four-Hour Toyshop, a ninety-eight floor skyscraper, each floor filled to the ceiling with toys. Anything that gets broken, the master of the toyshop, Old Mr McGranger fixes in his Twenty-Four-Hour Doll and Toy Hospital on site. He has the help of a family of squidgenflidges going back generations and there's literally nothing they can't fix between them. Squidgenflidges like to help out where they can in Thoughtopolis when they aren't ringing bells. I guess this is why they ended up on the flags!

- The Old Favourites Hotel, where Fred and I go to eat our favourite breakfast of pancakes and maple syrup, watch our favourite movies in their cinema room, jump on our favourite bunkbeds and do dance shows in the banquet room to all our favourite songs.

"Frankie?" Fred says, interrupting my thoughts. "Frankie, we've been gone ages. Do you think we should head back?"

I know the answer is probably yes.

But I don't want to go home.

"Just a little while longer, Fred," I say, noting how the sky overhead is getting just that little bit darker.

We run all the way to the end of the road, past a racoon in a tuxedo playing a saxophone while riding his unicycle right down the middle of the street.

"Wait for me, Fred!" I call.

At the end, there's a frog and a toad holding a signpost that reads:

> ## PIGEON EXPRESS AIRWAYS,
> ## TURN LEFT.

Bundlenugg promised to meet us here at Eighteen Minutes Past No One Knows When, and it seems like it's about that time now.

We lose track of time here in Thoughtopolis, and that's one of the things I love so much. Time seems elastic: it stretches and extends to suit us. Whereas at home it feels rigid and ordered like something made up of all its own rules entirely.

I wonder if anyone is looking for me at home. Time for homework. Time for school. Time to go to bed and get up and go to school again. Am I still on the bench in the park with Gr-Annie?

How long have I been gone?

I look at Fred. How long has he been gone?

As soon as I think that, Bundlenugg appears.

"Right, guys, we have you all booked on board the Pigeon 747 to take you on a trip around Thoughtopolis, departing soon and arriving some time before you need to go back and do your homework," Bundlenugg announces, looking at his pocket watch that doesn't appear to tell the time in any means or manner.

I look around the Pigeon Express Airways Terminal. Hundreds of pigeons in pilot hats stand along the runway, examining maps, flight paths and coordinates. Many of them are refuelling at the fuel dock, which involves pecking at leftovers from discarded takeaway trays. Pigeons will eat **ANYTHING**. One is even eating a green vegetable – gross!

An announcement rings out: *"Cooooooooooould passengers Frankie Finkleton, Fred Finkleton, Blue Brian Finkleton and Bundlenugg No Second Name please board Pigeon Number 135 as your flight is ready to depart."*

All pigeons emphasize their coos.

And yes, Blue's middle name is Brian. It's a long and embarrassing story.

"Cooooooooooould all passengers please dispose of their liquids before boarding the flight?" the announcer continues.

Blue trots over to a tree, lifts his leg and does a wee.

"That's me done," he squeaks.

"*A reminder that no weapons are allowed on board,*" the announcement continues.

Bundlenugg obediently reaches behind his head with one of his tiny hand paws and pulls out a large bow and arrow, then reaches into his coat and pulls out a spud rifle and a conker catapult.

"What do you need those for?" I ask, bewildered. There's nothing bad or dangerous in Thoughtopolis.

"Just in case, really," he says. "You can never be too sure with a magical mystery land that exists inside someone's brain."

"In case of what?" I ask.

He shrugs. "Worries, fears, dark thoughts, etcetera."

I shake my head. Worries and fears and dark thoughts don't belong in Thoughtopolis.

Right?

I focus instead on how on earth Bundlenugg has stashed an entire artillery in his coat.

Magic, I guess.

Our pilot is a lovely pigeon called Paul Peterson, which reminds me of the nursery rhyme. Do you know it? It goes: *Fly away, Peter. Fly away, Paul. Come back, Peter. Come back,*

Paul. Even though Paul Peterson is a pigeon and not a dicky bird and what even is a dicky bird anyway?

I think of Mum, lying on the floor in Fred's room next to the side lamp, making bird shadows on the ceiling. We had said that dicky bird rhyme together so often with her when we were younger.

I nudge Fred. "Do you remember? You jumped so high on the bed, Fred, trying to catch those dicky birds, you broke the wooden slat under your mattress and nearly fell through the floor."

Fred laughs.

"Mum makes the best hand shadows," he says. "She can make a triceratops from just a thumb and a couple of fingers."

A memory flutters through my senses but disappears before I can catch it.

I have an overwhelming urge to be lying on Fred's bedroom floor with Mum and him, making animal shadows on the ceiling just like we used to. I found her asleep in there recently, curled up on the rug beside his bed in the dark.

Parents with new babies are so sleep deprived, they fall asleep in the oddest places. I heard one of Mum's mum-friends had fallen asleep in the middle of the toilet roll tower display in our local supermarket a few weeks back. Which I guess was pretty comfy? It could have been worse. It could have been on top of the pineapples.

Paul Peterson has been doing the Thoughtopolis Whistlestop Tour for as long as he can remember, which was only back to last Tuesday as pigeons don't have the best memories.

"Would you like to fly, Frankie?" Paul Peterson asks me.

"Sure!" How wonderfully magical. "Have you ever flown before?" Paul asks, consulting a sheet of paper.

"Ehm, I've flown a kite?"

"That'll do," he says, signing something on his sheet and nodding his head. Pigeons nod their heads a lot and you never really know if they are agreeing with you or just being themselves.

Somehow we all squeeze on to Paul Peterson's back – the great thing about Thoughtopolis is how size changes according to where we are. And then, just like that, we're off!

"WAHOOOOOOOOOOO!" I cry as Paul Peterson flaps his wings. I close my eyes for a moment, feeling the fresh air on my face.

"This is **WOOOOOOOOOOOOOOOOOOONDERFUL!**" Fred shrieks and I shriek in delight with him before we all feel a sudden bump. Ooops. I've steered Flight 135 straight into the bum of Flight 278 AKA pilot pigeon Penelope Paisleyfeather.

"WATCH OUT, PLEASE!" she calls. "I had leftover curry for lunch and it could get nasty."

I feel a sense of calm wash over me as we fly over the familiar plains of Thoughtopolis. All the places we've discovered and adventured in so far. Everything looks teeny tiny from up here … like a zillion dots of colour.

"Frankie, look!" Blue exclaims, pointing a paw. It's difficult to know what a dog is actually pointing at exactly as they have no fingers, but I follow the general direction and see an entire flock of

brightly coloured orange and purple and pink and blue and yellow starlings flying just below our Boe-wing 747, like the most beautiful ripple of rainbow colours dancing across the bright blue sky.

"They are so beautiful," I say.

"Ah, yes, a fleet of fleeting thoughts," Bundlenugg explains.

As the birds pass us, slivers of thoughts run through my head.

Mum and Dad taking us to the beach, sand between our toes, twirling in a pool floatie with Fred, movie nights on the couch...

"They are the happy thoughts," Bundlenugg goes on. "The good ones. It's the murky ones you need to look out for. The herons of horrendous thoughts, or heronders. They hide among the reeds in the Overwhelming Quicksand Swamp over there."

My eyes narrow as I look over to where Bundlenugg is pointing. There's a bleak-looking marshland on the outskirts. I can't see the heronders, but even the thought of them makes me shudder.

An image of Monica, Veronica and Nell creeps across my mind, and I hear their mocking laughter. Other dark thoughts follow closely behind, so I shake them off quickly.

"Where to next, Bundlenugg?"

We fly over the Lemonade Lab where I've spent so many hours with Fred perfecting the ingredients to a lemonade that never loses its fizz.

Fred's lemonade is amazing. He is going to be such a brilliant inventor when he grows up. He already has loads of ideas, like Anti-Bully Face Spritz, a potion to make cabbage taste like pizza and a machine that removes knots from your hair without brushing it. I told him he could be an astronaut on bank holidays to fit it all in, and perhaps just have llamas as pets instead of running an entire llama farm.

"Llama think about it," he answers and I giggle. Being eleven and one month old is like a full-time job, but being eight and four twelfths is pretty hectic too.

We gaze down at the Stream of Consciousness coursing through the townland. Its currents ripple, curling in and out of all the different precincts and districts, tying it all together in a slinking watery bow.

Then plumes of steam mushroom into the air followed by a loud honking sound. This is the Train of Thought that threads all the different parts of the townlands together, stopping at stations along the way.

"Look!" cries Bundlenugg. "The train!"

Bundlenugg is absolutely fascinated by the train. Fred, Blue and I haven't been on it yet.

He looks from me to the train and then back again.

"Bundlenugg?" I ask.

"Today is for fun. I told you that," he replies. "But…"

"But?" I press.

"Butt!" Paul Peterson interrupts. "Gosh, sorry for that outburst. This is embarrassing, but I may need to go find a bathroom. A lot of the other pigeons just go when they need to wherever they may be. But my parents raised me with more manners than that. Not sure that green bean agreed with me."

"Yeah," Fred says, "I don't trust them. Never have."

Just as Paul Peterson changes direction in search of a bathroom, his feathers underneath me ruffle slightly in the breeze.

"Are you having a sense of something, Frankie?" Bundlenugg asks.

Weirdly, I think I sort of am. What is it? Is it to do with that train?

"You can tell us, Frankie," Pickle shouts, making Paul Peterson scream.

"Please," Paul pleads, "no sudden shouting. I'm doing my very best to hang on here. For everyone's sake."

"It could be the Sixthwisp, Frankie," Bundlenugg says. "Your own sixth sense. It's hard to know exactly what it is. It's not touch, sight, hearing, smell or taste. The sixth sense is harder to define because it's to do with your feelings, when you get a sense of something you can't quite figure out or explain."

"That sounds very mysterious," Fred says.

"The sixth sense can ruffle a feather, if you feel you can weather, or offer a balm for some much needed calm," Bundlenugg offers in a thought-provoking riddle.

Hmmmmm.

I make a note to:

- Get my magnifying glass out to look for more clues of the Sixthwisp.
- See if Fred and I can say Sixthwisp really quickly ten times because it sounds like a tongue twister.

That's it. Not all lists need to be long.

The Train of Thought hoots loudly again as we fly over Memory Lane and past the Worrisome Woods.

"What's *in* the Worrisome Woods?" asks Fred, but I interrupt him. *Worrisome Woods* doesn't exactly sound great, if you know what I mean.

"OK," Paul Peterson!" I say. "To the loo!"

"OK, for him to the loo, for you toodledoo," Pickle barks gruffly. "You need to go back now, Frankie."

"Awwwwww!" Fred protests, even though he knows it too.

"Can we—"

Bundlenugg stops me, and for the first time sounds stern.

"Frankie, you must go back now. You have been gone long enough. There are rules..." He is almost getting flustered.

"OK," I answer. "OK."

But I'm not sure I am OK.

I want to stay here.

What's the worst that could happen if I did?

CHAPTER SIXTEEN

THE FANTASTICAL FUNFAIR OF DELIGHT

WHOOOOOP.

"Candyfloss!!!!" I hear Fred shout suddenly. **"CAAAAAAAAAANDYFLOOOOOOOOOOSSSSSS!"**

And I can't help it

"Come on, Fred!!"

We chase towards the Fantastical Funfair of Delight. Just a little bit more time. We will go back soon!

"Fred!" I laugh. "Try and catch me!"

"Oh wimble bottoms!" I hear Bundlenugg call out after me. **"FRANKIEEEEEE! YOU NEED TO GO BACK!"**

Fred and I race into the funfair, weaving around all the amusement rides: the Obscure Octopus that gives you ten tickles with its tentacles; the Caramel Carousel, made literally of caramel; the Zipper; the Wipeout; the Flumper Cars with their marshmallow bumpers. We are running on brightly coloured tiles that light up and make noises like, **PAM!, BOOM!, WHOP!, YOU'RE DEADLY!** underfoot as we bound through the funfair towards Lillian Longstring, who is the tallest woman in the whole of Thoughtopolis and even taller than Stuart the Teenager on our road in the Real World – who grew so fast one summer that all his trousers became hot pants.

Lillian is *even* taller.

She is dressed in the suit that she is always dressed in, made entirely of striped twisted liquorice whips and straws. The buttons on her jacket are alternate pink and blue jelly spogs, those aniseed Liquorice Allsorts covered in teeny tiny round dots. I know this because I tried one once. And I am going to try another until Lillian Longstring says, "Actually, would you rather not, please, Frankie? I need to keep my jacket closed for when the lemonade rains come in from the east."

Lillian wanted to be one of those people who rescued cats from the top of very tall trees because it was an obvious career choice for a woman whose legs are the length of six ladders piled one on top of the other. But oddly for Lillian, she is quite scared of heights, and cats, which is quite problematic when you're looking into a career involving heights and cats.

"You see, Frankie, one mess can rather unfortunately lead to another if you're not careful."

I sort of understand this in a weird way. Even though my legs are only the height of one eighth of a ladder.

Lillian's profession found her in the end. Her head brushes against the clouds, which are made of candyfloss.

"Are you still scared of heights, Lillian?" I ask her now.

"Oh, yes, Frankie. But I suppose we're all frightened of something. It's doing your best to understand what that is so you can take the mystery out of it. Once the mystery has been taken out of the very thing you are frightened of, it no longer has more control over you than you have over it."

I think about what I'm frightened of. Spiders, maybe? Those guys really know how to creep up on you despite having **EIGHT** legs. A mushroom falling into my dinner? Nightmares perhaps. But I guess everyone gets nightmares, don't they?

"Now," she says, smiling at me and Fred, "what flavour of candyfloss would you like?"

"A rainbow candyfloss, please, Lillian Longstring!"

I say, my tummy gurgling in anticipation of that spongey crystal deliciousness.

"And one for Fred too!"

"What's the magic word?" Lillian says as she twirls floss around a stick.

"Please?"

"Try again."

"Spaflogamagdooooodleswipedypop?"

"Now you have it!" she beams, handing me two fluffy clouds of candyfloss on sticks.

I've only taken one bite when Fred tugs on my sleeve.

"We have to go, Frankie," he says. "We've been here too long."

Lillian Longstring nods. "I'll save them for you for the next time," she says.

"Yes, please," I say.

"FRANKIE!!!!!" Bundlenugg calls out; something in his tone is different now. **"ENOUGH!"**

He chases after us as best he can. Although it has to be said, heddies don't make the best runners. They are much better at hugs.

Pickle was at his heels. "Frankie, Fred, you *must* go home now," Pickle warns.

"I'm tired now, Frankie," Fred says.

"Me too," I say, fighting off a yawn.

The sky overhead is dusky now and the trees stand like statues around us, playing hide and seek in the dark.

"Frankie," Bundlenugg says, out of breath. "Have you had quite enough fun for now?"

I kick at the ground. It's getting harder and harder to leave Thoughtopolis after every visit. The temptation to stay longer is even stronger.

"It's time for you to go home," he says, bundling past us towards the same door we arrived here through. We watch as he tries to open it.

"What are you doing, Bundlenuggie?" Fred asks.

"I'm ... checking ... that ... it ... is ... still ... going ... to ... **OPEN!!**" he puffs rather laboriously, each word getting louder with every tug. On the final yank, the door flies open, almost knocking Bundlenugg on to his bum. As it does, everything around us flashes and crackles and sparks a little, as though there is an electrical wire blowing.

"I can see lightning strikes up there, Frankie," Fred says and I follow his gaze, spotting it in the sky too.

"Oh, wimble bottoms!" Bundlenugg says exasperatedly. "I was afraid this was going to happen."

He turns to me, serious now. "You need to listen to me, Frankie."

"I'm listening," I say.

"She's listening," Fred says.

"We're listening," Blue says. "And I can hear things seven times louder than humans so I'm really **REALLY** listening."

"Me too," Pickle agrees, and I wonder if Pickle might be in danger of making herself deaf seeing as her voice is so big and her ears are so small.

"I need to talk to you about … something," Bundlenugg begins.

Ugh! This *"something"* again.

"But," I say, "that's what I love about Thoughtopolis! I can escape! All the adults in the Real World want to 'talk to me about *something*', but here I don't need to!"

Another lightning bolt appears as if from nowhere and looks to almost split the sky in two.

I chuckle, trying to sound cool and not in the slightest bit anxious. But I am anxious and a little parp escapes.

I turn to blame Blue.

Having a dog to blame when puffs of air escape your body is very, very handy.

"Wasn't me," Blue says defensively.

Oh, yeah. Except when your dog can talk.

"Frankie, I'm giving you a warning. If you stay too long in Thoughtopolis at any one time, you will have trouble getting back out and back in again."

The door. I look at the door. Is that why it was so stiff? Have I been here too long?

The thought of not being able to get in here when I want to makes me feel even more troubled. I *need* Thoughtopolis. It's the only place where things make sense.

"That is why the sky is sparking. Your brain is getting overloaded, Frankie. Go back to the Real World. Get some rest. Hug your mum and dad. Eat a vegetable."

Ugh.

"You know we love having you here," Pickle says. "But you must tread carefully, Frankie."

They can't find out. No one in the Real World can find out! Bundlenugg and Pickle are right.

My goodness, in all the fun I had almost forgotten the responsibility I have keeping this very special secret.

And secrets about magic are even more doubly-triply-flipply special.

I nod with a renewed sense of purpose.

"OK, Fred! Blue! Let's go!"

We turn on our heels as the skies grow darker again.

"Frankie," Bundlenugg calls. I turn to him. He is twisting his hands together like he's worried about something. Pickle's ears are flat to her head.

"Scrub behind Fred's ears, I know, I know!" I say, trying to lighten the mood.

"You have figured out how *you* get to Thoughtopolis. Next, you must figure out *why*. And this will be the start of your true journey here. We've been having lots of fun, but ... it's time."

"It's time," Pickle repeats.

"There's a why you can't deny and there's always time for a rhyme when you do indeed know that it's time."

"Forgive me," Blue interjects, "but I *am* getting a clear sense that, perhaps ... it might be time?"

And then it's like all the leaves whisper it too as they shake in the breeze around us.

"IT'S TIME."

"IT'S TIME."

"IT'S TIME."

"IT'S TIME!"

A heronder squawks somewhere overhead, sending a shiver down my spine. I watch as its shadow drifts through the inky sky.

"Frankie? **FRANKIE?**" Fred calls in the dark. "I'm scared."

"There's no need to be scared," I say, reaching for his hand. "I'm with you."

And we leave. Out through the door, past some pink squishy brain matter, through the eyeball and **WHOMP!!!!**

"Frankie? **FRANKIE??**"

Dad is saying my name over and over.

"FRANKIE??"

He's closer now as I rub my eyes.

I look around. Where am I? Lying on the couch in our living room at home.

"Frankie," Dad says, sitting beside me. "You must have fallen into a deep sleep. You've been out cold!"

"Wh-where's Gr-Annie?"

"Gr-Annie?" Dad says, looking confused. I see him steal a quick glance at Mum. "She dropped you home hours ago, Frankie."

My goodness, how long have I been gone?

"She said you had been very quiet. Are you ... OK?"

"I think..." I mumble, "I think I'm just tired."

I feel Blue place a little paw on my leg, and I put my hand over it.

Not a word about the snorkling and the bubblebum balloon rides and the pigeon flight and the ferris wheel, OK Blue?

Blue blinks at me, because dogs can't wink. And it's definitely either a wink with two eyes (the best he can do), or he's simply blinking because that's what you do with eyeballs. I'll ask him the next time we're in Thoughtopolis.

"Come on, Frankie," Dad says. "It's bedtime."

I head up the stairs to my room, Blue following me. And I can't help thinking about a few things:

A) The lightning short circuit before we left
B) The heronders
C) The door that became stiff and difficult to open
D) Bundlenugg talking about the **WHY** of Thoughtopolis
E) The mysterious Sixthwisp
F) And the beginning of this even mysteriouser "journey"

I'm about to put **G)** on my list, which I'm pretty sure has something to do with pigeons, when I'm distracted by Mum and Dad mumbling in the kitchen.

They are talking in furtive mutters, but I can make out some of it.

"She's getting more and more distracted. It's like she's not here at all sometimes!" Mum says.

OH, WIMBLE BOTTOMS! Are they starting to suspect something?

"I know." Dad sighs. "Do you think maybe … it's time?"

I close my eyes and silent-scream.

Everyone is saying it's time!!

TIME FOR WHAT??!!!!!!!

CHAPTER SEVENTEEN

THE UNFORTUNATE SECRET BISCUIT MUNCHING INCIDENT

The best part of magic is how cool and awesome and exciting and wondrous it is. Obviously. The very worst part of magic is ... ADULTS.

Being an adult is an unfortunate condition that happens to kids when they are around for a certain amount of time. Sort of like a pear in a fruit bowl that goes all wrinkly after a while. And there is literally NOTHING you can do about it. All those creams they layer on their faces to help keep them young? They still end up with the same result: being an adult. It's the pits.

And the worst thing about being an adult? Apart from having to watch the news instead of cartoons and not being able to cartwheel in public? The worst thing, as I have noted before, is that they rarely believe in magic any more.

They believe in *facts*. Logic. Common sense. All of these seem like the opposite of magic.

I'm not sure at what point this happens. Perhaps it's when humans go through the teenage metamorphosis with the greasy hair and the grunting and come out the other end as adults ready to pay bills and organize play dates and watch the news even though it makes them miserable. Sort of like the life cycle of a butterfly, but backwards. Because the butterfly is the *best* bit, and that's what being a kid is like. Free and fancy and full of colour and wonder and adventure. No offence, but adults are more like the larvae. They have their butterfly moments, of course. Mum looks great when she brushes her hair and wears cool fun jewellery. Same when Dad shaves his stubble and wears a jumper that isn't grey.

I think about it all through dinner the next night, as I eat leftover lasagne and Dad says things like, "Did you see the news?" and Mum says things like, "Yes, wasn't it awful?"

Why does the news always have to tell you the bad bits?

The Thoughtopolis News Station run by anchor Felicity Joybubble only ever reports on good news stories

"And today, some wonderful news just in — a certain eight-year-old boy Fred Finkleton has won gold in the Keepie-Uppies Competition. Five hundred keepie-uppies! His knees must be wrecked, but we aren't going to focus on that, just on the fact that he won! Yahooo!"

Fred doesn't like lasagne as much as I do so he always has plain pasta with butter and cheese and mince which sounds a lot like a lasagne just split up into different bits.

"How's your lasagne, Frankie?" Dad asks.

"Uhmm, it's good, thank you."

"I always think lasagne tastes better the second night because there's no cooking involved." Mum smiles.

I look over at Flo, who locks eyes with me, grabs a fistful of lasagne and slowly reaches over the side of her highchair and throws it on the floor.

The savagery! I wouldn't even do that to a dinner *with mushrooms*!

I probably shouldn't call my parents larvae because I really do love them really. Like really *really*.

I've read about mean parents in books: parents who shout a lot and never allow things like hugs or laughter or flakes in your ice cream. But my mum and dad are fun and kind, with glinty bright eyes, squeezy hugs and loud bouncy laughs. Or at least they used to be.

They used to have a bit of sparkle to them. Way more than my friends' parents. My mum and dad used to be happy and funny and told jokes and made dens for us with duvets and cushions and brought us on adventures and just made life that little bit ... sparklier. They were like larvae with little teeny tiny butterfly wings. Not as magical and colourful and patterned as mine and Fred's, but still there nonetheless.

All of this went away when a certain Flo Felicity Finkleton arrived.

UGGGGHHHHHHHHHHHHHHH.

You see, Flo is at the egg stage of the metamorphosis. The most irritating stage of all. Babies are *not* like children. Not. One. Bit.

155

Their brains haven't developed enough to believe in magic. All they believe in is crying and not sleeping and throwing food across the room and taking all your parents' attention and destroying your life as you formerly knew it and pooing in their own clothes.

Honestly, whoever invented babies should take a long hard look at themselves. (I know I was a baby myself once, but I am choosing to believe I slept all day and all night from day one and silently got on with growing my teeth instead of shouting and whingeing about it.)

Anyway, I eat my lasagne and listen to my parents talking about the awful price of something and the awful way some guy who ruled a country spoke to the other lady who ruled a different one as I look at how awfully Flo is treating some poor innocent bits of lasagne. Then I help Mum clear up.

Everything seems normal, if a bit grey and boring, until Mum asks me a really odd question.

"Frankie, I was thinking..." Mum starts.

Uh oh. Bad things happen when adults do that.

I turn to look at her, dying to be upstairs doing some maths problems from my homework instead, which is really saying something.

"I was wondering if you might like to go to visit Granny for a bit?"

"Oh, yes! Can I go now? I was going to try and French plait the top of Granny's dog's hair. I think it would really suit her!"

"No, honey," Mum interrupts. "Not Gr-Annie. I meant Granny Doris."

Mic drop.

Silence.

And then Flo farts.

"I... why, I don't..." My words fall away to nothing.

"You haven't seen her in ages. And she misses you, you know. She's been asking after you."

"But she's really far away," I say, not even bringing the potato problem into the equation!

"I think it might be nice for—" Mum starts.

"I need to get my homework done," I say flatly, leaving the room.

I sit in my bedroom for what feels like ages. It really shouldn't take forty minutes to multiply forty-eight by twelve, but that's exactly how distracted I am.

First they talk about extra classes after school, and now they want to send me off to Granny Doris for goodness knows how long!

I give up on forty-eight multiplied by twelve and sneak downstairs for a snack. It has never been scientifically proven, but one of my ongoing investigations, "Chocolate Biscuits Definitely Help You To Do Your Homework Faster", has a lot of mounting evidence.

I know they definitely don't mean for me to overhear this next bombshell. They don't know I have snuck into the pantry while they sit over on the couch chatting.

I have performed many secret investigations in here over the years. All for different research purposes. Sometimes to investigate whether or not any biscuits are about to go off that need to be disposed of. Into my mouth.

I am very selfless like that. Fred often assists me on these investigations because sometimes he needs to stand on my shoulders so we can reach the top-tier biscuits.

We are incredibly nimble and stealthy.

Mum and Dad continue chatting as I continue munching. At first I assume they are talking about the awful fuel prices on the news again.

I feel bad for eavesdropping, but it's really difficult not to listen when you're stuck in a cupboard mid-biscuit investigation and the adults don't realize you are in there and they start having A Very Serious Discussion. Also, having carried out a number of these investigations, Fred and I KNOW how difficult it is to eat biscuits quietly.

There is no way out.

I bravely make my way through eight and a half chocolate hobnobs to pass the time while under cupboard hostage. That's how long and serious the serious discussion is. Eight and half biscuits long. And counting! I can't catch everything because chewing crunchy biscuits is a very loud operation as all the action happens RIGHT BESIDE YOUR EARS. But I catch enough.

Most of what they are saying I've heard before.

"... just that I'm tired."

"I know. We're doing our best ... trying to juggle so much..."

"It doesn't seem to be getting any better...'

"... she's getting more and more distracted..."

"I feel sorry for Flo in all of this..."

I silent-shriek. Flo and her pamper evenings? Me being signed up for extra classes after school?? And they feel sorry for HER?!

" ... if she wasn't finding things so hard..."

And then Mum says it.

"It's like..." She's sighing now: a heavy, weighted sigh. I stop crunching momentarily. "It's like ... something is missing. I know..." – crunch crunch – "Frankie feels it. It's like" – CRUNCH – "she's lost her spark. We all have."

CRUNCH.

No way! *Me*? I AM FINE! I'm one of the sparkliest people I know, apart from Fred. OK, maybe I'm finding it harder to show that on the outside, but I have *plenty* of spark! PLENTY! I'm so sparkly I'm magic, for goodness' sake! I want to burst out of the pantry to tell them that. I AM OK. But all my thoughts and words feel floaty like balloons on strings that I can't get a grip of as they drift out of reach. I also have a lot of biscuits in my mouth so it's sort of tricky to say ANYTHING.

Instead, I swallow hard. The backlog of chocolate biscuits is piling up and they suddenly can't get past a giant lump that has formed in my throat. The lump is causing a serious biscuit traffic jam.

And then the WEIRDEST thing happens. I START CRYING.

It's so weird because I don't even feel sad? Maybe a bit worried for Mum and Dad because they have this all wrong, but not sad.

It's as though my eyes are like heavily-soaked sponges that someone else is squeezing all the water out of. I have no power over it. And as soon as they refill, they are wrung out again over and over until I look down and what's left of the biscuits in my hands is one big soggy mess.

I think about how Tess is bored of me. And I think of Monica, Veronica and Nell laughing and whispering about me for ever and ever, until I'm an old lady eating scones in a rocking chair with noise cancelling headphones like the builders wear to block out the sound. But I'm still a little bit sparkly, aren't I?

Aren't I?

It's then I realize Mum and Dad have gone quiet. I can tell they are still there because I can hear them breathing and my mum is making funny snuffling sounds like she's crying very softly. Then my dad speaks.

"Our Frankie is not the same Frankie. Her spark has definitely been taken."

Silence.

WHHHAAAAAAAAAAT?!!!

Whoa now! This is new information!!

TAKEN??!!

I feel something/someone crawl in beside me in the dark. This might sound like the opening of a horror film, but I'm not scared; it's normally Fred or Blue.

A little paw creeps into my hand. It's Blue. And then he starts a high-pitched nasal whine. It's like he's saying, "Giiiiiiiiiiive meeeeeeee biiiiiiiiiiiiiiscuits!"

"Shhhhhhhh, Blue. Not now. I need to listen for clues," I say. "Someone has stolen my spark."

The great investigator of 34 Cottage Orchard Road has herself been ROBBED? I feel foolish and angry and confused all at once. Where has it gone? Who has it? More to the point: WHO has robbed it? Was it Flo?

Dun

DUN

DUUUUUUUUUUUUN.

This is the bit in the horror movie when the baddie is revealed. And in this case it's a tiny villain in a deceptively adorable pink fluffy bear outfit. THE WORST KIND. The kind that will trick you every time. *Especially* the ones whose hair twists into fluffy curls after a bath. Their excessive cuteness is their villainous superpower for getting away with doing all the shady stuff.

But she can't fool me any more!

Flo is my number one chief suspect.

Private investigators might sit the suspect down and deny rice cakes and bottles of warm milk until they start giving answers.

But there are a few obvious flaws to this plan:

a) Flo can't speak.

b) Flo can't sit on chairs without falling off to one side.

c) It's probably a bit illegal to question a ten-month-old.

I sit on the pantry floor, covered in soggy biscuit crumbs. I wonder how much longer I can sit here before the pins and needles climb up from my feet all the way to my brain.

162

"I've been thinking that maybe Frankie should go away for a bit," I hear Mum say. My tummy lurches as I crane to listen.

I start to feel a little bit sick, if I'm honest.

"Where to?" Dad asks quietly.

There's a silence.

"Granny Doris?"

GRANNY DORIS!!!! Not this again! Now she's told Dad, it feels like they might actually make it happen.

And what does she mean "go away for a bit?" FOR A BIT? I figured she meant a visit. Not a full stint! How long is "for a bit"??

More villain music. Granny Doris is not a villain per se, but she does talk about the weather for twelve and a half hours a day and eats potatoes at every single meal. EVERY SINGLE meal!

She has chopped up potatoes and milk instead of cereal in the morning. She says she only does that when she's out of bran flakes, but I think that's just a convenient excuse.

Everything in Granny Doris's house has a pattern on it: the carpet, the walls, the curtains, the ceilings, and it's hard not to look at them all without feeling a tiny bit nauseous. She obsesses about the right time to dry her giant knickers the size of tepee tents on her washing line and she has no toys or anything interesting to play with. She once asked me if I was bored did I think it would be fun to stack her plates in order of size from biggest to smallest?

163

I was so bored that I did exactly that, and I can confirm that it is not a very exciting thing to do.

Fred found an old pair of Granny Doris's tights once and we put them over our heads which made our noses squish up into two giant nostrils and we both laughed until we realized our faces were close to where Granny Doris's bum would be if she was wearing the tights and then we started to cry.

She rang my dad recently to say she had a very interesting book all about the different types of potatoes in the world and how to cook them, and perhaps we could sit down and read it together for something different to do.

I CANNOT GO TO GRANNY DORIS'S!!

I find I'm crying again. Really crying.

Crying quietly is difficult when you've always enjoyed running around giving in to loud wails with your arms flailing wildly, or flinging yourself on to a couch dramatically.

I've always been a believer in the idea that if you're going to do something, then you might as well give it your all.

They don't want me any more. They don't want me or Fred now they have their evil villain baby.

I have to fix this. I HAVE to.

"Let's give her another week, see how she is," Dad says quietly. "But maybe you're right. Maybe a bit of distance would do her some good."

"Why don't we wait until Friday and then make a decision?" Mum says, sniffling.

"OK, Friday it is," Dad says.

I feel my eyes fill up again, like my eyeballs are little baths and someone has left the taps on.

I REALLY REALLY HAVE TO FIX THIS!

I am practically a private investigator for goodness' sake!

OK, think, Frankie, THINK!

So a few things I know for sure at this point:

a) Flo has initiated stage one of her wicked plan to drive out the pre-existing and superior children from the home.

b) I am NOT going to stay with Granny Doris. It involves too many miles and too many potatoes.

c) In order for Mum and Dad not to send me to Granny Doris, I have to find my spark.

d) I have to figure out why my spark is gone.

e) I now know how to silent cry, which is probably a cool life hack thing anyway?

f) Do I need a warrant to search Flo's bedroom?

g) Probably not.

h) This is now a very long list.

i) Why was this all coming at the same time that Bundlenugg

had gotten all serious and said I needed to go on some
mysterious journey?

j) I'm going to have to put in some extra investigating
shifts, even though I already have a pretty packed
schedule as it is.

k) I need to figure out how to turn my eyeball taps off or I'm
going to get dangerously dehydrated.

l) I'M GOING TO FIND MY MISSING SPARK BECAUSE I
AM NOT GOING TO STAY WITH GRANNY DORIS A
ZILLION MILES AWAY.

CHAPTER EIGHTEEN

THE HUNT FOR THE MISSING SPARK BEGINS, BUM CREAM, STOLEN TEDDIES AND OTHER THINGS

Flo has *clearly* stolen my spark. And, in stealing mine, made Mum and Dad sad. Even though they will *still* take *her* side because she has chubby thighs and dimples in her knuckles which they seem to find utterly irresistible.

It must be her! Everything was fine until she showed up.

At last Mum and Dad stop their ominous conversation and go off and I can finally leave the pantry. I have to find Flo and discover what she's done with my spark.

I can hear her in the distance somewhere – laughing! Bouncing in her bouncy thing and cackling away because her plots to destroy EVERYTHING are finally coming good!

Fred will be in his room doing his homework and Blue has probably gone outside to do a nervous wee.

I creep down the hall, magnifying glass in hand, and peer around the corner into the living room. Flo is in her walker – I hear running water upstairs. It must be almost time for Fred's bath. Mum or Dad will be back any minute.

I shift closer. Flo turns around instantly, like she has the supersonic hearing of a ninja bat, and stares me straight in the eye.

We glare at each other in silence.

And then ... she *smiles!*

I whip back around the corner and pin myself to the wall, tucking my magnifying glass into the back pocket of my jeans and thinking about what my next move might be.

What a *BADDIE!* The baddies who try to befriend you are the WORST! That's no ordinary smile. It's the kind of smile the suave villain gives before he plunges you into a tank full of sharks or RELEASES A NEST OF WASPS IN YOUR FACE.

Power has clearly gone to her head. It's because she's encouraged to be lazy. She just sits in her buggy all day, being chauffeured around the place like a tiny bald queen in a onesie. Then she gets home, and it's: *feed me this, give me that, lift me up, wipe my bum, carry me across the room and place me on that cushion. Now!*

Lazy, power mad. And also a thief.

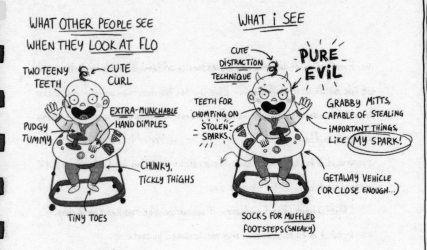

WHAT OTHER PEOPLE SEE WHEN THEY LOOK AT FLO

TWO TEENY TEETH — CUTE CURL

EXTRA-MUNCHABLE HAND DIMPLES

PUDGY TUMMY

CHUNKY, TICKLY THIGHS

TINY TOES

WHAT I SEE

CUTE DISTRACTION TECHNIQUE

PURE EVIL

TEETH FOR CHOMPING ON STOLEN SPARKS

GRABBY MITTS, CAPABLE OF STEALING IMPORTANT THINGS LIKE (MY SPARK!)

GETAWAY VEHICLE (OR CLOSE ENOUGH...)

SOCKS FOR MUFFLED FOOTSTEPS (SNEAKY)

This is too much.

This has gone too far.

However, I know where she is — and she isn't in her room. Which means I can search it.

I run up the stairs two at a time. I fling the door open and stare around the room. Cot, mobile, cuddly toys, changing mat. Weird sheep that plays a tune. So far, so innocuous. But that's what a villain would want you to think.

I comb the scene for clues. Nothing except bum cream, pyjamas and more fluffy teddies. Teddy after teddy—

Wait.

I recognize one of these teddies. It's *Fred's* teddy! Ms P! Old and battered but still cute and ready for snugs. I lift it to my nose. It smells of Fred.

SNIFF! SNIFF!

I shake my head, a grim smile on my lips. Not only has Flo stolen my spark, she's also stolen Ms P. Blue chases in after me and I bend down to let him sniff Ms P. Sniffing for Blue is a lot harder than most investigator dogs as his airways are so tiny, and he almost faints after giving the teddy a decent sniffing.

I should probably give him a raise. He is doing his best at the job. I'll up his doggie biscuits to three a day.

"That's right, Blue," I whisper. "Robbed. In broad daylight probably."

I stand in Flo's bedroom and think some thoughts:

a) Is it crazy that I am looking for a spark in my baby sister's room?! I mean, a spark is one of those things you *hear* about, but you don't ever really *see.* Like the Easter Bunny or everlasting gobstoppers.

b) I'm actually quite looking forward to Easter now that I think about it. I'm a big fan of chocolate.

c) What IS a spark? Sort of a thing inside you; a thing that makes you glittery in your soul?

d) Which means it's inside me. And what else is inside me?

e) Thoughtopolis is inside me!

f) OH MY GOSH, THOUGHTOPOLIS WILL HAVE THE ANSWERS TO WHERE THE LOST SPARK IS BECAUSE THIS IS ALL THE SORT OF STUFF THAT HAPPENS ON THE INSIDE!

g) I AM SPEAKING IN CAPITALS AGAIN BECAUSE THIS IS VERY SERIOUS AND URGENT BECAUSE...

h) GRANNY DORIS, ETC.

i) POTATOES, ETC., ETC., ETC.

j) NOT TO MENTION TIGHTS ON HEADS.

k) CHOCOLATE OVER POTATOES EVERY TIME.

l) I ONLY HAVE UNTIL FRIDAY TO FIND MY SO-CALLED SPARK.

m) ALSO, DOES BUNDLENUGG KNOW? IS THAT WHAT THIS JOURNEY WAS ABOUT? TO FIND IT?? WAS THAT THE WHY?

"Fred!" I call out, jumping to action. "GET READY! WE ARE GOING ON A VERY IMPORTANT MISSION!"

CHAPTER NINETEEN

TRYING TO SOLVE A MYSTERY WITH POST-ITS ALONE IS NOT AS EASY AS THEY MAKE IT LOOK ON THE TELLY

I, Frankle Finkleton, am on a mission. A mission against time. A secret undercover mission that no one can uncover.

Except me. But I think you already get that bit.

Well, and Fred. And Blue.

I gather my team around me to talk through the mission. I use a serious, tough voice so they know it's serious and tough. And we assemble in the Finkleton HQ tepee tent in the corner of my bedroom, which always adds an air of formality.

"I know we think Thoughtopolis is a fun adventure land that we can escape to when the adults get all serious and school is extra boring," I tell them. "But now we need to go there for another reason.

Other than fun, I mean. We have questions that need answers."

I'm out of the tepee now and pacing around my bedroom. I need to get things clear in my head before I go back to Thoughtopolis because it's so fun there that I might easily get distracted by watermelon candyfloss, flying on a pigeon, chasing tiny hedgehogs around the Teeny Tiny Forest, riding a llama down the main street or scuba-diving in the mouth of a giant whale. (He is a vegan and flosses quite regularly so this is not a) dangerous, or b) gross.)

"Bundlenugg said it himself," I reason, furrowing my eyebrows in deep thought. "Just last night. The next time you come back ... the real journey starts."

HE MUST KNOW SOMETHING!

I click my fingers.

"Fred, we've always thought that Bundlenugg was important. And now I think we were right – I think he might be our *actual mentor!* FOR A MISSION!"

If a light bulb could go off over my head, this would have been the moment. Where is the Thoughtopolis Lightbulb Emporium when you need it?

I look at my private investigator swivel lamp on my desk. It flickers slightly. Hmmmm.

Everything is starting to feel very mysterious indeed.

Right. Action!

"Fred, I'm going to write my clues on post-its and then stick them on the wall and stand back and look at them with my hands on my hips and say, 'Hmmmmmmmm,' like they do on TV when they are trying to solve things."

173

I did that, but unfortunately it didn't get me very far.

All I have is the following...

- My spark is gone
- Journey? ⟶ Bundlenugg
- Biscuits?
- When it needs to all be solved by: close of business FRIDAY
  or else ⟶ my own personal potato hell!

I check my magnifying glass is still in my jeans pocket, then I start shoving pens and my notepad into my backpack.

"Mum and Dad want to get rid of us. They want to send me away to live with Granny Doris because I've 'lost my spark'. You lost a fiver down a drain once and they didn't threaten to send you away to live with someone who was born when the whole world was black and white and everyone only ever ate the same beige vegetable. I know you like chips and chips are made from potatoes, Fred, but" – I pause and inhale dramatically – "I can't live like that!"

I zip up my backpack; it's full of everything we need for our expedition. I have one final thing to do before we head off.

I kneel down again, placing my head flat to the carpet and feel around in the darkness under my bed. Ah ha, there it is! My Incredibly Badly Named Secret Book Of Secrets I Still Haven't Renamed Because I Am Very VERY Busy.

I pull it out from under the bed, open it up and read over all my secrets again, making sure to add in one more.

Secret Number 14: *I am now on a secret journey, quite possibly to find my spark. Wish me luck!*

I slam the notebook closed and fling it back under my bed.

So many secrets.

So much magic.

So little time.

"Right! Fred! Blue! We are ready to go!"

I take a deep breath.

"Fred, we need to show them we are OK. We are still ... you know ... sparkly. Before they get rid of us both."

Something funny happens then. I start feeling an odd sense of doubt in my tummy. Fear creeps up my spine. I have never once been scared of going to Thoughtopolis before. What if nobody knows anything about my spark? What if I can't locate it? What if the heronders are around? What if the door gets stuck? What if this journey is ... scary?

I push away those feelings. Because right now? Right *now* I need to be brave.

I close my eyes and take another deep breath.

"OK, Fred, you ready? LET'S GO!!"

CHAPTER TWENTY

WHEN IT'S NEITHER DAY NOR NIGHTTIME, IT IS HARD TO SEE THINGS CLEARLY

Annnnnnnnd…

In through the eyeball, down to the right, turn left past the brain matter, second door on the right, three burps, "*Fibbleswizzle1234*"…

WE ARE BACK! I look around for Bundlenugg.

It's quite dark, like it's neither daytime but also not quite night, like a dusky haze is making it just that little bit more difficult to see things clearly.

For the first time ever, Bundlenugg isn't here to greet us as we come through the door. Where is he? Right when I really, *really* need to talk to him.

"Frankie?" Fred asks. "Do you think we'll make it into *The Spy Monthly* if we find the missing spark?"

"Hmmm, this is a good point, Fred. I would hope so. They might even take our photo so no bubblegum in or behind the ears for the next week, OK?"

"OK," he answers, like that might be a bit tricky for him.

I normally hate *The Spy Monthly*. That ridiculous spy magazine that Mum's friend Margery Lonergan brings over for afternoon tea on the last Thursday of every month. Margery Lonergan isn't even really Mum's friend. She's our neighbour!

Like when I sat next to Audrey Nolan in class one year, so everyone assumed we *should* be best friends, but all she did was wipe snot on the desk and rob my markers.

Not the foundations of a solid lasting friendship.

I'd be appalled if Margery Lonergan was wiping snot on our kitchen table; I mean, to be fair, that isn't really her vibe. She wouldn't have the time to pick her nose because her nose is always stuck in other people's business! Margery Lonergan is obsessed with what is going on in other people's lives. Being nosy is her main hobby, after being annoying.

The Spy Monthly would be a cool magazine if it reported on cool investigations like whether aliens ever land from the moon and sit on your window sill to look in at you while you sleep, or whether or not kids' toys have parties when their owners are in school.

Both are ongoing investigations of mine. I have set *a lot* of traps.

(So far Blu-Tack, double-sided sticky tape, half-licked lollipops do not work.)

Not articles like: *Local Man Suspected of Putting His Dog's Poo in Someone Else's Bin.*

Margery Lonergan writes in **EVERY** last Thursday of the month with stuff like: *I saw Basil Mungan and his dog down at the local shop and both of them looked very shifty. I said, "Mr Mungan, isn't the weather awful?" He replied, "It's cats and dogs, Margery Lonergan; I would go as far as to say it's **RUBBISH**." And if that, fellow scrupulous readers, isn't enough damning evidence, I do not know what is.*

She is such a snitch!

Imagine if Fred and I ended up on the cover of *The Spy Monthly*, though! For uncovering the case of the missing spark! That would be pretty cool. It wasn't Flo who took my spark after all, but I just know she's involved somehow. A criminal mastermind like her has to be operating other shady goings on. She put a tenner in the washing machine once and Dad joked that she was involved in "money laundering" and I wasn't sure what this meant exactly, but it sounded like a crime to me.

I bet Margery will be furious *she* wasn't the one to solve the mystery of the missing spark.

"Any news, Frankie?" she always says, stirring her tea slowly, her nose twitching, eyes like lasers. "What's going on in that little head of yours, eh?"

HA! Wouldn't she like to know?

"Frankie," says Fred now, digging the toe of his trainers into the golden sand of Thoughtopolis. (There is always golden sand at least once a week – the deserts like to move around.) "Can I ask you something? And will you promise to be honest?"

I remember another of Bundlenugg's riddles: *a jumble of feelings in the mind, like shifting sands to beat the bands, and never just one of a kind.* He says it's your thoughts and feelings that are constantly changing, and it can often feel like no two are ever really the same. I understand that. Especially when things feel particularly jumbled in my head.

"What's up, Fred?" I ask, putting an arm around him. I am just the right amount taller than him to rest my arm around his shoulders.

I hate it when Fred is solemn. It doesn't suit him. And it makes me worry.

Because the job I take most seriously in the whole world, way more than being a part-time private investigator or Blue's personal dancing skills trainer, is being Fred's big sister.

He hesitates, then says, "Is it OK if I smile on the cover of *The Spy Monthly* like this?"

He unleashes a huge beam and I burst out laughing.

Fred has more gaps than he has teeth and I sometimes wonder how on earth he manages to eat an apple.

He is a marvel of human science.

"Smile however you want! Come on, Fred! We need to find this missing spark! Then Mum and Dad might be happier and we can all be a happy sparkly family again!"

We shut the door behind us and I open it again, just to test it. It doesn't feel too stiff. Yet.

"LET'S GO!" Fred says.

"Bundlenugg? Bundlenugg, where are you?" we call, following the winding path deep into the heart of Thoughtopolis once more.

CHAPTER TWENTY-ONE

THE SHIFTING SANDS

"BUNDLENUGG?!" I call as we set off over the dunes. "Are you here?"

Things feel, sound and look different. Normally the sun is shining, drenching everything in a beautiful golden light. Today everything is blanketed in a grey fog. And the shifting sands have made the familiar landscape appear altered. I can't hear the birds chirping. And it feels colder now.

"Pickle?" Blue calls.

"Hello?" Fred shouts as I watch him leave footprints in the sand ahead. The sands shift again and the footprints disappear.

"OUCH!!" Fred suddenly yelps.

"What is it, Fred?" I run to catch up with him.

He has his finger in his mouth and when he takes it out I see a blob of blood on his fingertip.

"There are cactuses, Frankie, stuck in the sand. You need to look out for them."

I take a tissue out of my backpack and wrap it around his finger, grinning at him. This is what I've always known. Minding my little brother.

"Hey, Frankie, wanna hear a joke?" Fred asks.

"I do," Blue answers. "Things seem to have got a little serious around here."

Fred smiles. "I know there's something wrong with my cactus. I just can't put my finger on it."

"Boom! Fred Finkleton, ladies and gentlemen, he's here all week."

I smile at Fred. In his own way, he knows how to mind me too.

Just then I hear a familiar bell ring. Something ringing a bell in my brain!

"Hello?" I call into the twilight.

"Schnnnnoooogenfluuupleschmig!" the thing replies in the half-dark.

"Frankie! Look! It's a squidgenflidge!" Fred exclaims, pointing to the top of a nearby flagpole. The squidgenflidge is ringing the bell confidently.

So it is, I think. What just rang the bell in my head? That Fred is here all week? **ALL WEEK! I HAVE ONE WEEK TO FIND MY SPARK! LESS THAN ONE WEEK! I HAVE THIS WEEK! I HAVE UNTIL FRIDAY!**

"Come on, Fred, we gotta go," I say. I address the squidgenflidge up at the top of the pole. "Excuse me, Madam … squidgenflidge? Have you seen Bundlenugg?"

"*Bibblebobbledanglesnap!*" it replies.

Whatever does that mean?

"It means" – I hear a voice coming from somewhere – "he's over there behind that miniature watermelon gumdrop tree."

I turn and see Bundlenugg stepping out from behind a miniature watermelon gumdrop tree.

"Frankie!" he says. "You made it back OK."

"Of course we did." I feel my eyebrows furrow. "Is everything all right, Bundlenugg?"

"If you have painted things to be a certain way, they can often appear to be OK, that is until the very day, you realize that something is not."

"That doesn't—" Blue starts.

"Rhyme, I know," Pickle answers, trotting out from behind the miniature watermelon gumdrop tree. Her voice shakes the tree a little, loosening some gumdrops from the branches. We dust the sand from them and pop them into our mouths. They are delicious, like little fruity glass marbles. "It's been … busy here since you left. He hasn't had much sleep."

"I'm sorry I couldn't meet you at the door, Frankie," Bundlenugg fumbles in a fuddle. "I've been trying to, well … manage things." He takes off his hat and fans his face with it. **"WIMBLE BOTTOMS!!"**

Bundlenugg looks extra fumbly and bumbly.

What is going on?

"Bundlenugg, we need to talk," I say authoritatively.

"Indeed we do, Frankie," he answers with a sigh. "It's time."

WHAT'S TIME?!!!

"Come along, Frankie, and Fred, and Blue, and Pickle," Bundlenugg instructs before bursting into a scurry of flying sand as he scarpers off.

"Come on, Fred," I say, offering my hand. "It's *time* apparently."

I try to smile, but something stops me, or won't let me. And I can sense something else that I'm not entirely sure I understand. But it's there. Is this the mysterious Sixthwisp the others had spoken of?

CHAPTER TWENTY-TWO

SOMETHING BLEW!
(NOT BLUE!*)

*PHEW!

"Frankie?" Fred asks, trotting beside me. "I have a feeling we are not going to make it to the ConfooZ Zoo today, are we?"

"No!" I say. "No time for the zoo today."

"Pity. I have zotters to feed."

"Not today, Fred."

"And I have a meeting with the brain sturgeon to discuss my dreams."

"Not today, Fred!"

"*And* I need to test out my latest invention, the bubblegum that never gathers fluff no matter how long it lives in your belly button!"

"NOT TODAY, FRED!"

He sighs. I smile at him as we walk. Fred is always looking for the fun in things. What a fabulous way to see and be in the world. Like he's glued together with *joie de vivre*. I learnt this word in Gr-Annie's book. Even though it's three words and is actually French, I think it's used in English too. I wonder if the English language people were tired that day of making up words for things and one of them said, "Sure, we'll just borrow a French one; it sounds good!" Translated, *joie de vivre* means "an exuberant enjoyment of life". That's Fred's special spark.

But what's mine?

And more to the point, *where* is mine?

We run to try and keep up with Bundlenugg and Pickle, but it's difficult as the sands keep shifting and changing.

"What do you think is going on, Frankie?" Fred asks, running beside me.

I haven't the faintest idea!

I can feel the cactus — cactuses, cactusi? Never mind! — the cactus things scratching at my legs as we run. Uphill now. Against the pull of gravity as we charge forward behind Bundlenugg.

What's happening? Where's he going? Why does Thoughtopolis feel so … different?

I hear a heronder squawk somewhere in the distance and I grab Fred's hand.

"I've got you, Fred."

"And I've got you, Frankie."

Finally, after what feels like for ever and no time at all, Bundlenugg stops at the highest peak of the very tallest sand dune. We all hold each others' shoulders as we try to catch our breath.

This is more difficult for dogs as they have four shoulders and it gets awkward, so Blue and Pickle just sort of stand there panting.

We turn and look down. The dune towers over the whole of Thoughtopolis. Normally, even at night, you would be able to see the twinkling lights of the Thoughtopolis Metropolis below. But standing here now, we look down on to a pitch-black nothing.

I take out my magnifying glass and look around. Nothing but blackness as far as the eye can see.

I just want things to go back to the way they were. Why does everything have to change? Why does Thoughtopolis have to change?

"Frankie," Bundlenugg says, a worried tone linking his words, "we have a problem."

"Us too, Bundlenugg," I reply. "Us too! We came here to talk to you about it!"

Bundlenugg stands silently, blinking back at me.

"OK," I say cautiously. I'm not used to there being problems in Thoughtopolis. "What is your problem? And then I'll tell you mine."

"The problem with this problem is that there is a problem within the problem and it may be tricky to figure out where the problem begins and ends and therein lies the problem that lies within the problem," Bundlenugg says.

"Sounds about right," Blue agrees.

"Defo," Pickle echoes. I didn't know anyone else's echoes came back louder than they started.

"Hmmm," Fred muses, brushing his fringe out of his eyes.

"Pardon?" I say, feeling a little – well, OK, a lot – confused. Normally I can figure out Bundlenugg's riddles. They make sense to me, not like the ones the adults use in the Real World.

Is that going to start happening in here too? I wonder. This is where I come to make sense of things, not to feel even more confused.

"Well, Frankie, as you know, there is *in here* and there's *out there*." Bundlenugg points in the direction of the gold door, over the sand dunes. "Thoughtopolis and the Real World. And so far we've been separate and that's been great. But it appears something that has happened out there in the Real World has had a knock-on effect in here."

OH.

"It all went a bit haywire while you were gone last time. A few fuses blew, a lot of things got quite muddled, the bottom quite literally fell out of Thoughtopolis and then everything went very, very dark for some time."

"Whoa, that sounds pretty mysterious and serious," Fred says.

That is very odd indeed, I think to myself, listening intently.

"When did this start?" I ask.

Bundlenugg shakes his head. "Our engineers have been gathering the data. The current findings seem to suggest it might have been when ... you were eating biscuits?"

I think back to being in the pantry, shoving biscuits into my mouth, *crunch crunch crunch*.

"Must have been during one of our biscuit

investigations, Frankie!" Fred muses, still trying to blow his fringe out of his eyes. The wind up at the top of the dune feels much stronger than normal. It makes me feel cold and exposed.

I think back to the pantry moment as a squidgenflidge rings a bell somewhere in the distance.

Our Frankie is not the same Frankie. Her spark has definitely been taken.

THAT IS MY PROBLEM! That my spark is gone! So my problem is the same problem as Bundlenugg's problem? The problem *out there* has offset the problem *in here*?

"I ... I got really upset, Bundlenugg," I say quietly. "My mum and dad said that my spark is missing. And I don't have very long to find it. Until Friday, to be exact, or I am being sent off to the middle of nowhere to stay with an old lady who spends her days looking out the window for the right time to hang her knickers on the line or looking up recipes to cook potatoes."

"Hmmmmm," Bundlenugg replies. "Looks like what has happened to you is a **REALIZATION**."

"OK?" I press, hoping for more.

"A realization, Frankie, is usually something that you already knew but had told to shoo ... and then, well ...

something **BLEW**."

We stare out at the dark city below.

"Is a realization and a Sixthwisp the same thing?"

"They are related," Pickle says. "But more like fourth cousins twice removed."

"OK," I say again. "So … what happens now?"

CHAPTER TWENTY-THREE

THE BRAIN CELL-EBRITIES AND SYSTEM SHUT DOWNS

"I need you to have a word with them," Bundlenugg sighs. "You need to convince them to reboot the system."

We all stand staring at each other in the dark, our eyeballs like little moons in a night sky. Blue and Pickle's eyeballs are all black so they are like invisible ninjas, almost completely camouflaged.

"Who's *them*?" Fred enquires.

"Oh, you'll see." Pickle rolls her eyes. (I think) "Tricky little critters."

"Bundlenugg, is this a part of the journey?" I ask.

"No, no, Frankie," he answers, looking me in the eye. "You haven't even started that. Although ... a **REALIZATION** can kick-start a journey. But it's almost impossible to do it completely in the dark. Come on, let's go and talk to them.

Try to get them to reset things. We are already behind schedule."

"It's OK," Pickle shouts and I jump in fright, "we have a chap who's great at rewiring."

Once Bundlenugg has shown us the extent of how dark things have got inside Thoughtopolis, he leads us down the dunes and into the heart of the Thoughtopolis Metropolis and walks us through the dark empty streets.

I reach for the little torch in my backpack and click it on. It's helpful, but it also casts long shadows that appear to reach and grab me from afar.

"It's here somewhere..." he says, his paws patting about in the twilight darkness.

"What's where somewhere?" Fred asks.

"The switchboard of Thoughtopolis," he replies. "Always forget to ask where these things are kept ... they are usually tucked away behind something, the last place you look."

He continues knocking on buildings, hunkering down and checking along the skirting boards.

And then the strangest thing happens. He lifts the corner of a part of Thoughtopolis up, as though it were like the end of a curtain, and sure enough, behind it ...

is a switchboard!

"Ah ha!" he says triumphantly. "Found it."

We all strain our eyes to see. I point the torch under the hoisted edge.

A small round lady in overalls and sunglasses pokes her head from behind the switchboard under the edge of the little fold that Bundlenugg has lifted. She flicks her hair back nonchalantly, lowering her sunglasses down the bridge of her nose.

"Who is that?" Fred asks, peering at this miniature creature dolled up to the nines in formalwear overalls.

"That is a brain cell-ebrity. Famous around these parts."

"Please, please! Autographs later! We have important work to do. Everything is ... broken."

I inhale deeply.

"I think ... well ... that's..." I start.

"Excuse me, miss," the brain cell-ebrity interrupts. "I need to speak to the owner of this brain. If you are not the owner, I am asking you not politely to move on."

"I am the owner of this brain," I answer.

"Very well," she says. "Sign this waiver, please."

"What is this?" I ask, taking the tiny clipboard and

pen from her.

"It's your *brain waiver*. We can't be held responsible. Not being paid enough. We'll do our best if you endeavour to do the same, etc., etc. Different to a *brain wave* … one of those guys … different beast entirely…"

Suddenly a tiny cell rolls by, like a very small round octopus with a hundred nerve-like tentacles fanning its orb. It stops and waves, all its tentacles moving together like a Mexican wave. "Hey," it says, "I'm a brain wave." And then it rolls on.

The brain cell-ebrity rolls her eyes. "And they say we can be all fluff? Ha! All those guys do is literally wave."

"You've got some nerve!" it calls back to her.

"Looks who's talking," she shouts back and I watch as its nerve endings glow an electric blue.

I sign the waiver and instantly see a spark flashing. Another brain cell-ebrity pokes his head from under the curtain where the switchboard is.

"Should keep things going – for now," he says ominously. "These things do happen from time to time."

"What things?" Fred asks.

"Overthinking. You know, brain going into overdrive. The system can't cope." He sighs. "I've been dealing with this since you were born, Frankie, but things have got worse recently. I need a break too, you know." He sighs dramatically again. "Haven't had a holiday in years."

"Who is he?" I whisper to Bundlenugg.

"One of the brain cell-ebrities: Cognitive Function," he whispers back. "Good at his job but very pleased with himself. Self-important, you know."

"Howdy!" He tips his hat. "Happy to serve. Been putting the fun into cognitive **FUN**ction for eleven years and one twelfth now! It's been quite the career."

"So you're saying ... there was a glitch?" I ask. "But you've sorted it?"

Cognitive Function nods and adjusts his collar. "It was tricky but, yes, we have sorted it," he says.

"Oh, good," I say, relieved.

"*For now*," he says. "If this happens again, we might not be able to fix it so easily."

"Is this something to do with ... the missing spark?" I ask suddenly.

There's a silence. Bundlenugg looks very serious.

"Oh, Frankie ... this is what I've needed to talk to you about," he says quietly.

"When I overheard Mum and Dad talking. They said … they said my spark had been *taken*. I thought Flo had taken it initially, but I don't think she has the dexterity for that sort of crime yet. She can't even fit the square blocks through the shape sorter holes! So I realized it must be something to do with in here."

Bundlenugg nods. "I suppose it was only a matter of time before you found out. Frankie, we weren't sure how to tell you this – but, yes, your spark is gone."

The lights flicker a bit, then start to come on one by one throughout the city.

"Is it back?" I ask hopefully.

"No, Frankie," Pickle barks. "It's a different thing entirely."

"OK," I say. "But we can fix it, right?"

Bundlenugg gestures wildly. "Don't you understand? **YOUR SPARK IS GONE!** The very thing that glues you together! Sparks only disappear for very specific reasons, Frankie. And if we don't find it—"

"If we don't find it?" I repeat.

"Bundlenugg, what about the journey?" Fred asks.

Bundlenugg closes his eyes in fumbly frustration until a tiny pop of a squeeze escapes his nose.

"Bless you," Pickle booms.

"Thank you," Bundlenugg replies.

"A fneeze," Pickle whispers without whispering. "A fumbly sneeze. He gets them when the fumble feeling count in the air is high."

Bundlenugg pulls out what appears to be a thick manual from inside his jacket pocket and I marvel once more at just how much he can fit into it. He flicks through the worn pages and settles on a sheet towards the back. He folds the spine so he can focus on the page at hand and runs his paws along the text, murmuring to himself.

He then plucks tiny spectacles from a pocket within his jacket and places them on the bridge of his furry nose. He looks up at me and asks, "Do any of these things sound familiar?"

"One. Have you been in an accident that wasn't your fault?"

I shake my head. Fred shrugs his shoulders at me, unsure where Bundlenugg is headed in his line of questioning.

"Two. Have you been taking the people around you for granted?"

"No," I snap back. A little more defensively than I

mean to. "They have been taking me for granted."

"Three. Have you taken pleasure out of being mean to others?"

"Definitely not."

"Four. Have you broken a pinky promise?"

I shook my head.

"Then, five. Are you unsure how and why you have lost your spark?"

"Yes." And I nod as I say it. And so does Fred. And Blue.

Bundlenugg reads again directly from the manual. "In instances where a spark is lost due to unknown circumstances, it is likely that a buried secret will reveal the location of the spark." Bundlenugg looks up at me now and speaks his own words. "Frankie, to find your spark you must go on a journey through Thoughtopolis. This is what I was talking about. But you can only start it at the time you are ready. It may be darker than you're used to, and at times it may be treacherous. At the end of the journey you will find a secret buried very deep within you. Once you discover that secret, you will reveal the mystery of your missing spark. It is the *only* way to get it back! And to start your journey, Frankie, you need to be ready. Are you ready to start your journey, Frankie? **ARE YOU?"**

Bundlenugg pauses to draw breath. His cheeks have gone almost purple!

"EHMMMMMM..." I reply hesitantly. "I guess? I mean I am an investigator in my spare time so how hard can it be to find a secret that is hidden inside **ME?**"

And with that Bundlenugg sets off like a bullet, and we all shoot after him in a huddle of hurry.

My goodness, there is so much scurrying and flurrying and sometimes it feels as though we are getting absolutely nowhere!

Where is he off to now I wonder?

Am I ready?

I AM READY!!

"Bundlenugg! **I'M READY!!**"

Fred, Blue, Pickle and I chase after him.

"Tell me the facts, Frankie!" he gasps as he bolts along. "Everything that could help find your spark!"

"OK, so here is what we know," I shout after him, trying to keep up:

A) Mum and Dad say my spark is gone.

B) GONE! VANISHED! BOOM!

C) I can't seem to concentrate on much, I'm behind in school and my former best friend Tess has found a new best friend called Mindy who has a tortoise.

D) It feels like everyone is either laughing at me or whispering about me or **STARING AT ME WONDERING WHAT I'M THINKING INSIDE MY SPAGHETTI BRAIN.**

E) I don't know what to say or how to say it any more, so sometimes I think it's just easier to retreat and say nothing like a snail.

F) We don't in fact know if snails say nothing, maybe they do? But I feel this is one of the investigations I can come back to because:

G) All of this is worrying Mum and Dad (please see again point a) and they are talking about sending me away to Granny Doris if things haven't improved by Friday.

H) Flo has ruined **EVERYTHING.**"

Bundlenugg breaks into an even quicker sprint. Where on earth is he off to in such a hurry?

"Wait!" I call. "Wait for us!"

"WAIT FOR US!" Fred shouts.

"She's ready!" Bundlenugg is yelling. "Everyone! Assume positions! **SHE'S READY!!!**"

Whispers come from all around as Fred, Blue and I chase after Bundlenugg and Pickle. I feel a sense of excitement, intrigue and anticipation ripple through the air.

She's ready.

SHE'S READY.

SHE'S READY!!!!!

Small creatures with large eyes that look like mongooses poke their heads up from holes in the ground. Hanging bats blink out from the trees as they repeat it too. I can see the people in the city again now that the brain cell–ebrities have managed to turn all the lights back on. Dwellers of the Metropolis, people who pop their heads out of their windows as we pass.

"SHE IS READY!"

"SHE'S READY!"

"SHE'S READY!"

And it's almost as though the wind itself is wheezing

and whistling it too.

Wow, this is intense.

"Frankie," gasps Bundlenugg, "I'm so glad you're ready to do this. For a long time I knew you weren't quite there. Your head was upside down and you couldn't tell which way was up!"

Suddenly the whole world of Thoughtopolis turns upside down, like we're running along the sky. I grab a fistful of grass in the central park to steady me.

CHAPTER TWENTY-FOUR

THE CURIOUS JOURNEY JOURNAL

"GAAAAAAAAH!" shouts Cognitive Function behind us. "Careful! I've just fixed this!"

"Frankie!" yelps Fred. "What's going on?"

"Fred! Give me your hand!" I call, and clasp his little hand in mine, trying to steady us both.

For a moment, the world seems to pause with us suspended upside down. And then everything begins to wobble slightly and roll, like we are in a glass jar, placed on its side and nudged down a hill, gathering speed, gaining a hurtling momentum.

Colours, shapes, trees, houses, villages, fields spin in a blurred whir.

I hear voices, see a sea of faces looking on.

"SHE'S READY!"

"SHE'S READY!"

And then I'm standing again, feet in a little blue puddle.

We've come to a halt.

"Look, Frankie," whispers Bundlenugg. **"DO YOU SEE?"**

I look down and see my reflection staring back at me, distorted and wonky like a different version of myself. The water reminds me of my sponge eyeballs and all the tears I shed listening to Mum and Dad saying they were going to send me away. The lights around us flicker and spark once more.

I kick at the water, watching my reflection blur and disappear.

I look up, feeling a little dizzy. Thoughtopolis is the right way round again, and birds fly in and out of the trees.

"What's happening?" says Fred. "It's all changing, isn't it?"

"A bit," says Bundlenugg. "Listen, Frankie, Fred and Blue. We still want you to have fun here. But there's important work to be done." All three of us stand to attention. All eight legs. Like a really weird spider from the Real World, facing all six legs of our friends from Thoughtopolis.

This feels like the *Serious Bit* of a story.

Bundlenugg reaches into his jacket pocket and pulls out a small booklet. Different to the manual, smaller and shimmering in iridescent glitter.

"This is going to become the most important thing you own. This..."

Dramatic pause.

"Is your Journey Journal."

Another dramatic pause.

Fred and I look at each other. "Wow," I say at last. It seems the only appropriate response.

"Frankie, this is the very start of your journey."

"My journey to where?"

"SHHHH," Bundlenugg interrupts. "This booklet has room in it for **FIVE STAMPS**."

"Right, but what is this journey—"

"SHHHHHHH!"

"I think we need to *shhhhh*," Fred whispers.

"Are you listening?"

We nod.

"There is only room in this book for five stamps, Frankie. Each stamp relates to a different feeling and you get one for each stop on the Train of Thought once you've figured it out. You need to collect all five of them to move forward and locate your spark. The very thing that is missing. The very thing that is the essence of **YOU**."

"The Train of Thought that goes all the way through Thoughtopolis?" I ask.

"That's right," says Bundlenugg. "It stops off at all sorts of places, districts, precincts. It connects the entire land inside your brain. It loops and links all the ideas, the hopes, the fears, the memories, the daydreams. Indeed, they are the very engine of the Train of Thought."

Wow! That is pretty incredible, I think.

"But, Frankie?"

"Yes?" I reply, my ears glued to Bundlenugg's every word.

"The first thing to know is that sometimes the Train of Thought is more like a ... rollercoaster."

"Fantastic!" Fred whoops.

"That sounds ... fun," I say cautiously. Although, for some reason, it doesn't.

"It's certainly quite the ride," says Bundlenugg. "I also

need to warn you that the Train of Thought is fuelled on sleep and rest and at least five fruit and veg a day."

As one, Fred and I roll our eyes. **WHHHHHHHHHHHHHY** are vegetables responsible for so much hardship in a kid's life?

"It can also be refuelled at certain gas stations along the way. You must not let it run out of fuel. And when I say 'gas'—"

"Petrol? Diesel?" Fred guesses.

"Doggy nuggies??" Blue tries.

"By gas," Bundlenugg continues, "I mean FUN! We all want you and Fred and Blue to have *FUN*! You simply must! Must have gas and craic and fun! You must not let go of that. You are a kid, Frankie, and it is your moral duty, right and obligation to have *fun*."

I like the sound of that. This journey is going to be super. I can't wait to—

"But here is the serious bit," Bundlenugg interrupts my thoughts.

OH.

"The Train of Thought can also go off the tracks sometimes, so you need to be careful. And you MUST complete the full journey. Once you start, there is no going back."

That bit *does* sound serious. I feel my tummy whirl uneasily.

Fred and I exchange a look.

It all sounds exciting and intriguing but also … a little bit scary.

"To find your spark, you need to find out **WHY** you've lost it," Bundlenugg says. "That's a secret, I'm afraid. A deep, dark secret that has been buried somewhere in Thoughtopolis. You will need to be very brave and very courageous to make it all the way to the last stop. When, *if*, you finally reach the last stop, this Journey Journal" – he holds the journal out to me – "will transform into the *key* and this and *only this* will unlock your missing spark."

Whoa. This is a lot to take on. The only very serious task I've ever really been entrusted with so far in my eleven years and one month is to take the bins out on my own on a Monday night.

"A deep, dark secret?" I ask.

I think about my **SECRET BOOK OF SECRETS**. There is one more. And it sounds like it is the biggest one of all. What on earth is it?

"All of this isn't to do with the secret about Frankie

marrying Ross P. Rossdale one day, is it?" Fred asks, and my cheeks turn the same colour as the apples growing on the tress around me. To distract myself, I reach up and pluck one off and bite into it, tasting bananas and raspberries.

"Do I *have* to go on this journey?" I ask.

"Not at all," says Bundlenugg. "But if you want to find your missing spark, then you do."

"Will you be here to help?" Fred asks.

"As much as I can," Bundlenugg says. "And others from Thoughtopolis will try too. But this is your journey. A lot will come down to instinct and intuition; your Sixthwisp will sometimes guide you. There may be times when you feel very much on your own."

I gulp.

Fred gulps.

Blue gulps. But it might also be fur caught in his throat.

"What do you think?" Bundlenugg asks gently.

"Bundlenugg," I start, feeling nervous. "Do you … know *what* this great secret is?"

He looks solemn for a very long time before he speaks. "I do."

We stand in silence, feeling the weight of something

not all of us can understand.

"Then why can't you just tell me and save all this trouble?" I ask.

"Unfortunately, and you won't understand this right now, but it has to be yours to discover," Bundlenugg says. His little face is sympathetic, his little furry eyebrows softening. "The journey is your own journey, Frankie, if that makes sense?"

I shake my head. It doesn't.

"The further you go, the more you will know."

"Will it snow?" Fred asks, and I giggle.

"Hard to know," says Bundlenugg. "Hey, we're rhyming."

"Bundlenugg," I ask seriously. "What happens if I don't fill the journal, and I don't find the buried secret?"

"I am afraid, Frankie, that the fate of Thoughtopolis itself relies on you succeeding. You may notice that as you get closer to the end of the quest, the foundations of Thoughtopolis start to waver. Districts crumbling. Erratic behaviour. Creatures disappearing. More glitches. That sort of thing. Be warned, Frankie – cracks in Thoughtopolis will ultimately have an impact on you and how you feel. So try your best to stay focused. Fred will be with you to help. We all want you to succeed, but there may be hidden parts of you that don't."

I try to process it all. To make sense of the task ahead, the risks and the consequences. I feel a bit like an adult and I don't like it one bit. Was I going to start … playing golf and worrying about the price of a punnet of raspberries now too? Why do I have to do this? Isn't it my job to do cartwheels in the garden and build snail hotels and see how many bubblegums I can fit in my mouth?

Fred takes my hand. "It's OK, Frankie. We can do this. Together." I give his hand a squeeze. I honestly don't know what I would do without Fred – he is the single most important human in my life because he understands me exactly as I am.

He's your anam cara, *Frankie,* I hear Grampa Pinky whisper in my ear.

With Fred by my side, I can do it. I just know it.

"I'll do it," I say. "After all, I'll have Fred and Blue and all the creatures in Thoughtopolis behind me. I can do this!"

Bundlenugg claps his little hands. "Excellent. Your journey begins at the Tick Tock Grandfather Clock ride at the Fantastical Funfair of Whimsical Delightfulness."

"OK…" I say.

"At least that sounds like fun," Fred smiles encouragingly.

"When do we start?" I ask, taking Fred's hand again, gaining strength from his grasp.

"Yeah," says Fred, pushing his fringe out of his eyes. I think it might be time for a trip to Frankie's Salon when we get back to the Real World. Mum's not as keen on Frankie's Salon as Fred and I are. She says his fringe is never straight and once it ended up at a full diagonal line. But Fred doesn't even tip so he can't expect perfection.

"Would we have time for, say … a watermelon fizzing candy ice cream?"

There's a silence and Bundlenugg and Pickle look me straight in the eye before both shouting:

"Hey! You two!"

"Yes…?"

"YOU START NOW!!!!!!!!!!!!!!!"

CHAPTER TWENTY-FIVE

BRAIN FARTS AND JOURNEY STARTS

Fred, Blue and I run towards the Fantastical Funfair of Whimsical Delightfulness, where we've been many times before.

But this time? It's the very first destination on my Mystery Expedition!

There's no time to waste.

I take out my magnifying glass and shout, **"TAAAAHDAHHHH!"** to no one in particular. I just like doing that sometimes. It has a certain sense of purpose to it. And it makes you feel like you know what's going on even if you really don't.

And if I manage to figure out the first clue at this first destination, I'll earn stamp number one in my journal to bring me on to destination number two.

We have an awfully big journey ahead and not much

time to finish it before:

- I get sent away to live with Potato Granny. (Sounds like some sort of superhero. Definitely isn't.)
- Thoughtopolis implodes and causes irrevocable damage.

Yikes. This is the most dramatic list I've ever written, and it only has two points.

I need to lie down.

"ROLL UP, ROLL UP! GET YOUR TICKETS HERE FOR THE TICK TOCK GRANDFATHER CLOCK RIDE!"

A small barrel-shaped man rolls through the middle of the funfair, brandishing a wad of tickets in his hand.

"That's it," I say to Fred. "That's where we need to go."

I look around for Bundlenugg and Pickle. They are nowhere to be seen.

Just Fred, Blue and I. In the midst of a bustling crowd. It's so busy it's difficult to see anything or go anywhere with ease.

I see the Train of Thought pull into the platform just at the gates of the funfair. It's **ENORMOUS!**

Both Fred and I take a large inhale of breath. Carriage after carriage as far as the eye can see. Giant steel wheels screech against the metal tracks; large sheets of solid cast iron are interspaced with circular windows, while its tall cylindrical chimney lets off a colossal plume of steam as it comes to a stop.

I gulp, feeling suddenly very small.

"Knock knock," Fred interrupts.

"Who's there?" I smile.

"Alpaca."

"Alpaca who?"

"Alpaca my suitcase, and you see when the train leaves."

We both grin.

"Do we just get on, do you think?" I ask Fred.

"We need a ticket for the Grandfather Clock Ride first," Fred says, looking around.

The barrel-shaped man rolls over to us.

"You are just in time! One minute less, no tickets; one minute more, no tickets."

Well, that's good timing! I think to myself.

"We'll take two, please," I say, taking a step forward. But the man rolls back.

"Hey! We are trying to catch the train!" I say, but

he's gone again, disappearing into a crowd of happy faces.

"There he is!" yells Fred and through a couple struggling with a suitcase, I see his round head in the crowd, then his feet, then his head again.

"Wait!" I cry, pushing my way through the throng. "Please, we need to get on that train!" But the man is still rolling out of sight. He's like a giant marble that I can't quite grasp before he's gone again! I put on an extra burst of speed, reaching out and catching hold of the edge of his brown jacket. *Pouff.* I look at my hands as they grasp at nothing.

A whistle blows and a last flurry of passengers file on to the train. It's about to depart! We don't even have our tickets yet!

"I don't know what to do," I cry, frustrated. "We can't get on without a ticket and he won't give us one."

"Show him your Journey Journal," Fred says. This sounds like a good idea so I take it out of my pocket and wave it in the air.

"I've got a Journey Journal!" I yell. "I need to get five stamps. Please, I don't have time for this!"

The small roly-poly man appears at my side. This time he doesn't go anywhere, just hovers on the spot, waddling slightly from side to side.

"What is it with people?" he says. "Always worrying about not having enough time. Wanting to go back in time. To chase a feeling. To go forward in time, when they think things will be better. To chase another feeling. Suspending the *now* in favour of *then*."

"Right," I say, confused. "But I really *don't* have time for this—"

"Do you have a time machine, Frankie?"

"Me? Um. No."

"No one does. So the **ONLY** time you have is now! **NOW!** And *now* is the time that will eventually roll behind you and become your memories and *now* is also that imagined time somewhere far into the future that you can't quite grasp yet. People will always hide in the shadows of both. Never really existing in either before they have rolled out of your grasp once more. But you are here. *Now*, Frankie. And look – the sun is out! Isn't it about time you tilted your face towards it just a little?"

I stare at him, then do as he says. I lift my face to the warm Thoughtopolis sun and feel a strange sense of calm. I feel glad the sunshine has returned. That the darkness has been banished. For now.

NOW.

"Ahem," the little man says. "These tickets originally cost five Thoughtopolis sense, but the longer you leave it, the higher the price is, I'm afraid."

"Oh, for goodness' sake!"

"Clock's always ticking! I do hope you don't run out of time, Frankie! Tick, tick, tick."

I look around for Bundlenugg and Pickle. Still no sign. Panic rises up in me.

I imagine being back in the Real World, being driven off to Granny Doris's, Flo looking on from an upstairs window rubbing her hands together. *TICK!*

I imagine Tess arranging to meet me down a dark lane at midnight so no one else is about and telling me she is too mortified to be seen in public with me now because everyone else seems to be laughing and whispering about me and we can therefore no longer be friends. *TICK!*

I think of more and more glitches happening in Thoughtopolis and lights going out all over the city. And I think about not being able to get on this train and never finding my spark or leaving Thoughtopolis ever again while it slowly starts to fall apart around me. *TOCK!!!!!!!*

"Frankie," Blue says as kindly as possible, "time ticks on seven times quicker for me. We need to make a decision!" His nose squeaks a very urgent, very high pitched squeak.

This is followed by an even more urgent, even higher pitched SHRIIIIIIIIIIIILLLL of the train whistle.

I inhale purposefully, shutting down those thoughts. I'm Frankie Finkleton, aged eleven and one month, with all of my fantastic qualities. I have a magnifying glass and courage and strength. And I'm not afraid to use them!

"I'VE GOT THIS!!" I shout, stepping forward and grasping Fred's hand in mine as the crowd pushes against us.

The ticket seller is spinning away again and I race to him, feeling a new steely determination. "Hurry up, hurry up," he calls to the crowd. "Catch your moments before they're gone!"

I race alongside him holding my Journey Journal out and thrust ten sense into his hands. "That's for me and my brother," I gasp. "You might have a sibling deal, two for eight, but we don't have time to discuss it right now!"

"Oh, OK," he says. "Last thing. Do you have ID?"

"ERMMMM." I stall, thinking for a moment. I point at my own face. "Will this do?"

"Any proof you are who you say you are?"

"Eeeerm, my name is Frankie Finkleton and I'm

221

eleven and one month old and I got a magnifying glass for my birthday and I carry it around to look mysterious and I can do four cartwheels in a row before…"

"That'll do." He stops me, handing over the tickets. To use this ticket you'll need to jump on the Train of Thought to the other side of the funfair. "Tick tick, tick tock," he adds, before rolling out of sight. The moustache on his face looks like the two hands of a clock, I think, before he's gone entirely.

I stare at my ticket stub. It reads *N-O-W* in a swirly font, the O the face of a clock.

"Come on, Frankie! It's about to leave!" Fred cries as we inch through the horde on the platform and a final whistle blows as we climb aboard the famous Train of Thought.

"Bags the window seat, Frankie!" Fred says, plopping into an orange velvet bench. I sit beside him and place the Tick Tock Grandfather Clock Ride ticket carefully in my pocket. I steal covert glances around me.

There's a diverse mix of other commuters: passengers with long necks and tiny heads with giant blinking eyes; wizards and sorcerers stowing their baggage overhead. Small animals scurry along the carriages while a gazelle in shorts sits opposite us with her husband.

"It will be great to get away, Bernard," the gazelle sighs, lifting her sunglasses on to her head.

"Mary, it's been relentless. Being permanently chased by lions. We really need this holiday."

Fred giggles and I nudge him slightly.

A dolphin in togs sits down and Fred asks it if it's off to have a "whale of a time", but it doesn't laugh and I wonder perhaps if it's having a bad day. You never do know what other mammals are going through.

Tiny heads, large heads, furry heads, feathery heads … all with blinking eyes at everyone else in the carriage. Blue is having an intense stare-off with a tiny tarsier monkey.

"My eyes are larger," it says flatly.

"No. Mine are," Blue replies, standing his ground.

"Excuse me," I hear a voice say abruptly. We look up to see a dinner lady wheeling a trolley of snacks. Her hair is pinned into a net and she wears an apron knotted in a bow around her waist. "Would you like to try anything from the trolley?" she asks.

"What do you have?" Fred says.

"We have all sorts, young boy … you can sample lots of things on the Train of Thought – happiness, anger, jealousy, love, regret, denial, hope, sadness, confusion,

223

daydreams, experiences, memories. It's a robust menu –
but we do have a deal on realizations today. Two for the
price of one and you get a free cup of tea with a biscuit."

"**OHHHHH**, Frankie, you like realizations, don't you?
You had one today!"

"**SHHHHH**, Fred," I whisper and before I can think
any more about it, we're suddenly thrown back into our
seats as the train shoots forward at high speed down the
track, looping around and up and down, taking sharp
turns left and right. Everything out of the window is a
blur of colour and sound and flashing whips of light. I
feel dizzy and giddy all at once! The carriage we're in
lights up with a dazzle of different colours. And then, it
all comes to an abrupt and sudden **HALT**.

Fred, Blue and I all dismount the Train of Thought
and then sure enough … *there it is*.

The Tick Tock Grandfather Clock Ride, so towering
a tower that the tip of it is buried deep in a tuft of
surrounding clouds. Stacks upon stacks of wooden blocks,
like an enormous Jenga pillar, topped with a big moon
clock face over a giant golden swinging pendulum.

My tummy lurches at the sight of it.

I puked a tiny bit on the teacups when the local

fairground came to our village in the Real World. Can I manage this one?

My bottom parps a nervous little noise and Blue coughs to disguise it. Or again, it could have been a furball. Either way, Blue is a good friend.

It's odd that a brain fart in the Real World is when you forget what it was you are just about to go and do. Whereas a brain fart in Thoughtopolis is simply just a fart in a brain.

"The trick is, Frankie," Fred says, "to keep focused on one thing. Just stay focused on **ONE THING** when it feels like a hundred things are jumbling around."

"Good luck, Frankie," I hear Bundlenugg whisper, even though he's nowhere to be seen. "You have to work out what feeling you feel to get your stamp and get back on the Train of Thought and move forward to the next stop of your journey."

I nod purposefully. Not porpoisefully, which is something a dolphin off on a holiday might do.

Fred and I look at each other, then square our shoulders and walk towards the towering ride.

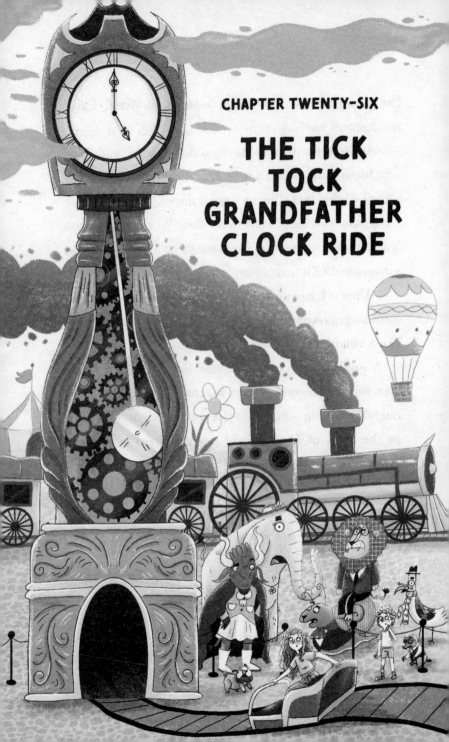

CHAPTER TWENTY-SIX

THE TICK TOCK GRANDFATHER CLOCK RIDE

The grandfather clock is even more intimidating close up. It is a vast tower of wood and clogs and gears, disappearing into the clouds.

"What's going to happen, Frankie?" asks Fred. He sounds a bit scared, like he's beginning to lose his nerve a little too.

I have no idea, to be honest. But I'm certainly not going to tell him that.

"What is happening, Fred, is that we are going on the most … interesting … funfair ride **EVER!** You and me! *That's* what! Now let's go!"

A green ninja burp escapes my mouth. I narrow my eyes at it, not wanting it to give the game of my worry away and watch as it tumbles and kicks off into thin air. I was thankful at least the brain farts didn't make themselves so visibly present.

I don't normally feel nervous at the funfair. But this all feels very different now. And why is it exactly that we've never been on this particular ride before?

I look up at the giant tower of coloured metal wheels all slotted together. It looks so intimidating as we stand like three little dots down below.

Lots of people bustle about in a carefree manner and

I think that Fred and Blue and I might be the only ones feeling a little scared.

I hear a squeak from Blue and I'm not quite sure if it escaped his nose or bottom.

I'm wondering if any safety checks have been done for dogs on the metal pull down seat restraints.

I offer Fred a reassuring smile. "We've done plenty of fairground rides in Thoughtopolis."

"But none of them have been *that* tall," Fred says, clutching his tummy worriedly.

"One second too late, one second too early! Everything in your life can change in just one second!" a voice booms from the inner mechanics of the ride.

I lock Fred into his seat with the metal bar, double checking it for safety before we take off.

It's something I always do with him.

Check his shoelaces are tied.

Check his coat is zipped up so he won't get cold.

Check he doesn't have a toothpaste beard before he leaves the house.

Run back to check he's OK if he falls off his scooter.

"I'm OK, Frankie!" he assures me. "Don't fuss!"

Suddenly the giant machine clanks into action and

I hear the sound of metal cogs and wheels folding and clunking into one another.

I assume this is ... safe?! Because everything in Thoughtopolis is safe. Isn't it?

I've never questioned all the things we can do here. I haven't needed to before now.

I feel the pull in my tummy as the pendulum draws backwards. We look down. Our feet look tiny dangling in mid-air over the edge of our seats.

Blue's hind paws poke out next to ours, rigid as pokers.

"If this all ends badly, tell my mother I love her," Blue says. "Actually, I never really knew my real mum. My gosh, I have so many regrets. That ball you kicked under the shed, Fred, that I still haven't recovered. A bone I buried under the hydrangeas in the corner of the garden I still haven't got around to—"

"It's OK, Blue," Fred says, placing a hand on his trembling paw.

I look at Fred. And although I hate him ever to see it, I blurt out, "I'm scared!"

Fred offers one of his finest gap-toothed smiles.

"Don't be scared, Frankie! I'm with you!" He places his other hand over mine.

And then, as if being released from a catapult, we are off! Soaring through the air! Warm and refreshing and fast and oh so high!

We screech with laughter.

It's the strangest thing, it feels almost as though we're gliding in slow motion, but really *quickly*! The giant pendulum swings over and back, over and back, until it suddenly pauses mid-air on the draw back and then ... the weirdest thing ever to happen so far in Thoughtopolis so far happens...

We float up out of our seats and—

Fred and I are **BABIES!!!!** Blue is a puppy!! Weeing everywhere and chewing everything.

Fred and I are actually ... babies! Crawling around in nappies cooing and laughing. Free from our seats, but also in our seats. It's the most peculiar and unexpected thing!

"Goo goo," Fred garbles.

"Gaa gaa!" I answer. And we understand each other perfectly! I blow a raspberry on my lips, and he replies immediately. Oh my gosh, Fred was so cute when he was a baby!

"Goooo gagaaa gaa goo!" If there had been subtitles they would read: *Fred! Look at your squishy baby thighs and your squashy hand dimples and the* **ADORABLE BABY CURL ON YOUR FORHEAD!**

"GAA GGGOOOOO GOO GOO GAHHHH," Fred replies and I know he means: *Frankie, I think you need to get Mum to change your nappy.*

I can understand him, the way I always have. The way I've never understood Flo.

And then we're floating through the air again, and we aren't babies any more – we're a bit older and I'm holding Fred's hand in his cot, combing his springy curls (he has five now!) with the soft bristles of a brush. I am reading to him about all the different animals there are in the zoo. And then it's bath time and Mum's there! Hi, Mum!!

She's smiling. And laughing. It is so lovely to see her *laughing*.

She's squeezing warm soapy water over our heads and dotting buttons of suds on the end of our noses. I can smell her perfume. Wow, this interactive 3-D ride is so realistic!

And instead of making my tummy dip and swirl, it makes my heart sing and swell.

I'm on Dad's shoulders now, racing through long

grass, Fred running in welly boots to catch up. We're laughing; the breeze is making our hair dance.

This time travel ride is the best ride ever! How have I never done this ride before? Perhaps I was too scared to go on it before now!

I'm suddenly racing in a different field, my legs longer, my hair longer too. I look down; oh, whoa! Am I? **AM I A TEENAGER?** Uh oh! I'm flooded with emotions, one after the other. And the most peculiar thing… I can't help rolling my eyes. **AT EVERYTHING!**

"THAT IS SOOOOO UNFAIR!!"

"UGGGGHHH I AM SO BORED!!!"

"OH MY GOSH I AM SOOOOO EMBARRASSED."

I float past a park bench and is that … Tess?! Haha! Tess has a lump of metal through her nose! Suddenly I'm sitting on the bench and our heads are close together and we're talking about how annoying our parents are, getting us out of bed before one in the afternoon—

And then I'm in college, sitting in a class that isn't that boring and … Ross P. Rossdale is sitting next to me! My tummy does a weird dip, but it's probably just the funfair ride and oh my goodness … he has a beard!

"HI, FRANKIE," he says and his voice is as deep as

Pickle's. It sounds so odd and funny as Ross has a really high voice in the Real World. It's something that Monica, Veronica and Nell do **HAHAHAHAHAAAAAAAS** at. But how can you **HAHAHAHAHAHAHAA** at a voice that only ever says nice things like, "Hi, Frankie, how are you today? Want my apple?"

And then I'm walking along the pavement and I'm wearing a suit and then I'm older again, maybe even older than Mum? And these little children, are they mine? I'm laughing with them, holding their hands and dancing round and round in a circle as we sing. Their little faces, I can't see them properly, but I know I love them. Love them the way I love Fred. I'm telling them to eat their vegetables and get a proper night's sleep. I guess that's just what happens when you turn into an adult. But, oddly, I don't feel bored or that everything is dull. And I don't even have an urge to do a cartwheel or have fizzy lemon sours for my dinner. How odd.

"Mummy?" a voice calls out as I pick a little boy up into my arms.

"Yes, Fred?" I answer.

Oh, wow! I call one of my own children Fred! He is going to be so chuffed!

233

I feel the pendulum swing. Over and back. Over and back. It's starting to make me feel a little bit sick now. I know I'm still locked into my seat. But I'm also here. Here in the future.

My eyes fall on a group of old men, all wearing braces attached to their trousers and flat caps on their heads. Some have beards, some have round bellies, all of them have warm kind smiles.

Who are they?

CHAPTER TWENTY-SEVEN

A GAGGLE OF GRANDDADS

"FRANKIE!" one of them calls.

"Sit down, join us," another offers. "Do you know how to play Uno?"

"Who are you?" I ask, bemused.

"Us?" they answer in unison. "Who do you think we are? We are the Grandfathers of the Tick Tock Grandfather Clock Ride!"

I look around and all of a sudden there's a full chorus of them! Hundreds of grandfathers smiling, arms folded on their bellies, chortling jovially.

"Frankie?" one asks suddenly, standing out from the crowd.

"Granddad?" I say, squinting my eyes at him.

"Yes, Frankie!"

Oh my gosh, that's my granddad! The only granddad

I have left in the Real World as Granny Doris's husband – Grampa Pinky – died a few years ago from being ancient. But Gr-Annie and Granddad with the second best dog in Dublin are alive and well in the Real World and only eat potatoes once a week like most normal people.

"Granddad, you look so old!"

He laughs. "Why, thank you, Frankie! So do you."

Well, that was true. "Oh, no, sorry, I mean..." I stutter.

"No, really, thank you! We feel lucky we are old! Lucky us that we got here, eh?"

They all chuckle again. "How are you, my little pet poppet? Or can I call you that now?" he asks.

"Oh, Pop," I sigh. "It's a bit of a mess at home. Mum and Dad are so tired from Flo and they think I've lost my spark, but I really think it's them who have lost *their* spark! And I have to find mine by Friday! It's buried somewhere with a secret. Do you know anything about that?"

Granddad looks quiet for a moment and I'm not sure if he's thinking or if he just hasn't heard me. Gr-Annie says he has an old age condition called "Selective Deafness", but normally he only gets that when it's time to do the washing-up.

"I have to figure out a feeling on the Train of Thought. I have five feelings to figure out! And hopefully they will lead me to this buried secret and I can get my spark back or they are going to send me away to Granny Doris!!"

"Oooooohhh, Granny Doris does a lovely potato gratin. Don't worry, love. Come here."

I take a step towards him, then stop. What's happening to Granddad?

"Come on, Frankie, it's OK!" he says, his hair almost snow white now, more and more wrinkles splintering from the corners of his eyes.

"No! **NO!!!**" I scream. "I don't like this! I want to get off now!"

The wheels creak and groan again. In the distance I hear the screams and bustle of the fairground.

I look around. Countless grandfathers with their Uno cards.

Fred loves Uno—

Hang on, where *is* Fred?

I look around. Around and around and around. All I can see is grandfathers everywhere.

"I WANT TO GET OFF!!!" I scream again, louder,

panic charging through me.

"GET OFF, THEN, FRANKIE!" Granddad calls. **"GO! GO BACK WHERE YOU ARE NOW, FRANKIE FINKLETON, AGED ELEVEN AND ONE MONTH. THAT WILL HELP YOU FIGURE THIS OUT. THAT IS THE ONLY PLACE YOU CAN EVER REALLY BE. GOING INTO YOUR PAST, OR YOUR FUTURE IS ONLY EVER REALLY A MIRAGE, FRANKIE. IT CAN HELP YOU PIECE THE PUZZLE TOGETHER BUT THE TRUTH IS WHERE YOU ARE NOW. AND THAT IS WHERE YOU NEED TO BE."**

Granddad's blue eyes are fading now. The Uno cards fall to the floor, spilling about in slow motion.

I remember something then. It was Fred who taught me to play Uno. Fred and I once played Uno every night for a week with a torch under our duvet, way after Mum had ordered lights out.

And now I can't find him. Where is Fred? I feel a familiar panic rising.

"Frankie," whispers Bundlenugg. He appears out of nowhere just when I need him. The ride has stopped; the grandfathers are gone. It's just me, standing outside the enormous grandfather clock ride. "How do you feel?"

"Confused. Lost," I say.

"Why?"

"Because – because Fred isn't here."

"And that makes you feel lost…"

"Yes."

"You did it." Bundlenugg nods. "You've got your first stamp, Frankie."

CHAPTER TWENTY-EIGHT

THE BORING OLD REAL WORLD

It's Wednesday already. *How* is it Wednesday?

The school week normally drags on for aaaaaaaaaages and takes for ever to get to Friday. But now, when I'm under pressure to solve the biggest mystery of my eleven-and-one-month-year-old life, the week is racing along like an Olympic gold medallist!

"Well," I say to Blue the next morning. "That was seriously odd."

I'm packing my magnifying glass into my school bag this time. I need to be on the lookout for more clues in the Real World too. If what happened in the biscuit cupboard has had a knock-on effect in Thoughtopolis, I need to be even more "private investigatory" for the rest of the week.

I pull on my familiar itchy woollen jumper and knot the tie around my neck.

Chase around the garden, then dig a hole, up pops this guy to dive down past the mole.

I taught Fred how to knot his school tie. My rhyme doesn't really make sense, but it makes sense to us.

I think about Bundlenugg and the riddles. Both here and there. And I think about the first part of "the journey".

I pad across the landing to Fred's room and push open the door. The familiar creak makes its familiar creak noise. I had been so terrified, so worried for Fred.

I'm relieved everything is OK. Fred has already left for school. He has drum practice every Wednesday morning before classes start and always leaves before me to get in there on time.

I close his bedroom door and sit on the top step of the stairs. And think some more.

"That grandfather clock ride was quite something, wasn't it?"

And then I think even more.

"We were all babies for a while – do you remember that, Blue?"

Blue sits staring at me, like he has done for the last ten minutes, so I take that as a yes.

"Then we got stuck. I got stuck. But somehow I got out, and I got my first stamp in the Journey Journal. When I told Bundlenugg I felt confused. Lost."

I pull on my socks and buckle my shoes closed.

"And then Granddad told me I need to be in the Now. And that's what my ticket said." Hmmmm.

So a list of things I now know but which make absolutely no sense to me at present:

    a) I got my first stamp in my Journey Journal: Lost.

    b) But only when I said I felt lost without Fred.

    c) Being in the NOW is a help.

    d) Old people can get seriously wrinkly. I will buy Granddad a
        moisturizing face mask for his birthday and tell him to
        start using serums like Mum.

I zip up my bag and slide down the stairs with my back against the
wall. I mean, there's no real need, but I'm feeling particularly private
investigatory this morning.

"Frankie," Dad says, making me jump. He's standing at the
bottom of the stairs with a slice of toast in one hand and a
hairbrush in the other and he doesn't look afraid to use either.

"Frankie, you need to eat," Dad says, handing me the slice
of toast. A decoy as he attempts to run the brush through
my hair.

"You look like you've been dragged through a bush backwards!" he
remarks.

*Or flung back and forth on a giant Tick Tock Grandfather Clock ride
in a magical world called Thoughtopolis inside my own brain!* I think before
smiling and scarpering out of the door.

I look at the piece of toast Dad's given me, and before I go to take a bite, I spot two tiny teeth marks in the crust.

Ugh! Flo!

Does she have to ruin *everything*? Toast included?

I pick up my speed, not wanting to be late for school. I know I've been *even* more distracted than usual lately and I don't need to be giving any of the adults more reasons to scrutinize me *even* closer, wondering about my spaghetti brain. Not now that I need to sneak off to Thoughtopolis more than ever before.

Hmmmmm.

I'm *hmmmmm*—ing a lot more lately. I find it really helps when I'm trying to figure things out. And a *hmmmmmmmm* goes together really well with a magnifying glass. I bet detectives have to pass a *Hmmmmmmmmm*—ing exam in Private Detective College before they are fully qualified. It must be a part of their finals. (It is very different to humming. Detective hmmmmmm—ing is traditionally not at all musical.)

"I was worried about Fred," I say to Blue as he follows me down the path. I don't like admitting I'm worried, but I can't help myself. "He just disappeared. That ride was really fun, but then it got really scary. But we do all need to get back to Thoughtopolis as soon as we can. We are making progress! Our first stamp! We need to go to the next destination and then the next and the next and then we'll find the buried secret. Or else."

243

I gulp.

Blue trots with me to the end of the road and waves me off with his tail.

"Good boy, Blue," I say, patting his head. "You have a nice day for yourself. Sleep all morning, even though you've slept all night and then maybe bark at some trucks and then have another nap and then I guess just repeat all that until I see you later. You'll need your energy for our next adventure to ... *you know where*."

I whisper the last bit in case anyone is listening.

I pass all the people I usually do on the way to school. No one seems any the wiser about the mission that is underway. And that is the way I need to keep it.

There's Sally O'Malley sitting on top of her garden wall swishing her tail, watching the world as it starts to bustle and hum and settle into the day ahead.

Sally O'Malley is, in fact, a cat. Not a woman with a tail who sits on the very top of her garden wall. She follows me with her gaze every day.

"Sally O'Malley," I nod.

"Meeeeeeow," she purrs, looking down her nose.

Poor Sally O'Malley leads such a boring life. Although she did make it into our local paper once for being able to meow to the letter "b" in the alphabet, which isn't that impressive, but when you consider she is a cat, it is impressive enough.

Either way, she isn't as special as Blue. And she only lives in the boring old Real World. Blue gets to have very cool adventures.

We walk past the feral triplets, Gary, Larry and Barry's house. I can always hear them before I see them.

Where's my hockey stick? Where's my water bottle? Oi, give me my toast! I'm telling! I'm telling! I'M TELLING!

And then they spill out of the house in a tornado of arms and legs and accusations and freckles and elbows and bits of toast and sticky uppy ginger hair and I quicken my pace to try and avoid getting sucked in and caught up in the tumbling tornado all the way to school.

Same as every day.

Mum once asked if I wanted to go and play with them seeing as they live on our road, and that might be better than sitting in my room all day by myself, and I was genuinely insulted.

I have far more interesting things to be doing in Thoughtopolis than hanging out with Gary, Barry or Larry in the Real World shouting about toast right into my face.

Down past the twitching curtains of Margery Lonergan's house on 24 Cottage Orchard Lane.

I see the curtain twitch and one of her beady eyes looking at me through the glass. *I wonder what is going on in that odd little*

245

girl's head, I imagine her thinking.

Wouldn't you like to know, Margery Lonergan?

"Act as if everything is normal, Frankie," I tell myself.

Then I pick my nose as I pass her house. I'm not exactly proud of doing it. I grew out of nose picking about two years ago, apart from special occasions, but I do it now as a cunning decoy. She will be so appalled and shocked that she'll stop wondering what's going on inside my head for just about long enough to go and report me to *The Spy Monthly* where a headline will follow along the lines of: *Local Girl Picks Her Nose Walking Down The Street But Finds Nothing At All There As She Had Only Blown It Recently.*

I walk towards the village and pass by Mr Gordon's Sweet Shoppe. Why it has an extra P and an E after "shop", no one really knows. They say it's an old-fashioned spelling and I try to use this excuse myself in spelling tests on Fridays when I've guessed some of the letters. But it never works. They are all still "worried" about my grades.

Gr-Annie keeps suggesting we go to Mr Gordon's sweet shop some time soon and she will treat me to a quarter bag of jellies. But the last time we did that, her dentures got stuck in a toffee penny and Mr Gordon had to prise them out with a set of tongs. Gr-Annie didn't seem embarrassed at all and I marvelled at how strange it was to be able to laugh along when you are mortified and everyone is laughing at you. Then Mr Gordon had fainted. And Fred got an apple drop stuck up his nose. It was quite the trip to the sweet shop.

But that was ages ago.

Also, if I'm honest, the sweets in Mr Guzzleworth's sweet shop (with the far easier spelling) in Thoughtopolis are far more interesting and exciting. I'm not going to let Gr–Annie know that, though. Or that I've hung out with Granddad in the future.

I turn the corner of Windy Ridge Street, near Doctor Hilda Stitch's practice and I wonder when doctors finish practising and started actually *being* doctors. But this seems like a rude question to ask. And anyway, Doctor Hilda Stitch isn't the *worst* of the adult herd.

We agree on a few things, the doctor and I. That the red lollipops in the waiting room are the very best flavour, and that of all the plasters she had in her practice, the rainbow ones are probably the nicest. That's two things. Even though I know very well that a multicoloured rainbow plaster is going to do absolutely diddly–squat for a worry pain.

Oh, and we also agree that Flo has the loudest cry in Ireland. That is just a scientific fact that absolutely no one could disagree about whatsoever.

This morning, I pass Doctor Hilda Stitch's door as she's unlocking the bottom bolt. I've nearly made it past when she catches sight of me.

"Morning, Frankie! How are we today?" he asks, one eyebrow raised like he's also attempting to unlock the bottom bolt in my head.

Nuh–uh. I hope Bundlenugg bolted the golden door good and tight until

247

the next time we're back!

"Good, doctor, thank you!" And I scurry on. Like I always do.

No one seems any more suspicious than they normally are about the goings-on of my spaghetti brain. Even though the goings-on have even more goings-on going on! And Fred and Blue and I are on a mission to find the buried secret and get my spark back.

No biggie. And I almost smile to myself.

I pick up my pace so as not to be late for school, and so I can slip into class as inconspicuously as possible.

CHAPTER TWENTY-NINE

RUNNING IN CORRIDORS AND SHARK TEACHERS

I see Mr McNogg the school principal standing at the gate ahead, surveying the children under his thick bushy brows as they enter the grounds. I wonder which poor unfortunate child he will reprimand.

"There is no nutritional value in that, Stuart Monkton," he says to Stuart Monkton, whose finger is halfway up one nostril. "And a banana tastes better, you know."

"Ugh, bananas are so gross," Stuart Monkton answers, looking like he might be sick.

Mr McNogg's eyebrows are so bushy that I often wonder how he can see out from under them. I imagine his eyeballs shouting, "Help us! We are trapped back here: come and save us!"

But now I know those eyes are staring at me from behind the bushy eyebrow fence. He's zoning in. On me.

I speed up, even though I'm not allowed to run at school. Running is a weird one because it is highly encouraged in yard, in fields, on sports day, but when a kid runs in a school corridor it becomes an illegal crime.

I don't want to get told off by McNogg, partly because that might lead to a conversation about how I am, and partly because of the spit. Mr McNogg is the worst for spitting when he talks. I wish I could wear my rain jacket with the hood up and cord pulled tightly around my face so that only the tip of my nose is left exposed. But I don't want to appear rude. Adults are obsessed with not appearing rude. To them it's the most important thing. When everyone knows that manners rank below:

a) Watermelon fizzing exploding candy
b) No Homework Fridays
c) Videos of cats riding bikes on the internet

"Frankie Finkleton," he says now, almost like an accusation. "I've been meaning to talk to you about—"

"Sorry!" I mumble. "Running late for, um, roll call!" I scurry past. This is not what I need first thing in the morning. Or, let's be honest, at all.

I look down at my shoes click-clacking on the tile corridors as they head to my classroom. I am like a well-trained ant, marching through the gate, saying goodbye to Fred at the top of the corridor to the junior classes (when he's not in early for drums) turn left, down the corridor to the senior classes, into my classroom: eyes to the floor, avoiding making eye contact with anyone in particular, not drawing too much attention.

Today is even more important than usual. The less noticeable I am, the more unremarkable and unassuming, the better chance I have of sneaking off to Thoughtopolis. We are running out of days; it is already Wednesday! We need to get back ASAP.

When are we going to go? Fred loves drums so he should wait until his lesson is over. Perhaps I can do it in yard when everyone is playing freeze tag. I can just stand there, as still as a statue, totally zoned out and no one will be any the wiser where I've nipped off to.

When I arrive, my class teacher — Ms Hammerhead — is already at the board writing something in chalk.

The chalk squeaks like a chorus of mice out of tune. She eyeballs me like she always does, and I dart my eyes away quickly.

"Good morning, Frankie," she says. "How are you today?"

What does she mean by *that*?

"Fine," I mumble and slip into my seat.

I have learnt — interestingly from Ms Hammerhead herself — that very often someone's surname comes from their ancestor's profession, yonks and yonks of years ago.

Like Timmy Baker in my class. His family probably made and baked bread in the olden days. Timmy adores sandwiches, and he *even eats his crusts*, so this makes a lot of sense. Even Fred's music teacher is Ms Drumm!

I wonder what the Finkletons might have done many moons ago. I haven't a notion what a *finkle* is.

Could it possibly have something to do with magic?

Which brings us to Ms Hammerhead and her family history. I think it might really be possible that Ms Hammerhead's great-great-great-great-great-great-grandfather was ... a *hammerhead shark??*

It would explain how her eyes seem to be on either side of her head and yet somehow she can see everywhere in the classroom – which means all the students, both in front of and behind her – ALL at the same time.

She also has a gold medal for swimming in the inter-county championships, which is further evidence of her shark heritage. Not to mention she will eat you alive if you don't have your homework done. All very shark-like behaviour, if you ask me.

As well as possibly being related to a shark, Ms Hammerhead is also obsessed with:

a) Saying, "*Shhhhhhhhh.*"

b) Facts about things from yonks ago.

c) Maths sums and carrying the 1.

d) Manners. (No surprises there.)

e) Spelling. Oh, and ruling out made-up words like "fizzlesniz", which is a very specific type of sneeze that you cannot keep inside your head because it fizzes up your nose and suddenly explodes out of your mouth. Or "wurp". Which is a specific type of worry burp that has not yet officially been recognized by medical science. But Dr Hilda Stitch has said she will make a note of it for when he next talks to all the other doctors. If they aren't "actual" words then perhaps they should be because I can't see anyone else coming up with any other words to describe them.

f) Not eating the crayons. This is the only thing myself and Ms Hammerhead agree on. They give me terrible indigestion.

g) Keeping an extra close eye on me. No matter where Ms Hammerhead's other eye is looking, her other one will always, at some point, circle back to ... me. Which makes it tricky to slip off to you-know-where.

h) Speaking of you-know-where, all I can think of now is Ms Hammerhead in the ConfooZ Zoo, half-shark, half-fifth class primary school teacher eating tuna and bold pupils for lunch.

I stare at my desk and wonder if perhaps Ms Hammerhead was off sick during teacher training on the day they were taught how to make all our subjects fun for students to learn. Or maybe it is because sharks aren't known to have the best sense of humour in the animal world. Hmmmm.

I just really want to head back to Thoughtopolis with Fred, where at least exciting things happen and things are, well, a bit more exciting.

A lot more exciting.

Ms Hammerhead takes the register:

"Monica?"

"Ha!"

"Veronica?"

"Ha!"

"Nell?"

"Ha!"

They are probably answering "Here!" but it sounds like "Ha!" to me.

I look at our class goldfish Finn as she reads through the names, and I wonder how Ms Hammerhead has not eaten him yet.

And then all of a sudden I think of Vinny Finkleton.

He's dead now.

When he died, all the adults said things like:

"Death is a natural part of life."

"You don't need to understand it, Frankie, you just need to accept it."

And then to each other they would say things like:

"She doesn't really understand."

And I would think to myself: *of course I understand!* Vinny was really old, and of course he wasn't going to live for ever. Little bits of him had started to fall off, his eyes had gone white and he couldn't stay the right way up without flopping on to his back and floating about belly up.

Sorry, I should mention that Vinny was the family goldfish. He died aged seven, though in goldfish years this is about four hundred and fifty-six and therefore he was actually older than anyone I know. I was only little at the time, but I understood.

When we flushed him down the loo I made Granny Doris promise we wouldn't do that to Grampa Pinky when it was his time to go. And to be fair, she kept her promise.

"Copybooks out!" Ms Hammerhead shouts, cutting through the classroom noise and chatter like a shark fin slicing through the water, still squeaking her chalk on the blackboard.

As I take out my book, I accidentally catch Tess's eye. I'm not expecting her to acknowledge me – after all she prefers going to Mindy Morgan's house now to shout "LETTUCE!" at her tortoise – but to my surprise, her face lights up in a smile and she waves awkwardly.

I used to feel lucky in my choice of best friend. That she was kind and daring and wise and silly in the very best way because some of the other kids in my class were annoying and nosy and silly in the very worst way. We used to find fun in so much – eating our sandwiches at lunch, looking at the concrete in the yard and finding shapes in it like frogs or clouds or hamburgers or Mr McNogg's side profile.

But the last time we hung out we just sat on the bench kicking the ground, not knowing what to say.

"Any news, Frankie?" she'd ask.

"Erm ... nothing really," I'd answer awkwardly

255

"Want to come to the park today to hang upside down on the monkey bars?"

"I'm... I can't, Tess. I'm too busy."

And then she'd sigh, as though she already knew the answer before I had said it.

"But you're probably going to be hanging out with Mindy anyway," I added.

"Well... Probably. If you're too busy..."

And then we'd just sit there in silence, and I couldn't make out any shapes in the concrete, and I couldn't find any words that would make the situation feel easier.

It's less complicated to avoid her altogether.

I look away. I don't need friends who prefer to hang upside down with other friends at the park — not now I have Thoughtopolis.

Ross P. Rossdale, the noisiest person I have ever met in person and someone I would never marry, enters the classroom in a bustle, late; he throws his books on the table and sits down noisily beside me.

"Hey, Frankie," Ross bellow-squeaks. It's a rather strange combination. He's clutching a large apple, his mouth wide open like a lion about to eat a goat in one go.

CRUNCH!!!!!! That poor apple never stood a chance. ARGGGGGH, why can Ross P. Rossdale not eat quiet fruits like overripe pears? Or mandarins?

Ugh. Like I am literally never marrying him. Definitely squefinitely.

"Hey," I reply, and my cheeks go red, like they always do.

Having to sit beside Ross P. Rossdale is not helping my plan of going

256

under the radar, because EVERYTHING HE DOES IS LOUD. He always draws attention!

He reaches for his copybook and slaps it on the table. I didn't realize sheets of individual paper bound together could even make that much noise.

A little scream is up and out of my mouth before I know it. Maybe not a scream — more of an *eek*. A *meep*.

"Meeeeep," I meep.

"ARE YOU OK, FRANKIE?" Ross shouts as his words get louder and higher-pitched until he almost roars the word *FRAAAAAAAAANKIEEEEEEEE!!!!!*

I feel everyone's eyes dart over and then hear an eruption of *HAHAHAHAHAHAHAHAHAHHHAAAAs* and *pssshhhhhhhhhhhsss* from Monica, Veronica and Nell.

NOT GOOD.

I stare down at the desk, focusing on all the knots on the wood, the way they marble and swirl around each other, hoping everyone will get bored soon and look away again.

"I go really red sometimes too," Ross whispers, even though he cannot physically whisper and it comes out like someone speaking at a normal volume.

I sneak a glance at him and I notice that Ross P. Rossdale has really kind eyes.

"Thank you," I whisper.

More *HAHAHAHAHAHHAHAHHAAAAAAAAAAAAAAAAA*s mixed in with *PSSSSSSWWWWWISSHHHHH*s from the back of the room.

I really, really do not want to be here.

Ms Hammerhead says, "Come on, everyone, stop messing around, we have so much to do!" Does she know how much *I* have to do?

I get paid a little bit of pocket money, but I should probably start charging double time for being an eleven-year-old.

"RIGHT!" she bellows. "I want this finished by lunch!"

The whole class groan but are silenced immediately with one look — well, two. A glare from BOTH eyes.

"Everyone get to work. This morning's project is up on the board."

I look up at the board to see the words: *FAMILY TREE.*

Ugggghhh.

So boring.

I take out my pencils and colours. The clatter of everyone else's seems very far away.

I hear Ms Hammerhead's shoes, *clack, clack, clack.* And extra sheets of paper slapping down on the desks, *whack, whack, whack.* Getting louder, getting closer, as I seem to drift further and further. Monica, Veronica and Nell staring at me harder and harder. Ross, crunching crunchier and crunchier. Everyone's eyes darting over and over.

And then I see Ms Hammerhead circle my table like a predator about to gobble a little fish doing its best to mind its own business.

258

"Frankie," she whispers. "Come on, Frankie, just get your pencils and papers together and—"

And that's all it takes. As everyone around me crunches and stares and colours, I slip right off to Thoughtopolis.

CHAPTER THIRTY

DESTINATION NUMBER TWO WITH FRED AND BLUE

We're on the Train of Thought and travelling fast. Fred and Blue and I cling to our seats as the train flashes blue then green then red then orange then purple then a bright burst of golden. We loop sideways this way and that way. Then we climb upwards slowly, our tummies churning with anticipation.

"Frankie?"

"Yes, Fred?"

"Why don't French people like going on roller coasters?"

"I dunno," I answer.

"Because they are afraid they will do a *OUI!*"

And then we plunge downwards again at full speed. Giddiness, excitement, worry, doubt, fear. Different colours, shapes, noises whipping past.

"This is exciting," Blue says, gasping. "But you know, sometimes I miss getting my kicks from just 'walkies'."

Then we screech to a sudden halt.

"We must be at the second stop," Fred declares.

I can't help feeling a mix of excitement and nerves.

I look out of the window. But as I press my face to the glass, all I can see is Bundlenugg's squished face on the other side. And Pickle's little face coming and going as she jumps up to look in and says, "Hi!" Jumps up and bellows, "Hi!" Jumps up and says, "Hi!"

Pickle looks very excited.

"Frankie and Fred," Bundlenugg shouts through the glass, "I'm just going to press the giant red button on the side of the carriage that says, *DO NOT PRESS, OK?*"

"Sounds good!" Fred shouts back.

"What?" I interrupt. "That does *not* sound good!"

I watch Bundlenugg scarper towards the door near the gangway and start to reach up to a giant shiny red button that reads: *DO NOT PRESS*.

"ARRRRGGH!!" What are you doing, Bundlenugg?" I cry, chasing out of the carriage. "Don't do that! It says *DO NOT PRESS*."

"It's fine, Frankie," he answers calmly. "Sometimes your brain tricks you. It tells you to keep going, that it's *better* for you to keep going: ducking and diving, racing through your mind, never stopping. Never processing your feelings."

"It's a survival tool really," Pickle advises in her deep gravelly voice.

"But sometimes," Bundlenugg says, offering a hand down with his tiny furry paws (which actually makes it more difficult even though it's a nice thought), "you simply need to just **STOP AND GET OFF THE TRAIN.**"

"You really do," Pickle hollers. "All this dillydallying. You'd think you were not under any pressure whatsoever to find the secret buried in Thoughtopolis and uncover the missing spark before you get sent away."

I gulp.

No, thank you very much.

"Are we at Stop Number Two?" Fred asks excitedly, climbing off the train. We're standing on a platform covered in grey rock. I can see pinpricks of stars overhead. It's dark, but not in the same way as when the glitch happened.

It's calm and beautiful. The Train of Thought isn't as

busy as the first time either. A few passengers disembark at the platform and trickle away into the night.

"Yes, we are," Bundlenugg says. "Pickle and I are not coming with you, but we we will be waiting when you get back."

I look at Bundlenugg and Pickle on the platform. I already miss them before we've even said goodbye. I can't help feel bubbles of worry fizz in my tummy like I'm made of lemonade.

"It's OK, Frankie, we are still here. It's just we don't fit the height requirement for where you are going. We could end up floating away and getting lost for ever. And who wants that?"

Floating away and getting lost for ever. Weirdly that sounds both tempting and terrifying.

"We do hope that doesn't happen to you," Pickle barks. "And that we meet you on the other side when you get your stamp. Good luck, I guess." She shrugs with all four shoulders, which really must be a lot of extra work.

"We are excited for you, though," Bundlenugg says. "Where you are going is really ... *out there.*"

Hmmmm, cryptic.

I grip my Journey Journal. Crikey, where on earth are

we going that we could float away?

"Nowhere on Earth," Fred answers, reading my thoughts.

Ahead of us is a small metal container, just big enough to fit two children and a small dog with large eyes. It stands on the end of the platform like an elevator connected to nothing. Bundlenugg and Pickle nod, and Fred, Blue and I step inside. The doors slam closed and we look out through the portholes at our friends. Then before I know it, we shoot right into the sky at a billion light years an hour, a trillion stars whizzing past!

CHAPTER THIRTY-ONE

TO THE MOON
AND BACK

I close my eyes tight and hold on to Fred and Blue.

"**WAHOOOOOOOOO,** Frankie!" Fred calls. "Frankie, look at me!!!"

I open my eyes cautiously, blinking and squinting in the strange celestial light. We've come to a stop, and Fred is already outside the metal tin.

"Hahahahahahaaa! Frankie!! This is so fun! Try to catch me!!" His voice sounds echoey and far away.

What's going on? Hang on a second... Is he...? Oh my gosh! Fred ... is he?

YES!!

Fred is **FLOATING!**

Fred is floating ... in a space suit!!!

I go to rub my eyes, but my hands clunk off the glass of my own space helmet. I look down at Blue: his huge

eyeballs look even more hugey and eyebally from inside his fishbowl glass helmet. He's *also* floating. And so is something else.

"Oh my gosh, Frankie, I am mortified," Blue says. He's obviously nervous and who could blame him? He's done a little poo. We both stare at it as it floats away slowly.

"Would be handy if that happened at home, Blue. Would save Dad going out with the pooper scooper at the end of every day."

"Yeah," he sighs, sounding both amazed and humiliated.

Where *are* we?

Miles and miles of glowing rock surface stretch out before us, puckering in a thousand pockets of different cavernous craters and cavities. Some that are large mountainous swells that reach up out of the ground

grab the pitch black atmosphere above them. And others that are dug into the surface creating deep, dark endless pits. All around is pitch dark, like a giant sea of spilt ink. But because the surface we're standing on is so bright, everything is illuminated in a silver glow. Somehow the light manages to press against the weight of the heavy darkness surrounding us, and wins.

I look at Fred floating in thin air.

It's so quiet. So eerily calm.

I can't remember the last time anything was so still inside my own head. Or if it ever has been.

I look at Fred again and giggle.

"Frankie, I'm cartwheeling! You said I'd never get the hang of it! **WEEEHHEEEEEE!**"

Fred is a notoriously bad cartwheeler. I guess that's the reputation you earn after smashing Gertrude Gonnigle's glasses during a cartwheeling extravaganza down Conker Hill in the Real World. Fred did manage to put them back together with slime, Blu Tack and football stickers, though, and I really thought Gertrude Gonnigle's mum would have been more impressed with his fixing skills.

I push out of the metal tin and reach for Fred but my hands sail through thin air, moving slowly like they aren't

268

even attached to my body. I'm also … floating!

I am! **I AM FLOATING TOO!**

I'm dressed in an identical suit to Fred: a sort of padded white moon suit with big marshmallow moon boots.

I wriggle my toes in my boots, feeling so light and free! Our feet are not on the ground! We are *actually* **FLOATING!**

"Hahahaha!! Fred! This is incredible."

"I know! This is so fun! Waheeeeee! Watch me, Frankie! Are you watching?"

I nod, not knowing how exactly we are able to talk to each other through our helmets.

"There's no gravity, Frankie! It's like we are flying! **WEEEHOOOOOOO!**" He swirls around again, landing softly on his feet before taking off once more. I laugh and try it myself, my head light and woozy as everything around me tumbles slowly.

Now Fred is jumping, bouncing his moon boots on the surface and floating in the air, before landing on the surface again softly.

BOING!

Off he goes again, chuckling inside his glass helmet. It looks like he's wearing an upturned fishbowl on his head. His hair fans out in all directions like a mess of floating spaghetti.

269

His hair makes me think of my spaghetti brain, the adults back in the Real World and the task at hand.

I remember why we've come. My quest to find my spark. Surely there is a clue floating around up here. I reach for my magnifying glass, hearing a **CLINK** as it bashes off my glass helmet.

"Fred?"

"Yeah," he replies, floating past my face.

"I think ... I think we **ARE ON THE MOON!**"

It's the only place we *can* be: the space suits, the floating, the stars, the stillness, the celestial glow—

"WHY CAN'T PEOPLE CLEAN UP AFTER THEIR DOGS?"

Huh? Fred and I turn, hearing a strange voice. It sounds ... hoarse but also squeaky. Sort of like Mum first thing in the morning before she has her coffee.

I follow Fred as he bounds over to a curious-looking figure in the distance.

It has its back to us, and the shape of its form doesn't look human; it's taller and ganglier with a long oval-shaped head.

"Excuse me!" Fred calls. "We are here on our holidays! Well, actually that's not true. We are here to find Frankie's spark."

"It's a long story," I add.

"She's going to get sent away to eat potatoes, and be kept back after school for extra classes. You haven't seen Frankie's spark lying about, have you? We've been told we can find it once we figure out where the secret has been buried. Somewhere in Thoughtopolis?"

The figure turns slowly to reveal ginormous almond eyes: long, glinting ovals of beetle-black glass. It has no other discernible facial features except for the smallest mouth I've ever seen. Like a nail clipping from a baby finger. And its entire body emanates a gentle silver glow from within.

Blue's giant round eyes blink back.

"Is it ... a dog?" he whispers. "Cross breeds are so popular right now. But I'm pretty sure that's not a cockapoo."

It stands there as still as a pillar, only moving its eyelids to blink.

None of us says a thing.

And then a shriek escapes my mouth and whirrs around inside my helmet, trapped and panicked like a small purple tornado, and I lift the glass slightly to let it out. It disappears into the ether in an echoey scream.

Sometimes that happens in Thoughtopolis. The ninja burps are green, but the shrieks are like a spool of purple steam rising out of a kettle. Bundlenugg told me it's how we literally let off steam.

No way. I continue to stare at the thing that is definitely not a cockapoo.

NO WAY?!! Could it be…?

"IS THAT YOUR DOG?" the figure calls angrily, extending a narrow pointy hand with one long finger. **"I'M TRYING TO SELL MOON CHEESE HERE. I KNOW EVERYONE THINKS ANYTHING GOES IN OUTER SPACE, BUT WE DO HAVE BASIC HYGIENE AND HEALTH AND SAFETY, YOU KNOW."**

"Sorry," Fred says as Blue's tiny space poo floats past the figure's face.

My tummy whirrs nervously again. How is Fred not in any way frightened?

Because … that creature standing right over there in the distance is surely…

AN ALIEN.

CHAPTER THIRTY-TWO

MOON CHEESE WILL GIVE YOU NIGHTMARES

"Fred! Fred, stand back. It's an alien! **AN ALIEN!!**"

Fred seems completely unperturbed as he boings and tumbles some more in slow motion.

"**SHHHHHHH**, Frankie, I don't think that's the politically correct term any more." He begins to bounce after the alien. "I want to try some of their cheese."

We bound past a flagpole and Fred spins around on it. "Come back! Come back!" The American flag at the top refuses to droop with no gravity pull.

I look at the handwritten note pinned to the surface of the moon. "Oh my gosh, Fred, I think this is where Neil Armstrong landed?"

"Haha! Cool!" he replies. "What does it say?"

I read it out loud. "That's one small step for man, one giant leap for mankind."

I smile, thinking how cool this is.

I've always thought astronauts must be really lazy, floating about all day doing everything really slowly. But I guess it involves a lot of work and organization and it makes me think that not everything appears like it does from far away.

Oh, and don't forget to sample the moon cheese. It's **DELISH!** *Neil* **XOXXO**

And then I look down at the ground where *Buzz waz 'ere* is scratched on the surface.

We *are* on the moon, I realize. Only this is Thoughtopolis's moon! How cool that we share the same one!

I finally catch up with Fred and the alien.

I'm moving so slowly. Like Gr-Annie making it back up the hill after visiting the park.

"Excuse me," says Fred politely. "I'm Fred. Could I please try some of this moon cheese?"

The alien nods slowly. "I'm called Martin," it says.

"You're a ... martian?" I ask.

"MARTIN!" he replies in annoyance. "Honestly, you earthlings, we've been trying to tell you for like a billion light years that we are called Martin. **NOT MARTIANS.**

274

The genius who discovered us wasn't actually listening when we told him."

"Maybe he couldn't understand you?" I say.

Martin nods. "Communication can be hard sometimes. That's why we cry when we are sad."

The creature starts leaking fluid from his large eyeballs, but instead of the tears plopping downwards, they float in slow motion through the air and crystallize like snowflakes, free-wheeling in the atmosphere around us.

"And why we go red when we're embarrassed," he continues, his entire head glowing as red as a cherry.

"And why we shrink ourselves when we are shy." The creature's head shrinks to the size of a raisin, and his voice gets all high and squeaky like he's been sucking helium.

"And why we let off steam when we're angry." His head grows again and purple steam flies out of his non-existent nostrils.

"And why when we are happy we laugh." The creature's face explodes in colour as giggles rise out of him in a stream of bubbles from his mouth! They float around us like tiny moons before popping into explosions of colour.

"There are a zillion ways to communicate other than just words, if only others could read them properly."

I think of Tess in the yard at school, kicking the ground with her shoe aimlessly without talking.

I think of Mum turning away when she found me in the fort Fred and I had built from blankets and pillows that I wouldn't let her take down. Probably disappointed I was in there rather than at my desk doing my homework.

I think of Dad, sitting on the end of my bed, trying to start a hundred sentences before abandoning them all and getting up to walk away.

There is often so much hidden in the silent gaps between words.

"The thing that confuses you earthlings the most," Martin continues, "is when a feeling is dressed up with words that don't match it."

"Like what?" Fred asks.

"Like saying, 'I'm fine, I'm fine,' while these are leaking out." Martin points at the tears floating from his eyes.

"Or saying, 'Go away, go away,' when you want to do this." Martin extends his arms for a hug and Blue jumps up in slow motion to meet his embrace.

"I forgive you for pooing."

"I can't help it," Blue answers.

"I understand," Martin replies and they hug.

"Hey, Fred," I say, feeling for some reason that this is the perfect time for a joke. "I like my water like I like my emotions … *bottled*."

He doesn't laugh.

"So you're called Martin," I say, filling the awkward silence. "My name is Frankie, pleased to meet you. This is my brother, Fred, and this is Blue."

Martin extends a long skinny hand as Blue jumps out of his arms and floats about for a bit. I reach out to shake it.

"No, no," he replies, sounding exasperated. He turns to Fred.

To my astonishment, Fred sticks out his hand and waggles it. Then Martin and Fred perform an incredibly intricate and impressive hand greeting routine that ends in an elbow bump.

"How on earth did you know how to do that?" I ask Fred.

He chuckles. "I just did. Instinct, I guess. And we *aren't* on Earth now, are we?"

"I should introduce you to Martin," said Martin.

"Wait!" I say. "Are all of you called ... Martin?"

"YES."

I look around.

Hundreds of large glassy black almond eyes are blinking at us.

Whoa! How did we miss them?

"We are all called Martin!" they say in unison.

There must be hundreds, thousands, thousands upon thousands of these moon beings, almost blending in with the moon's surface; their black eyes are like a vast pattern of oval polka dots.

"Is that not ... confusing?" Fred asks.

"Not in the slightest!" Martin says. "I always think you Earth creatures must get confused – all those different names, first names, second names, double-barrelled names, nicknames…"

I think about this. Martin has a point.

"I also thought that you guys were supposed to be…"

"Don't even say it!" another Martin answers. "**GREEN!** Go on! You thought we were all green with three eyes, didn't you? **DIDN'T YOU?**"

Fred and I nod guiltily.

"Not gonna lie, absolutely," Blue says.

"See how rumours can start?" Martin sighs.

I think about the time when Monica, Veronica and Nell told everyone I was a space cadet who couldn't concentrate and a rumour went around row D and E in the classroom that they reckoned I was an actual alien.

Ha! Wouldn't they like to see me now?!

"Sorry," I say. "I did think you'd all be green and possibly shooting lasers from your fingertips."

"No, you have us confused with superhero aliens. They all live on a planet called Sporganoff in the outer reaches of your imagination."

I look around at the sea of identical, shiny Martins. "Are you … all the same?"

Martin snorts. "Because we look the same? That's not a very higher intelligence way of thinking, Frankie. It's easy to label people the same when you don't know them, or you think you won't understand them. But when anyone takes the time to look, to see, to really try to understand, to read the different ways we communicate, they will see that everyone is exactly the same in different ways."

I think of Bundlenugg and his riddle. *We are the same, you and I, inside and out, whether you are small and furry, have a beak or a snout.* He says that despite us all being different on the outside, we have the same jumble of feelings on the inside, just in different ways.

I think of everyone at home in the Real World – Mum and Dad and Monica and Veronica and Nell and even Margery Lonergan – and wonder if, like me, there are other things going in their heads other than wondering what is going on in mine. I'm starting to think people communicate in very different ways, but that doesn't mean they don't feel the same things.

"Like when your feelings are playing fancy dress in different words entirely," Blue offers, digging at the moon ground, and I think how clever he is.

"Hey, Martin, can I dig a really cool hole here for no reason?"

"I'd prefer it if you didn't."

"OK." And then I think Blue is clever just sometimes.

"I do get it," Blue adds as an afterthought. "But we could just say I'm looking for Frankie's spark...?"

"Oh, you won't find it there," Martin scoffs.

I sigh again. Where is it, this spark of mine?

"Monica, Veronica and Nell call me a weirdo," I say to Martin.

"Of course they do. It's a defence because they don't understand you. Because you are not exactly like them. Because you don't think exactly the way they do. And for some people, that is a threat. There's no space for you in their world. Here? Here, there is lots of space."

Martin busies himself with his moon cheese samples as I stare into space. Like I do in the Real World, only in a different, way cooler way.

I look around, spotting Mercury, Venus and Mars in the distance, rotating in an endless black sky dotted with twinkly stars that light up like a blanket of fireflies. Martin's words echo into the distance for miles and miles and miles.

"Come on, weirdo," Martin says and his voice is kind. "Have some cheese."

"I'm starving!" I say, suddenly realizing I am.

Fred chimes in too, "So am I!"

"Then please help yourself to our moon cheese, freshly mined today."

"Mined? You mean you get your cheese from…"

"From moon rocks, yes. Why – have you ever seen a cow on the moon?"

I haven't, to be fair.

I lift my fishbowl helmet and take a curious sniff followed by a tentative bite.

OOOOOOOOOOOH! Delicious! It melts on my tongue and is both sweet and tangy all at once.

"Yum!!!!" Fred grins.

"Is it true that you control the tides?" Fred asks, still chewing.

"It is. When you are next in the sea, jumping the waves. That is us saying hi."

"What about when kids moon out of car windows? Is that you too?"

"Not any more," Martin replies, picking up a piece of moon cheese and popping it into his own tiny baby fingernail mouth. "It was giving us quite the bad reputation so we handed that job over to Uranus. A much better fit, if you ask me."

Fred giggles. And then I giggle at Fred.

And Martin giggles. And then Martin and Martin and Martin and Martin. And Martin. All the Martins. Until we are all giggling. Until it feels like the whole moon shakes a little.

"When you go to sleep at night, who is shining down on all of you?"

"The moon! You are, Martins!" Fred giggles.

They all nod in unison. It's hypnotic.

"We sit on your window sills and make sure your brains are resting. Rest is very important, Frankie. Particularly at night. It's the only time your head can figure out the day's thoughts. Your mind processes them as dreams."

Sometimes I don't let myself fall asleep, because that's when the nightmares creep in.

Sometimes, even though my eyes are heavy with tiredness, it's easier to lie there and stare at the ceiling.

If you live with a small villain who could possibly crawl under your bed at any given moment, nightmares are common.

"I had a dream once that I was a giant shoe. It was after Frankie taught me how to tie my laces," Fred recalls. "I was in a right knot."

The Martins laugh. I love how Fred makes everyone laugh.

I feel my face glow a lovely shade of pink with the pride.

"The only problem is when things go wrong. When earthlings aren't communicating with each other properly."

"When they dress up their feelings?" Fred asks.

"Yes, it can make things go awry. And that's when …

283

nightmares can happen."

My tummy squirms suddenly. I don't want to think about nightmares.

If it is all about communication, how on earth am I supposed to communicate with a lazy baby bandit who only ever says **"BLLLLLLLAAAAAAAADEBLOOOP"?**

"We want to help you, Frankie," said Martin quietly.

I feel like so many people have been saying this to me lately. Now even the aliens are at it. Sorry, the martians. I mean, the Martins.

"How?" I reply. "How can you help me?"

"By facing the scary things that are coming out in your dreams. Bringing them into the daylight."

I shake my head. *No*, I think. "I don't remember them so I can't do that." I bite my lip.

Flo is only the tip of the iceberg. I have *a lot* going on right now. But what else is in the nightmares? I stop staring into space for a moment and look at Martin, remembering why we are here. Destination number two! "Do the nightmares have something to do with the missing spark?"

And just as I say it, it's as if the skies darken. Which is almost impossible as they're such a deep inky black already.

No one answers. I inhale, thinking of all the times I've woken in the night with a bad dream. My dad pacing on the landing. My mum crying. Padding into Fred's room to watch him sleeping.

That's always where I go in the middle of the night. To watch Fred sleep.

"You need to go now, Frankie," says Martin. "You've had your moon cheese. This will help you face your worst nightmare on your journey."

My worst nightmare, I think. What could that be?

Far into the distance I hear a heronder squawk. I lean over the edge of the moon and look down on Thoughtopolis. It looks so small from up here. I squint. Is that the Worrisome Woods rippling slightly? The wind forcing itself through the trees?

Maybe they know about next week's spelling test and that the word *misscellanyous*. I mean, *miscsellanious*. I mean, *mistleayynyous*, is going to be on the list.

And I see a bird's-eye view of Proud Palace, and it looks from up here as though the turrets are … crumbling? Are the King and Queen in there? Are they OK?

I giggle, trying to show I'm not nervous. But I know the emotion on the outside doesn't match the feelings I have on the inside.

"Take this," Martin says, handing me a small glass bottle of iridescent blue and silver powder. I study it as it shimmers and glows within the bottle.

"It's moon dust. Use it sparingly and only when you really need it. It glows when it gets very dark and helps you see."

"Incredible," Blue says. "You'd think with the size of these bad boys I'd be good at seeing in the dark. Nope. False advertising."

"I've never seen moon dust before," Fred marvels, peering into the bottle.

"Wow! Moon dust," I study it closely too. Seriously cool. "How will I know when I really need it?" I ask.

"You will know when you know."

Ugh. My life is one entire riddle right now!

"You need to find another stamp," Martin continues. "Another stamp on your journey to the secret. But remember what Bundlenugg said: you must also have fun. It is your moral obligation. Go and explore outer space."

Does Bundlenugg know the Martins? Bundlenugg knows everyone I figure.

"Off you go!" all the Martins chime in unison. **"OFF**

YOU GO!!"

I reach for Fred's hand as we make our way to the very edge of the moon, looking back at all the Martins one last time as they wave us off.

"We will send you all our very best dreams. But you must face what's in your nightmares first, Frankie."

"And do watch those emotions, won't you?" another Martin offers. "You will get better at figuring out which one goes where."

"Like sorting out a sock drawer," a Martin adds.

"That's true, Martin," Martin says.

"Good luck, Frankie. Try and figure out the feeling; it will be another clue. It will get you another stamp," another Martin entirely says.

"Thanks," I whisper, feeling as untethered on the inside as I am on the outside. At least that's a match, eh?

Fred, Blue and I turn towards the outstretched dark abyss, the moon shining its light for us like a torch.

And then...

We jump.

CHAPTER THIRTY-THREE

TWO SPACE CADETS AND THE FIRST DOG IN SPACE

We land with a thud on the first planet from the sun.

Mercury.

And it is **BOILING.**

Is there going to be a clue *here*?

Fred and I are suddenly in swimming togs. We're still wearing our helmets as there's no air to breathe on Mercury either. And it rotates so fast that we have to race to keep up. It's like being on a treadmill, in our togs! In space!

This is so wild!

We write our names in space dust in the sky – **FRANKIE** and **FRED** – and Blue does a paw print and it reminds me of camping in Dad's car in the front garden one night and writing our names in the fog on the windows.

"Fred!" I call. "Wait for me!" He is jumping to

the next planet and Blue and I chase after him, soaring through the twinkling skies.

We are on Venus.

Which I am happy to report is not as boiling as Mercury. It is also one of the most beautiful places I've ever been. Even nicer than the secret tuckshop cupboard in school behind Mr McNogg's office and that's saying something, as he keeps red liquorice swirls and sherbet dip dabs in there.

Everything here is **GORGEOUS**, like a giant bright big sparkly red and silver Valentine's Day card or something. It's like being inside a huge hug.

"It's named after a goddess lady person whose job is to love everyone," Blue says, and I think how fascinating it is that Blue is into the Classics.

"Sounds like Mum," Fred answers.

"Totally!" I agree. Then, because we are, after all, on the planet of love, I say, "I love you, Fred!"

"I love you, Frankie!"

We giggle, our cheeks turning the deep red of the planet's glow. Even though Fred knows I love him and I know he loves me – sort of like knowing how to breathe, or to eat when you are hungry – we still get embarrassed when we actually say it out loud.

But out here, out on Venus, it's like it takes over and you have no control over it.

"I love you!" we shout at each other again, laughing every time we get louder. We chase after each other, kicking the heart-shaped confetti into the air around us like fresh leaves in the park. We laugh and laugh. Our giggles bouncing in endless echoes into the vast galaxy around us.

"I MISS YOU!!!" I shout suddenly, stopping in my own tracks, my feet not touching the ground, hovering in the nothing.

Fred looks at me for a minute. Then he turns, jumping away, just out of my reach.

We land on Mars next. A giant orange-red ball.

"It's orange, Frankie, because Mars is full of iron!" Blue informs us. And there I was wondering if all the toys got up in the night and had parties while we slept, while it was actually Blue who was up by candlelight, studying all my schoolbooks.

He's right, though. All around us are teeny tiny irons on teeny tiny ironing boards plugged into the surface and ready to go. We crawl around on the ground, weaving in and out of them as best we can. I really do not like doing laundry!

"This is where the Martins get their ironing done apparently. Great service. Light years ahead of other places." Fred giggles. "Do you get it, Frankie?"

"I get it," Blue answers. "A unit of astronomical distance equivalent to the distance that light travels in one year, which is 9.4607×10^{12} km (nearly six million million miles). But also in joke form, it means something is way ahead."

"Thank you, Blue," I say.

"Any time," he replies.

Fascinating.

We catch a shower of asteroids straight to Jupiter next, the most efficient way to travel in space after rockets apparently. It's comfy enough, if a little bumpy on account of all the … well, rocks. Jupiter is even more **HUMUNGOUS** again…

But when we get there we can't even land as the entire planet is gas! Fred and I float above the surface, laughing uncontrollably because the planet is made of … laughing gas!

"This is good, Fred!" I yell. "Bundlenugg told us we needed to have fun, remember?"

Fred squeaks his nostrils against the glass of his helmet and I burst out laughing.

"Fred! How do the Martins get their baby to sleep?"

"I dunno," Fred replies, trying to wipe the laughter tears from his eyes, forgetting the glass shield of his helmet which stops him.

"They **ROCKET** to sleep."

"*HAHAHAHAHAHAHAHAAAA*"

"What's an astronaut's favourite key on the keyboard?" Fred asks. "The space bar!"

"*HAHAHAHAHAAAAAAAHAHAHAA*"

"Why is it better to bring a dog into space rather than a cat?" Blue jokes.

"We don't know!" Fred and I call together.

"To avoid any cat-astro-phies!"

"*HAHAHAHAHAAAAHAHAHAHAHAA*"

We laugh even more, our chuckles propelling us around the planet like little engines fuelled by giggles.

Underneath the laughter, though, I can't help thinking about my mission. My missing spark. About Flo. About Mum and Dad. It gives me a feeling of unease. The sky grows inkier. I push the thoughts away. I chase after Fred instead. Getting further and further away on to...

Oh, woweeeeeee, Saturn is **THE BEST FUN!** It has a giant ring around it and we slide the whole way round, our arms up as we fly through the air, shouting, **"WHEEEEEEEEEEEEEEEEEEEEEE!"** into the endless twinkling skies. The flying space ring around Saturn is made entirely of icicles and popping candy dust, sparkling a million different rainbow colours under the light of the stars.

Uranus is the strangest planet; it makes Fred and I fart uncontrollably! The more we fart, the more we are propelled around the planet. The sheer force of our farts makes us go even faster.

"Whooops! Sorry, Frankie!" Fred apologizes, zooming past me.

"No need to apologize!" I reply, zipping ahead of him loudly.

"Don't mind me!" Blue mumbles, whipping past.

"I'm glad I'm wearing a helmet, Frankie. That moon cheese really does not agree with you!" he says, wincing and waving his hand in front of his nose. "Should we move on?"

Neptune is cold, but beautiful, like a magical frozen ice world. Snow glimmers in the moonlight, while shards of ice glow like giant illuminated crystal statues. We make ice sculptures and have snow fights. Then we lie on the surface and make snow angels. Except for Blue as pugs aren't really bendy enough for that.

"Have you ever wished on a star, Fred?" I ask.

"I have, Frankie. Have you?"

"A million times," I say, looking back at the stars.

Ginormous pale blue clouds creep over our heads, changing the wintery weather once more.

"Frankie!" cries Fred. "I think it's going to hail!"

We race to pluck a large umbrella each from the expansive umbrella patch growing on the ground around us like toadstools, and we open them as the clouds overhead crash into each other and start raining showers of asteroids. The asteroids aren't hard like stones, but soft like foam, and they burst into crystal-coloured water particles as they fall. It's like standing under a melting rainbow.

"Remember when Mum let us splash in the puddles in the park for three hours once, Fred? Normally she'd bring us home when it started to rain. I remember how tired you were. But you didn't want to go home; you were having too much fun."

"Yeah," he says, kicking the asteroid puddles at his feet. "She said some things were more important than rules, or common sense. We were **SOAKED**."

"We haven't done that in the longest time," I say. I look up at him. "Why haven't we done that, Fred?"

I remember Mum looking sad as she watched us splash about. I think it was probably because she had blow-dried her hair straight and then curled it again just that morning and now it was ruined.

Thinking of the Real World makes me think of what is planned this week if I don't find my spark on time. Where is this clue? How do I get my next stamp??

Fred smiles at me, then turns and heads for a large asteroid puddle. I see that his moon boots have been replaced by a pair of wellington boots with space rocket patterns on them. I recognize those boots. They're Fred's favourite wellies.

I go to follow him.

But he keeps jumping forward.

I lumber after him in my space suit. Eventually I catch up with him, sitting beside a large frozen lake.

"What is it made out of?" Fred asks. "That's not water, is it?"

We scrape our fingers along the surface, gathering little frozen fluffy velvet snowball scoops on our fingertips. Then Fred lifts his helmet and pops his finger into his mouth.

"Frankie, it's ice cream!" Fred says. "Raspberry ripple!" We look out over the lake: soft custard-coloured ice cream with splinters of deep raspberry swirls throughout.

I smile at him, beaming and eating ice cream. But I feel sad in a way I can't explain. Fred looks so teeny tiny small sitting on the edge of the lake, on the edge of the planet, on the edge of the furthest place we can ever go together. And my heart stings at how much I want to protect him always.

He winces slightly. "Frankie, I don't feel too good."

Suddenly *everything* around us starts getting darker. The sun is doing its best to squeeze some remaining light out before losing its range entirely. Long shadows stretch along the surface of the ground around us. The planet starts spinning so fast it must have been turning from day to night much faster than on Earth.

"Fred, I think you've eaten too much ice cream," I say.

Fred burps. A tiny shooting star flies from his mouth

and lands in the ice cream below in a dissolving hiss.

"Well, that was cool!" I reply, attempting to distract him.

We burp. And burp. And burp. **AND BURP!** Lots of little shooting stars fly out of our mouths and sink into the soft yellow and pink velvet lake below us.

"Oh, Frankie," Fred grumbles, holding his tummy and wincing. "I *really* don't feel well."

"You're OK, Fred, it's just too much ice cream, and all the spinning. And all the burping."

But Fred slumps over to the side and then he curls into a little ball.

"Fred?"

He doesn't answer me this time.

"Is he OK?" Blue asks, his nubbin tail still now.

Double uh oh. Like uh oh times two multiplied by twelve.

I take off his helmet and touch his forehead. It is icy cold. All of a sudden a giant thermometer grows from a crack in the planet's surface, so high and tall like a giant thermometer sky scraper!

"FEVER! FEVER!" it bleeps, flashing red. This is so weird; he's cold, but he's also hot.

Quadruple uh oh!

"Fred! Come on, we gotta get out of here!" I order,

popping his helmet back on and pulling him to his feet.

"I'm so hot, Frankie," he mumbles weakly. "I don't feel good."

CHAPTER THIRTY-FOUR

THE VERY DARK DARKNESS (OR ... AFRAID OF THE DARK)

How is Fred so hot when he's also so cold? It doesn't make sense.

I start to feel hot too with panic. Even though we are on a giant frozen ice rock planet. The lake! I think. We need to jump in the lake! I grab his hand and in we dive, feeling the refreshing hiss as we plunge into the icy water.

It helps for a bit. Until we start to feel too cold! The sunlight is gone completely now, everything dark. And grey. And **FREEZING**.

Our eyes blink bright white, reflecting the celestial glare from the nearby moon.

Even in the cold, Fred still feels roasting!

Blue whimpers. "Sorry, habit; what I mean is I'm a bit worried and I don't like this."

"We need to get out of here, Fred!" I look around to see where the shore is. When I look back, Fred seems suddenly very far away.

"Frankie! Frankie! I'm sinking!" he calls and I watch in horror as he starts to disappear into the depths of the rippled ice-cream lake. I reach for his hand, but my fingers slip through his. Blue tugs at my moonboots to help anchor me.

I try again. And again. But I can't reach him. I'm losing him. I'm losing Fred!

My heart beats in my chest as my legs kick in the thick frozen lake.

THINK!

THINK, FRANKIE!

I stretch out, while reaching with my other hand for the bottle of moon dust. I flip open the lid with my thumb and shake it. Specks of precious iridescent powder rain through the air in slow motion and I finally feel a flood of relief as my hand closes around Fred's.

This time I won't let go,

We find ourselves on Pluto. The furthest away.

It's dark and quiet here. As though the whole galaxy has turned the lights out and gone to sleep.

I shiver, zipping my coat over my space suit and pulling the fluffy hood up over my helmet. Blue huddles close to me.

Fred sits on the very edge, the furthest spot away in the whole solar system, his back facing me, his shadowy outline just about visible.

"What are you doing?" I whisper in the dark.

"Fishing!"

"There are *fish* out here?" I ask, tiptoeing towards him.

"I'm not fishing for fish, silly. Although did you know that Real World starfish came from Mars? They dropped out of the sky one day and ended up in our seas!"

"Really?" I say.

"Really," he shrugs. "In Thoughtopolis, anyway."

"It's true," Blue adds quietly.

"What are you fishing for?"

"A star, Frankie. You keep wishing on a star. I'm not sure the dandelion fluff wishes get as far! This *one* wish. I'm trying to get it for you."

I squint my eyes and see him clearer now, sitting with

his knees tucked under his chin, holding out a fishing rod with an endlessly long line dipping down into a sea of stars below.

He looks tired and pale.

"Are you OK, Fred?"

He doesn't answer me.

I look over my shoulder in the direction we've come from, suddenly feeling very, very far away.

I can see Earth in the distance, just about, the Earth that holds Thoughtopolis. And it's as though the seas are swirling and the land is twisting.

A storm is coming. I can see it gathering momentum from all the way out here.

Bundlenugg told me the storm will get stronger and stronger as we go along; that I have to find the buried secret and my spark before the storm gets out of control and Thoughtopolis becomes under threat.

OK, we've had our fun; we said we'd do that too. But we need to find out why we are here to move forward on the journey now!

But where to?

I've come as far as I can possibly go.

And it's lonelier than I had imagined it would be.

I have Fred and Blue with me. And a billion stars to wish on.

But all I feel is completely alone.

And just like that, a wind whips up from around my feet, scattering dust and particles like mini tornadoes gaining momentum. I can hardly see a thing.

"Fred!" I call. "We've been gone way too long, Fred! They are all going to ask where we've been! Fred? **FRED?**"

I can't see anything. And I can't move. I'm stuck. Blue is beside me and I hear him whimper.

I know Fred is close, but I can't reach him. Is this the nightmare that Martin meant? It feels familiar somehow.

"FRED?" I call into the abyss. "We've gone too far, Fred. We can't stay here. We need to go back. NOW."

And then all my fear bubbles up and out of me.

"FRED! I'M SCARED! I CAN'T LOSE YOU AGAIN!" I start crying. "Fred, I promised. I promised I'd love you to the moon and back and now we've been to the moon and we need to go back."

I think about the first time I ever met Fred. He was one day old. He was so small in his crib. "Is it ... a guinea pig?" I had asked Mum. (I was only three, you'll have to ignore my immaturity.)

"It's your baby brother," Dad whispered.

I peered in through the glass. He was so tiny, so delicate. He looked like he might need my help.

"He's one of the greatest gifts you'll know," Mum said softly, running her finger along my nose.

And he is.

"Can I help you mind him?" I asked.

"You can!" They smiled back.

And I have done. Every day when he was small, and when he grew bigger, and when he got sick—

"FRED!!!!!"

And with that not even my echo returns to comfort me.

There's nothing.

Nothing except an all-encompassing darkness.

Blue places his paw on my space suit. What's he doing? He scratches a little, and I remember the moon dust. Have I used it all?

I reach into my space suit and pull out the glass bottle, opening the lid and scattering the last few iridescent grains into the void.

CHAPTER THIRTY-FIVE

AND THE OSCAR GOES TO ... FRANKIE FINKLETON!

"Fred?" I whisper in the dark. "This journey is getting so intense. I'm pretty tired. Are you tired?"

I'm hunkered on the rug beside his bed in the Real World.

Mum and Dad are downstairs, probably dreaming up ways to send me to other relatives who only eat one type of vegetable. Apparently I have a great-aunt in Scotland who is obsessed with parsnips, and that sounds even worse. Flo is in her cot in the next room pretending to be one of those nice compliant babies that sleep at night-time and give everyone a bit of peace.

Compliant is an interesting word in Gr-Annie's word of the day book. It means you agree with everyone and obey the rules. But if you look at it closely with a magnifying glass, the word "lie" is right there in the middle.

That's Flo in a nutshell.

"I didn't know Thoughtopolis could get so out of control," I tell Fred.

"It was scary. But we have the next stamp. That's two out of five. We must be getting closer."

I look out of his bedroom window at the moon and think about the Martins. They said I need to face my nightmare. Is the nightmare I faced that I would lose Fred?

Where will I lose him? I wonder. And the feeling of being lost, stuck, floating in a blanket darkness, my feet not feeling grounded, not able to reach him? Unable to take him home. Terrified of losing him.

I'm scared. That's what I'd said. It was then that I'd got the next stamp in the Journey Journal. The final sprinkle of moon dust had helped at the very last moment.

And then the golden door had opened up and we had run out and got home safely.

Blue stares at me now in the dark.

"Don't worry, Blue. I won't tell anyone about your floaty poo."

He blinks back. It's annoying that he can't talk in the Real World, but I'm pretty sure that eyeblink was code for: *Thank you so much. I am still utterly mortified. I would very much appreciate it if you kept it to yourself.*

When we got back to the Real World it was business as usual in 34 Cottage Orchard Road. Dinner time, homework, cartoons, glass of milk, brushing of teeth, brushing of hairs (why we don't say hairs when there are loads of them is beyond me).

"How was your day, Frankie?" Mum asked and I shrugged a "fine" like

I usually do. And Mum and Dad stole a quick glance at each other over my head which they usually do. A secret nod to imply that Operation Granny Potato is well on target for Friday.

And then Flo roared, "Ha!" or "Whaaa!" like she usually does too.

"Get some sleep, Fred," I whisper, patting Blue's head and rubbing my eyes. "We have a lot of work still to do and we need our energy."

Even though I know I'm going to crawl back into my own bed and stare at the ceiling until it's time to get up again.

I lie in the dark in my bed, looking at the shadowy outlines of everything in my room. Thinking of my Secret Book of Secrets hidden in the dark under my bed. When Dad comes in to kiss me goodnight, I pretend to be asleep. I am getting really, really, REALLY good at pretending.

I'm so good at it that I'm starting to wonder if a person can be awarded an Oscar randomly. Like maybe it could just be presented out of the blue in school assembly at the end of the year.

I'm good at acting like everything is normal and I have no secrets whatsoever and I'm not on a very intense mission against time to get my spark back, save our family and avoid being sent away to Granny Doris and eat potatoes for the rest of my life.

Yeah. I think I could get nominated for Best Performance by an eleven-and-one-twelfth-year-old in a true story about their own life.

I might start writing a speech juuuuuuuust in case.

Pretending to be fine is pretty exhausting, though. Pretending that school is fun and that I'm committed to learning how to divide ginormous numbers into even more ginormouser numbers. Or pretending to find boring history stuff interesting. All that olden days stuff. Those soldiers in medieval castles that were pouring the boiling oil over the other guys who were trying to break into their castle and wreck it? Time out on the naughty step, medieval castle guys!

They didn't have screens back then so their parents couldn't threaten to take away their screens if they didn't stop pouring boiling oil all over each other or running around with spears shouting, "ARGGGGGGGGGGGGGH!!"

Mum would be so annoyed if someone ran into our house and poured boiling oil all over our couch. The cushions are new!

The triplets, Gary, Barry and Larry, once had a massive argument over the last red wine gum and it was so bad that Gary wedged the wine gum up Larry's nose and none of them spoke for a week and Margery Lonergan said it should be reported to *The Spy Monthly* and that Gary, Barry and Larry's mum would be *mortified*. And Mum wants me to befriend these savages?

I guess the angry castle people couldn't have been arguing over wine gums because it was the olden days where there was nothing to do all day except collect stones for fun and eat potato—flavoured sweets and run away from lions. And the boiling oil, I guess.

Yes, I'm great at pretending. So great I'm basically a COMP—LIAR. I know this is technically dressing my feelings up in a fancy dress costume of other emotions and the Martins did warn me about that. But I'm doing it for the good of my family and sometimes private detectives need to be all mysterious to get the facts and solve the conundrum.

Some things are just a work in progress.

I pretend not to mind not hanging out with Tess. Or that Mindy Morgan and Karen the tortoise are her new favourite things. I pretend I don't miss putting rainbow chalk in our hair and in Blue's and I tell myself that even if Tess and Mindy are doing that together, at least Karen doesn't have hair and I won't be missing out on that.

The thing is, I know Tess would *love* Thoughtopolis, and I feel bad that she can't come with us or that I can't even tell her about it. But she once went to Wexford for a long weekend with her cousins and forgot to tell me for a *whole* month!

I pretend to like lasagne. And fish fingers. And beans on toast. It all tastes like mouldy cardboard.

I'm not sure cardboard can go off, but if it could, then that's what all my food tastes like.

Everything in the Real World is soooooooo much duller than in Thoughtopolis anyway. Give me a marshmallow, caramel chocolate toasted sandwich on rainbow pastry bread any day!

I pretend to Doctor Hilda Stitch that I'm absolutely fine and that I'm getting loads of sleep at night. Even though I lie awake for hours most nights staring at the ceiling, making lists and trying to go over all the clues in my head.

Trying to figure out what the stamps are leading to.

When she asked about the dark circles under my eyes, I said I like them like that. That I want to dress up as a panda for Halloween and I am making sure to get the practice in.

Don't get me wrong, pandas are cute. But so are squirrels, bunnies, seals, elephants, giraffes and lemurs. And I'm not sure I want to look like any of them. But like I said, all of this is a work in progress. Missions can be full on when you're in the middle of one.

I pretended to Margery Lonergan that I found her story about repainting her hall light bluebell blue after it had been medium bluebell blue for twelve years FASCINATING. I smiled at her when she ate all my pink wafer biscuits and pretended I didn't care in the slightest.

I deserve that Oscar so much.

I pretended to find Mr McNogg's story about ordering new paper for the printer machine RIVETING. He told me it had a shinier look to it than the last batch and I pretended to almost pass out with the excitement.

I have to keep pretending to throw my enemies off the scent.

Not that Mum and Dad are my enemies — I don't think you're supposed to love your enemies until your heart hurts — but still. They can't find out how I really feel about anything. And they certainly can't find out about Thoughtopolis.

Flo is still very much my enemy. Her artillery is getting more sophisticated now. Only this evening, she flung a pooey nappy at my head from the upstairs landing. She's getting sneakier and grosser in her forms of attack. She's like a medieval avenger using molten poo instead of oil, and I would honestly prefer boiling oil over liquid bum vegetables.

I had looked up at her, her face mushed between two wooden balustrades on the staircase.

"Dankie!!!" she shouted, and then she had ... *waved* at me.

Dankie? DANKIE?? Now she's mocking me to my face. Well, I'm not having it, dankie very much!

And Monica, Veronica and Nell are definitely still my enemies. They might not be flinging dirty nappies at me across the classroom, but I think I would prefer a fresh warm nappy on my head over their cruel words and laughs and whispers.

"Frankie is on Planet Zog again! Haha! She's like an alien weirdo!"

After class today — I didn't manage my family tree, but it seemed like a boring task — Monica got up and walked around like a zombie, arms outstretched and talking like a robot. "I'M FRANKIE AND I AM AN ALIEN AND I WILL EAT YOUR BRAIN."

"Frankie, is your great granny an alien?" Nell had asked and then laughed some more.

Well, now I know that they are Martins, not aliens. And they eat moon cheese not brains. And there's no planet Zog. I've been to them all.

"Hey," Ross P. Rossdale said. "Stop being so mean."

There was a pause and Nell had shouted, "OOOOOOOOOOOOH, WHY DON'T YOU JUST GET MARRIED TO EACH OTHER, KISSY KISSY KISSY."

Honestly, I thought I could even *hear* his cheeks going red.

I pretended I didn't care who was saying what, but then I think I said some stuff back that I don't really remember. And that was how I found myself in Mr McNogg's office. Again. For the second time this week.

Pretending.

More pretending.

Pretending to hear him bleating on like a sheep in a field.

"*Blaaaaaah, blaaaaaaah, blaaaaaahh,* falling behind in schoolwork, *blaaaaaaah, blaaaaah,* unacceptable language, *blaaaaaaaah, blaaaaaaah,* fractions."

The bits of spit were flying about this way and that and it reminded me of being at the water slides in Thoughtopolis with Fred. Except way

312

less fun and way more gross. And a thousand times more boring.

I sat there pretending that this wasn't a complete waste of time. I need to get back to Thoughtopolis and my mission ASAP.

I have:

a) A lot of work to do.
b) None of which involves fractions.
c) Unless you consider I have only a fraction of time to find my spark.
d) And even though this is a fraction I can't tell Mr McNogg.
e) BECAUSE I HAVE TO KEEP PRETENDING AND NOT TELL ANYONE ANYTHING.
f) AT ALL.
g) WHATSOEVER.
h) The End.
i) Actually not The End at all, I still have three more stamps to get in my Journey Journal!

So when Mum asked me how my day went? *That's* how my day went.

And now tomorrow is Thursday.

Just one day before Friday.

CHAPTER THIRTY-SIX

SOME TRICKY MAGIC ISSUES

The next morning I wake early and get dressed really fast. I didn't sleep much, what with all that thinking, but I want to try and visit Thoughtopolis before breakfast and school and all of that boring stuff.

Tomorrow is Friday!

My fate will be sealed. Like a potato in tinfoil.

And what will happen to Thoughtopolis? I can't afford any more glitches!

I need to get back there right away!

Except...

I can't get back in.

I can't get back into Thoughtopolis.

I close my eyes. *Whomp.*

Through the eyeball, down past the brain matter, second door on the right, three burps, "*Fibbleswizzle1234*".

Nothing. The door is there but it doesn't open.

Is it stiff again? I try the door knob one more time. Nothing.

"Bundlenugg?" I knock. "Are you in there?"

Absolutely nothing.

I take a deep breath and wiggle my toes in my socks, in my shoes, on the ground. I touch the hard knot twisted in the school tie around my neck. I smooth the woollen grey jumper down the front, my fingers running over all the bobbly bits I usually pluck off in class while I'm pretending to concentrate.

I put my hand on the cool hard wall of the hallway.

I'm still here.

In the Real World.

"Frankie! Hello, Frankie! Come and have some breakfast, will you?"

It's Mum, calling from the kitchen. I wait as her footsteps clack closer and closer, getting louder and louder. I feel the warmth of her hands on my cheeks.

"Don't forget your lunch for school," she says. "And please eat a slice of toast for me now, will you?"

I look at her and smile. That invisible fuse from my heart right to hers buzzes and flickers and lights up in a warm glow. I stare at her tired face, at the sad pools that collect in the black wells of her irises and seem to leak out a worried expression that spills down the rest of her face.

I steal a glimpse down the hallway towards the kitchen where Dad is holding my arch—nemesis, the deceptively adorable—looking Flo Finkleton in brand new very cute dungarees, in his arms. She looks me straight in the eye and says something, probably: "*Mwahahahahaa!!* I am the favourite child and you are being sent away because you are boring and dull now without your spark, Frankie, and they feed me raspberries — *raspberries!* How wonderful! And play endless 'Horsey'. And all you will eat is potatoes and the only game you will play for the rest of your life is Old Granny Tights on Your Head, *mwahahahahahahah.*"

Or she could be saying, "Blahhhdahblah blah blah."

They both sound pretty much the same to me.

Gosh, babies are such hard work. I'm never going to have one.

Or if I ever do, I'll order one that is already two or three years old and properly house trained because at least by then they might actually sleep through the night and have stopped crying manically if a banana is not mashed in the *exact right way.*

"Where do you go?" Mum asks me now. She brushes back a lock of hair from my face. I turn away from Flo to look at her again.

Thoughtopolis, I whisper in my own head.

"School?" I reply to Mum with a wry smile, hoping this answer might satisfy her. Knowing it won't.

"Yes, but where do you go?" she asks again, quietly now.

We are looking at each other closer than we have in some time.

Where do you go? I think in return, looking into her deep navy eyes.

I don't know how to reach her. Even though we are both standing in the hallway together locked in a stare, with my freckled cheeks cupped in her warm soft hands.

Maybe adults have their own version of Thoughtopolis. Maybe they have a world in their heads they can escape to where punnets of raspberries are only two cents, they can get the washing dried in any weather, it never matters if you forget to turn the immersion off and car clamps are made of goat's cheese pizzas. Adults are the only people I know who actually like goat's cheese; all the children I know are *obviously* allergic to it, and hold the shared understanding that goat's cheese is the quickest way to destroy a perfectly innocent pizza.

I feel sorry for goat's cheese that it's not moon cheese, but hey ho.

Where do you go, Mum?

Where do you go, Frankie?

Mum kisses me on the top of my head and I hold on to her hug.

I wish I could ask her to help me.

But I'm getting there. And she'll be so proud of me once I've completed my mission.

I'll show her I can still be sparkly.

That things can be the way they were before.

And then off I head to school.

CHAPTER THIRTY-SEVEN

MORE "SERIOUS" CHATS, SOME MORE ISSUES ... AND A NEED FOR TISSUES

I make it through an entire day at school. We work on our family trees again. Monica says something about her granny having invented the Macarena dance and I think that is impossible, but I don't say *HAHAHAHAHAAAAAAA* to her.

Tess is giggling with Mindy and I look over at them. They don't even notice me as they swap different coloured markers and pencils.

We always used to do that.

My purple marker was always used up first as it's my favourite colour. And Tess's blue one was always used up first as that's her favourite colour. So we would swap!

Well, we used to.

All I think about all day is getting back to Thoughtopolis. Finally, I make it home and through dinner — fish fingers. Fishy cardboard, but I manage them. I didn't think fish had fingers and I think maybe the supermarket people have got this wrong, but I don't have time to tell them right now. Then, at last, I'm back in my bedroom. At home. In the Real World. In my pyjamas. In my bed. I pat the duvet around me just to double treble snebble check.

Yup. I'm here.

Still.

Fred can't figure it out either. Why can't we get back in?

I stare at the ceiling blankly.

I'm not sure how long I'm looking at nothing, trying my hardest to get back to Thoughtopolis, when I hear a little knock on my bedroom door. I look over to see Dad walking in and padding across the carpet towards me.

"Night night, Frankie," he whispers softly.

"Night, Dad!" I answer, doing my best to sound chipper and like there is zero need to ship me off to an old grandmother with a weather forecast obsession and limited interest in a varied vegetable diet.

Normally he would head off, but tonight he lies on the bed beside me, scooping me into one of his warmest hugs. I feel an instant lump in my throat that I can't explain.

"How are you, Frankie?" he asks in a way that feels layered with a thousand questions.

"I'm good. How are you? Is Flo asleep?"

"Mum is trying to get her down now," he says. I know what he really means is that Flo is the most annoying baby ever to have been made, and if she were to enter the National Annoying Baby Championships she would surely win first place or if not get a Highly Commended certificate for effort and consistency. But he's just too blind to her charms.

I should ask them if they got a receipt when they got her, and if so maybe they could return her and get credit or something.

Perhaps we could get a bunny instead.

"Frankie?" he starts, hesitating slightly. "Is everything ... OK at school?"

My tummy takes an instant dive. Like jumping into a deep dark pitch black diving pool.

"Frankie?" Dad asks again.

"Err, yes ... Dad ... everything is fine in school."

Silence.

"It's just that ... Mr McNogg phoned us today and said there had been an incident..."

I feel panic sweep over me. An incident? Had something happened? Something other than me "daydreaming", "zoning out", "not listening" as per usual?

Perhaps something had happened in the Real World while I was in Thoughtopolis yesterday. Had I accidentally ... I gulped ... done a wee I had been gone so long?? Right there in my seat? The thought was too horrific to even comprehend! I would have to move to Australia immediately! And never come home! Actually, scratch that, at nearly ten thousand miles away Australia is far too near. Mars? Too close too! Pluto? That was a cute little planet; I could make a perfectly happy life for myself there!

Pluto it is.

The breath I've been holding in my chest suddenly escapes in the form of a high-pitched squeeeeeeeeeeeak!

"Mr McNogg said that yesterday Ms Hammerhead had left you all to complete a project on family trees and when the two hours were up you had done nothing ... absolutely nothing?"

I gulp.

Wow. Two hours. Two whole *hours* I was gone. I know time in Thoughtopolis slows down compared to time in the Real World. Sort of like dreams. That's how we get so much done in the time we're there. But *two whole real life hours?* That's *days* in Thoughtopolis time!

This is getting dangerous. The adults are going to start worrying even more. And the more they worry, the more they scrutinize, and the more they scrutinize, the less opportunity I have of magicking away to Thoughtopolis to complete my mission before ... before ... I'm sent away, before Thoughtopolis crumbles and disappears for ever!

"We were wondering, Frankie, Mum and I. We wondered if maybe ... you might like to ... spend some time at Granny Doris's. Just to get away for a bit, somewhere different. Have a break from school. Sometimes a change can do us a world of good. She has loads of space down the country and—"

"I really need to go to sleep, Dad," I say. Then I yawn and rub my eyes.
Where *is* that Oscar?

There's a silence. Then: "OK, Frankie," he whispers. He leans in and kisses
the top of my head.

"I love you."

"I love you too, Dad," I croak, squeezing the words out around the lump
lodged in my throat.

I hear his footsteps shuffle out and I curl up towards the wall.

They want to get rid of me. Because I haven't found it yet. My spark.

I feel tired and frustrated, flat and empty. I don't want to feel like
this all the time any more.

I need to get it back! For them, but also I need to get it back for me.
I suddenly feel the weight of what's ahead of me. And all that's against me.
The tears start to trickle out of my eyes.

I NEED TO GET BACK TO THOUGHTOPOLIS. NOW!!

A little high-pitched breathing squeak interrupts my thoughts and I see Blue
beside me. He hops up on the bed and rests his stubbly little chin next to mine.

"Oh, Blue," I say. "There's so much to do."

He exhales sadly, like he's thinking the same, then rests his paw on my
hand like he always does, just when I need him to.

And we both close our eyes, willing, trying, doing everything we can
to get back in.

CHAPTER THIRTY-EIGHT

DESTINATION THREE, IS IT TIME FOR A NERVOUS WEE?

"Frankie! Frankie, we were worried about you!" Bundlenugg cries as he run towards us, little fuzzy legs moving like lightning.

"We couldn't get back in!" I say, relief flooding through me. We close the door to Thoughtopolis firmly behind us. "What happened?"

"Something *not* good," Pickle barks.

"What?" asks Fred.

"Woof," Blue chimes in, before saying, "my gosh, sorry, I always forget I can actually speak in here. Still blows my mind, to be honest."

"EXACTLY, BLUE!" Bundlenugg quips, raising his small fluffy arm in the air. "The mind was blown! *That* was the problem."

"What do you mean?" Fred says, looking shocked.

Bundlenugg pauses momentarily, does a quick yoga pose, then inhales purposefully. "Frankie, it went wrong again."

"Thoughtopolis?" I gasp. "What happened this time?"

"The lights went out all over the Metropolis. All the half-broken toys escaped the toyshop and were roaming the streets like zombies; the one-legged, one-armed dolls with no eyes were quite alarming. The lightbulbs in the Lightbulb Emporium smashed, the merry-go-round was flying about, hitting off everything like it was in a pin ball machine and several zoats escaped from the zoo!"

"My gosh!" I exclaim.

"But why?" Fred asks.

Bundlenugg waves his little arms around, trying to find his words. "Our engineers have been working on it all day. The brain cell-ebrities have been on to their agents and their findings indicate that all of this 'pretending to be OK' has made your brain short circuit again. It's overloaded. They've done what they can, but there's talk of strike action if this continues."

YIKES.

I'm not really sure what this means, but it sounds serious.

"But I have to pretend," I protest. "Otherwise I can't come back here and find the secret and get my spark back!"

Bundlenugg shakes his head frantically. "That is a very dangerous course of action, Frankie. Masking your feelings means they will eventually leak out at the surface, whether or not you want them to. And as much as you try to stay in control of them, or fight them, or will them to be anything other than your own true feelings ... well, sometimes ... you simply can't. If you ignore them, that's when things can start to go wrong."

"Your brain is a wonderful place, Frankie, just wonderful," Pickle says in her deep voice. "A definite five-star review on Tripadvisor. There are so many things in here which make it fun and work really well. Take, for example, the library over there."

We all look to the left to see the local Mind Reader Library, a cute little building the shape of a crystal ball dome. Fred and I have spent a lot of time in there. It's crammed full of books about what other people may or may not be thinking. There's a whole book called

Are Monica, Veronica and Nell Only Mean Because They Feel Lost? and another called *Is Margery Lonergan So Nosy Because She's Lonely?* That one is a trilogy. The librarian says the prequel due out next spring really explains the full story. You get a library card when you join that says:

Remember: never judge a book by its cover.

As I look closer at the library, I see there are cracks in the façade and the paintwork around the glass looks shabby.

"That library is an amazing thing your brain did," Bundlenugg says warmly. "It shows just how thoughtful and big your brain is. But lately you've been tiring your brain out, Frankie. Dressing your feelings up as something else all the time can be exhausting. Haven't you felt that?"

I nod slowly.

"If you don't give your brain a rest by letting those feelings out, things will only get worse in Thoughtopolis."

Perhaps I'm not going to get that Oscar, after all.

Fred and Blue and I look at each other nervously. I notice something running in the gutter below – different coloured trickles of liquid, racing in little slipstreams at our feet. Some are bright, some are muddy.

"These are your feelings, Frankie. They are confused,

they are muddled, they do not know where to go."

I watch as little rivulets break away from the trickles and disappear down the drain, while others spill out through cracks along the surface.

The wind begins to pick up. A tree branch smacks against the library window, and the glass fractures.

"A storm is coming," says Pickle sadly. "Another one. But this time…"

This time, *what?*

"Frankie, you must get back on the Train of Thought *now,*" says Bundlenugg over the growing hum of the wind. "Just remember to hold on extra tight. Things might get extra bumpy." He gives me an encouraging smile, but his expression is worried. An expression on the outside that doesn't match the feeling on the inside. Perhaps I'm getting better at reading that.

"Go on. Collect that third stamp. It might be hard to stay focused. It might feel at times you will drown in it all. Try to stay afloat. Try your hardest to focus. We'll be here when you get back.

"When you are trying to be brave, just remember who to save, because when it all feels like it just might cave, you will know how to behave."

I swallow the lump in my throat and grab Fred's hand in mine tightly, Blue already at our heels. We leave Bundlenugg and Pickle and head back towards the station as a heronder caws overhead, and then another, and another until it sounds like there's an entire flock up there. I suddenly feel very small and very lost in Thoughtopolis. Everything is unfamiliar and threatening.

Like I suddenly don't know where I've really been after all this time.

Just as Bundlenugg warned, the Train of Thought is more turbulent than before. It sways as it navigates the tracks and screeches around the bends, the carriages shudder against the winds and I think the windows might crack.

"Oh, Frankie," Fred moans.

"I know, Fred, it's OK," I say, even though I feel sick in my tummy. "Hold on!" I shout as we dip and loop, the whole world of Thoughtopolis turning upside down before our very eyes.

Focus, Frankie.

Focus.

"HOLD ON!" shouts Fred, his eyes wide.

"HOLD ON!" shouts Blue, his gums flapping in the full force of the ride.

HOLD ON! I think to myself. *Just hold on!*

And then as we slow and begin a steady ascent, I feel my fear turning into something else. ANGER. It gets stronger and stronger, rising higher and higher up my throat as we climb higher and higher up the tracks. The train feels heavy and sluggish. Have we fueled it properly? Are we going to make it?

"Frankie?" Blue says nervously.

"Are you OK?" Fred asks.

NO. *No,* I think, *I am not OK.* This all suddenly feels too much. It all feels so unfair.

Why?

Why do I have to find this stupid spark?

Why did it have to go missing? Normally kids my age misplace their homework notebook or their water beaker! Not their entire **SPARK!**

Why am I collecting these stamps?

Why do I need to dig up a secret? Why can't it just stay buried? Why am I responsible for what's happening in Thoughtopolis?

I am **SO ANGRY**. With Mum and with Dad and with Fred! I never get mad at Fred!

I feel the anger pool and swirl in my tummy, swelling and swelling like it might explode and rip right through me. An anger that feels like pure fire.

"Frankie?" Fred asks worriedly again. "Are you sure you're ... OK?"

"I'M SO MAD, FRED. I AM SO SO MAD," I explode. **"WHY? WHY, FRED, WHHHYYYYYYYY?"**

My head is a pot on a hob, steam hissing and rising, pressure building, needing to escape.

"This is all your fault!"

"Why are you mad, Frankie?" Fred presses.

I AM SO MAD THAT YOU LEFT ME, FRED. I AM SO MAD YOU LEFT ME! I shout in my head. But I am in my head?

"Frankie, you've been holding on so tightly. Now let go," Fred whispers. "Let go, Frankie."

Then my frustration and confusion and seething anger screech to a sudden halt and we are thrown off the train in an unravelling wheel of slow motion.

Through the ripping wind, I grab Fred's hand and pull him close with all the might inside me.

And then we land, with a thud, right in the middle of what feels like a thick grey swamp.

"Where are we?" Blue blinks sleepily.

We all look up to read the sign overhead:

YOU ARE NOT VERY WELCOME TO THE LAND OF EXHAUSTION.

CHAPTER THIRTY-NINE

THE LAND OF EXHAUSTION

"You know you could have let me go there, Frankie," says Fred. He yawns, picks himself up and dusts himself down.

"Yeah, right," I sigh, relieved to be off the Train of Thought for now.

"I love that you always want to save me. Just..." He stops, like he's deciding which words to choose.

"Just what, Fred?" I ask, poking at what he's trying to get at.

"Just make sure you don't..." He pauses again, like something is caught in his throat. "Don't hurt yourself too much trying to save me."

"PFFFFF!" I grin. "Not much can hurt me. I'm your big sister." He yawns again. "Are you OK?" I ask.

"It's just ... it feels like we've been at this so long now. I know we've got two stamps, but it's like we are no closer to finding the secret." He breaks off to give another enormous yawn. "I'm getting so tired."

I'm suddenly tired too – exhausted. I smile sleepily. I guess that's because we're in the Land of Exhaustion!

I shake Fred's shoulders as his eyes start to close. "Come on, Fred, we can't sleep! Did you not hear Bundlenugg and Pickle? We need to keep going!"

"I know, I know… I'm just so…"

"Come on, Fred!" I yell impatiently. Can he not see how hard I'm trying?

"Stop it, Frankie, OK!" he snaps at me. "Can't you see this is hard for me too?"

We stand there looking at each other sleepily as drifts of fog encroach around us. I feel a lump in my throat.

I hate fighting with Fred. We argue so rarely, I'm not sure I can take it now.

He turns and walks away, hunkering down on the ground, his head in his hands.

Blue pads over and curls into Fred's lap, snuggling down and closing his eyes.

Everything is shrouded in a thick fog. I rub my eyes to try and see things a bit clearer, but it only makes me feel even more tired.

This isn't like feeling tired after swimming or staying up late to have a midnight feast. This is … like a tiredness that's snuck into my bones. All I want to do is close my eyes and sleep for four hundred and fifty-eight years. I drop to my knees. Darkness closes in like a heavy blanket.

A figure floats past slowly, right in front of my face. I can't make it out properly, but it's almost like a blurry misty blob. A foggy grey ghost with no shape.

If I wasn't so exhausted I would have jumped in fright. But I'm too tired to be scared. I'm too tired even to be angry any more.

"Excuse me?" I call groggily, my words sounding muffled. "What exactly is this place?"

It's a struggle to even talk. I hear Fred yawning beside me, over and over.

Focus.

FOCUS. I think of what Bundlenugg said. That almost feels like a dream now.

"You are in the Land Of Exhaustion, Frankie, you

know that right?" the figure says. Its voice is slow and drawn out.

I do know that. But the tiredness is making it harder to make sense of things. I narrow my eyes, trying to see who I'm talking to a little more clearly. The figure is vague, like it's made of mist and haze and swaddled in a gauze. I can see its sunken eyes staring at me. Its mouth is fixed into a permanent gaping yawn.

"Wh-what? Where is that?"

"Oh, it's down the Slippery Slope of Your Emotions right at the edge of Thoughtopolis. You end up here when you've gone a bit too far. Not quite over the edge yet, but close."

"Where is the edge?" I ask nervously.

"Over there." It points. I can't even see through the fog.

"It's hard to see it coming," the figure replies, as if reading my mind. "But if you stay here too long, you can get pulled into a current of exhaustion, and slip right over."

That does not sound great.

What's out there? Where is the edge exactly, in the mire of this swamp?

"Why are you here?" the figure asks. "You shouldn't be. It's far too dangerous."

I feel frustration puncture my exhaustion. I need to get the next stamp – but I can't move.

"I can't leave without a stamp," I reply, trying to stay awake.

"Ah, I see. Well, then, you need to figure out why you are here. Why the train brought you down the Slippery Slope."

"Because … I'm tired…?"

"Indeed … but *why* are you tired?"

Why am I tired? I would laugh if I wasn't so, well, tired. Because being eleven and one month is, as I may have mentioned, practically like a full-time job! And that's on top of my part-time job as a private investigator on a secret mission to save my family!

"What are the feelings that are making you tired? You have exhausted yourself, Frankie. But watch out, because you could fall over the edge if you don't look where you are going."

How am I going to navigate my way out of all of this? This journey seems to be getting harder and harder.

I feel a sudden spark of anger again. But it's quickly diluted by another deluge of tiredness.

It's like all of my rage, all of my emotions are drowning

in tiredness. I can't process one from the other.

"Come with me," the figure says. "But mind your step, and whatever you do, do not disturb the jesters that hide out here in the shadows of the fog."

"The jesters?" I query, but the figure is already moving away into the haze.

It's trudging towards a building barely visible in the distance. Small Lego men and women lie on the ground outside the building, curled up and fast asleep on the ground. Their little snores drift into the mist.

"What's that building?" I ask. "What's happened to them?"

"Come with me, Frankie," the figure calls, lumbering towards the building.

I look down at Fred and Blue. Is it better to let them rest? Or should I be waking them?

"I'll be right back," I whisper.

CHAPTER FORTY

A HERD OF YAWNS AND A FLASK OF NOTION POTION

We enter the building and the figure reaches out to switch on the light. A ceiling pendant blinks and flashes momentarily before blowing into darkness once more.

"IT'S BROKEN," the figure yawns. "No surprises there. The entire factory has stopped working. It ended up here after the last Thoughtopolis glitch."

The figure's speech is long and drawn out, like he could fall asleep at any moment.

"What is it?" I ask. I strain to see what's in the large cavernous factory building. Are they conveyor belts? I reach out and run my finger along the tracks of one; inches of thick dust gather on my fingertip like everything here has been out of action for some time.

"It's the Thoughtopolis Thought Processing Plant. It's

normally right in the heart of the downtown Metropolis, and all these workers go about their business day and night, putting in the shifts to process all the feelings that you have, but it was scrapped here during the last glitch. Everything went a bit haywire. Systems shut down, things got muddled…"

"What is going to happen to it? Can we get it back to where it should be?" I ask, stepping over the bodies of the little sleeping figures in hard hats and overalls, snoring softly.

"I don't know," it answers. "It's not working right now, and it's *here* because, well, you're too exhausted. It's causing quite a few … complications."

The thought of being too exhausted to process any of my thoughts properly makes me *even* more properly exhausted!

"They can't figure out one feeling from another. You keep telling them you're OK, but the thought won't process, because, in fact … you are not."

I am silent for a long while. My instinct is to say that I'm fine, that Thoughtopolis is wonderful and I'm happy here, but I can't find the energy to say any of it.

"Who are you?" I ask, changing the subject.

"Me?" the figure answers, sounding flattered. "No one usually asks – they just assume we are too boring."

"Oh?"

"I am a yawn, Frankie."

"A yawn?"

"Yes," the figure yawns. "We're everywhere. Yawns have invaded the Land of Exhaustion, settling here in droves."

I look around me: more grey blobs hover in the darkness. Herds and herds of them.

"You need to get out of here, Frankie. Yawns are contagious. If you start you will never stop. You found it hard getting back into Thoughtopolis?" It pauses. "What if you never get out? What if you get taken over by the yawns? What if you can't find your way out and finally fall over the edge?"

A wave of yawns from a nearby yawn herd breaks the silence.

I don't like the sound of this either. What about Mum and Dad? What about everything I care about in the Real World?

I didn't know I *could* get trapped in here. I know I need to find the buried secret to find my spark or else I'll be sent to stay with Granny Doris. I know Bundlenugg said Thoughtopolis could be in danger of crumbling. But getting trapped here *for ever*?

I suddenly ache for Mum and Dad. I want to go to them, tell them everything, curl up on their laps and have them tell me it will all be OK.

WE CAN'T GET TRAPPED IN HERE!

The herd of yawns is encroaching on us through the fog.

YAWN.

YAWN.

YAWN.

"You need to get moving, Frankie. I am one of the lighter yawns, but *that* is a weariness of yawns."

"What's a weariness of yawns?" I say. Do I even want to know?

"It's the collective noun for multiple herds of yawns. Nothing you want to get too close to. Go and collect your stamp, Frankie, and then **GET OUT OF HERE**," it says as energetically as a thing possibly can before lying on the ground and yawning itself to sleep.

Where? **COLLECT THE STAMP FROM WHERE?!** I look around, feeling like I'm moving in slow motion. Everything looks grey and bleak. With no way out.

As hard as it is, I drag myself back to Fred and Blue, scared now, afraid of getting stuck here.

Out of the corner of my eye, a brightly coloured shape moves with more energy than seems possible here. I rub my eyes again.

A tiny court jester is in front of me. He is no bigger than a thumb, dressed in a multicoloured diamond-patterned outfit, with a spritely bijou hat on his head complete with bells that jangle in little echoes through the fog.

"He's funny," Fred whispers sleepily, waking up.

The jester trots over to us, dancing from one foot to the other as his bells jingle jangle.

"You look so tired. All of you. Even your dog."

"We are," Blue answers almost in his sleep. "I mean, I can sleep a lot, but even for me … this really is *a lot*."

"Take some of this," he offers kindly. "It's Notion Potion. It will help you, I promise."

"Really?" I ask, remembering that the yawn warned me about something to do with the jesters. If only I wasn't too tired to think what.

"Thank you so much," I answer, taking the small metal flask. "We are so tired."

"I know." He smiles again. "Drink this. Drink up."

Blue whines slightly, lifting a paw before getting distracted by his own yawn. I can see his mind drifting. The way it does when someone is eating chicken.

"Frankie, I don't..." Fred says, then trails off, his eyes closing mid-sentence.

I look inside the bottle; the fumes of blue frothing liquid make my nose tingle. I bend down to Fred and let him take a sip, then Blue, before I drink what is left.

"Thank you so much," I say to the jester.

"Frankie!!" I hear the yawn call behind me. "Do not listen to him! He is one of the Thoughtopolis court jesters, sent to play tricks on your mind. **DO NOT TRUST HIM!**"

Uh oh, I think as the Notion Potion slips down my throat.

It tastes sweet at first, but the aftertaste is sour and stings my mouth a little.

"That's it, Frankie, that will help you. That will help you go the right way. Or at least you'll think you're going the right way." The court jester smiles unscrupulously. Unscrupulous is another good word from Gr-Annie's word book, if I could remember what it meant. Is it when something is scrumptious? Or is it when someone isn't very honest? The two feel muddled

343

together in my mind.

"Frankie?" Fred calls drowsily, and I hear the court jester laugh before scuttling away into the fog, the bells on his hat jingle jangling in hollow echoes before disappearing completely.

"What ... what does it do?" I asked the yawn, struggling to find the words now.

"It tricks you, Frankie," the yawn answered. "It makes you feel you can do something when you can't. Or you can't do something when you can."

"But..." I say sleepily. "How are you to know...?"

Before he can answer I drop to my knees into the marshland and the bottle slips from my hand and lands with a *thunk* in the mud.

I feel more tired than I have ever felt in my whole life.

Like I'm a cake of tiredness iced in thick layers of more tiredness.

I am so endlessly exhausted. Like I'm breaking from the inside out, bits of me fragmenting and cracking. But I feel too bone weary to know how to put myself back together again.

I think of going to Mr McGranger's Doll and Toy

Hospital. Could he help me fix this?

But I'm too worn out to move.

Could we make our way back to The Old Favourites Hotel, and get our energy back by drinking bowls of blueberry fizzy pop and margherita pizza with the crusts cut off?

No. I'm too tired to eat.

I want to be with our friends in the Teeny Tiny Woods. Fred and I love chasing the Teeny Tiny animals, especially Harold, the miniature hedgehog, who bounds over mounds of leaves and burrows under large fallen branches, the breeze in his squinchy bristles.

I want to sleep so I don't have to think about any of this ever again.

But then there's Fred.

And it's as though my last fighting instinct is the only thing left battling my fatigue, helping me wrangle a way out of it.

I need to find a way to fight for *him*.

I curl in beside him now, trying to find any remaining strength in him to spark courage to my own.

"Fred, please," I whisper. **"WE CAN'T STAY HERE ANY MORE. I CAN'T DO THIS ANY MORE."**

I hear Bundlenugg in my ear: *When you are trying to be brave, just remember who to save, because when it all feels like it just might cave, you will know how to behave.*

Focus.

FOCUS.

I will not let this win! I will not let the jesters play tricks on my mind so I think I can't when I can! So that I get stuck here for ever!

I shake my head, trying to dispel the effect of the Notion Potion.

I look at Fred, curled in a ball with Blue on his lap. And with every last fading ember of energy I have left in me, I gather us both up off the ground, collect Blue in my arms too, and somehow manage to trudge forward out of the Land Of Exhaustion, bearing the weight of Fred, the weight of everything: my emotions, my feelings, my exhaustion, this journey.

Fred's hand cups inside mine gently as we forge our way further from the herds of yawns behind us, and the rolling fog, ready to swallow us whole.

And it's then we get our third stamp in the Journey Journal.

CHAPTER FORTY-ONE

VANISHED

I tumble through the golden door and back into my bedroom.

"Phew," I whisper. "That was close, wasn't it, Fred? Just in time for school as well."

There's silence.

"And it's Friday! D-Day!"

Nothing.

"Fred?"

I look around. Blue's there, sitting to attention beside me. But Fred is...

GONE!!!!

I go and check his room. Nothing.

I run back to my own room. He's nowhere.

I look under my bed and in the cupboard in case he's still asleep somewhere.

But I simply cannot find him.

Has he got stuck in Thoughtopolis? Did the Notion Potion somehow keep him there? Trapped? But we'd all left together, hadn't we?

My brain still feels a little foggy.

347

"Fred?" I whisper, tiptoeing back into his bedroom to double triple whipple check. I take my magnifying glass in with me. I stare at his bed.

Nothing.

The bed is made, apart from an indent in his blankets.

But where is he *now*?

Ms P sits next to his pillow and I lift her to sniff her worn-out fluff.

Where are you, Fred? I think, rubbing the teddy's nose. *Where are you?*

I try not to panic. Fred told me he would be OK on his own, without me looking after him. If he's stuck in Thoughtopolis, Bundlenugg and Pickle will be keeping him safe.

But I'm going to be in *so much* trouble with Mum and Dad.

They were cross that time I accidentally locked him in the downstairs loo. How am I going to explain accidentally locking him in my own brain?

I wonder whether Mum and Dad know anything yet. I get quickly changed for school. Jumper, tie, socks, hairbrush through my hair(s) and grab my bag, then creep down the stairs as quietly as I can, my back against the cool hall wall.

I creep out of the front door and into the back garden. I see Mum and Dad and Flo in the kitchen. I creep as quickly as I can to the treehouse in the corner of the garden. The place Fred and I go to talk about very serious things. And read comics and drink hot chocolate. And get away from Flo. Once she masters how to climb the ladder, though, we are goosed!

I look in the treehouse.

Fred isn't there.

I go back in the front door and put my coat on.

"Frankie?" I hear Mum call from the kitchen. "Come and get some toast before school."

"DANKIE!!" I hear Flo squeal in ... *delight?!* Ugh! Why does she always take such pleasure in blowing my cover? And when is she going to get better at pronouncing her "F"s! I guess it's a hard letter to grasp with only two tiny teeth on a little bottom lip. But still. I eyeball her briefly, just out of sight of Mum, before Blue and I sneak out of the front door and close the latch behind us.

I say goodbye to Blue at the gate.

"Keep an eye out here in case he comes back," I say, patting his head. "I'll look for him at school."

Blue whimpers at me and lifts his paw to my hand. He's trying to communicate something to me, but I can't understand.

"I know, Blue," I say, not really knowing anything at all.

Is Fred mad at me? We'd had an argument, I remember now.

I walk to school. I feel Sally O'Malley's eyes on me as I pass her wall. I really hope in that moment animals don't have a secret language and Sally isn't saying to Blue, "So I heard Frankie lost her brother. And she was supposed to be looking out for him. She said she would always make sure he was *OK*. Well, where is he? *Meeeeeeow!*"

I keep my eyes down as I pass Gary, Barry and Larry rolling down the hill to school in a giant human wrestling ball.

"Oh ... hey ... Frankie! Wanna ... come ... play ... at ours... – Gimme my toast! – after school?"

"Er, no, thanks," I mutter, my head down.

I feel Margery Lonergan's eyes on me. Dr Hilda Stitch's. Everyone in the village is watching. A gallery of eyes following me.

If I could disappear back to Thoughtopolis right now I would.

But I can't.

"Printer paper is so amazing. I love filing cabinets. I only ever read boring books about all the boring things in the world like how cardboard is made. My favourite book ever is *101 Interesting Things About Mud*," Mr McNogg is saying at the school gates.

Well, perhaps he isn't saying that. Perhaps he's telling us all to walk and not run, but it doesn't matter. I don't care what he says.

Nothing matters when Fred isn't here.

I whip my tie in front of my face like a windscreen wiper to shield myself from the splats of flying spit as I scuttle by. Gosh, Mr McNogg even *smells* boring. I bet he wears *Eau de Maths Books and Vegetables for Men*.

"Don't forget to ... boring, boring, boring..." he continues to bleat as I walk past. Maybe Mum and Dad could rent Mr McNogg as a means of getting Flo to sleep at night. Honestly, all he'd have to do is start talking about the school heating system and she'd be out like a light.

Could be worth a try. The dream star mobile clearly isn't working.

The bell rings for us all to go into our respective classes, but I slip into a flow of younger students filing up the junior corridor the other way, and then hide around a corner and wait as they settle into their classroom.

When I think everyone has had enough time to get into their seats, I creep up to the small porthole window in the classroom door and peer into Fred's classroom.

I look over to where he always sits.

His seat is empty.

Back in my classroom, Ms Hammerhead is standing there saying strings of words together in sentences that presumably I am supposed to be listening to.

I hear snippets. Things like, "Go to page thirty-four in your books." I hear, *HAHAHAHAHAHAAAAs, PSWSHHSHHHHHHWWWHSHHSHS.* I hear pencils being sharpened, chalk scraping against the blackboard, rulers thwacking off desks, I hear Ross P. Rossdale *thinking.*

Can I? Can I hear what's going on inside his head when I don't even know what's going on inside mine?

Ms Hammerhead is talking again: "Questions one to ten in your copybooks." "The olden days." "I am a shark."

"Frankie?"

"FRANKIE?"

Uh oh. Me! That's me. She's talking to me!

351

"YOU ARE A SHARK!" I say loudly.

The entire room bursts into laughter. I feel my cheeks burning.

"Sorry ... sorry..." I mumble, wishing I could climb right inside my textbook and become as flat and unremarkable a page as all the other hundreds of pages bound together. All I can see in front of me are eyeballs. An army of eyeballs poised and beady.

Lucy Judge is staring at me like I've committed the worst Criminal Act Against Classrooms and am going to detention for life without parole.

Ross P. Rossdale is staring at me. For once, he's quiet.

Timmy Baker's mouth is open, eyes wide, looking like he's about to take a bite out of a baguette. But there's no baguette. This is just the look of shock someone might have when another person in their class just called the teacher a shark.

I catch Tess's eye. She turns away, like she can't bear to look at me. Like she *pities* me.

And then the *HAHAHAHAHAHAHAAAAS* from the back of the classroom start up again and I gulp, wishing this was all over. Wishing I could get out of here and get away.

Anywhere.

Anywhere but here.

Thoughtopolis.

I want to go back to Thoughtopolis so badly! Fred is there and right now I want Fred.

I close my eyes shut and concentrate hard. I wish and wish and wish and...

I...

Just...

Need...

To...

GET BACK IN!!!

Nothing.

I open my eyes again. I am still at my desk and people are still laughing.

I want to cry. But not sad crying like when you stand on a snail in the dark accidentally or drop your last sweet down the loo by mistake.

Angry crying.

No one in my class understands. They don't have a clue about responsibilities! No one has told *them* they need to dig up a giant massive humungous great secret.

They can all just do their homework and hang upside down on the monkey bars in the park with their mates.

But not me.

The hot angry tears well up. But the last thing I need right now is to start crying. That would be game over. Monica, Veronica and Nell would laugh at me for ever and I would be sent to the Hall of Shame Of Most Embarrassing Things to Happen In The Classroom in everyone's head for ever more. Right beside everyone who has accidentally done a wee in their seat or fallen asleep at their desk and farted.

I hold in my tears, imagining a fleet of beavers stopping a dam from bursting in my eyeballs. Perhaps they're in there. From the Teeny Tiny Forest. Harold's friends. Helping me. Knowing I need saving.

Just then, something drops on to my copybook. It's a little slip of white paper. I shield it with my sleeve and open it very carefully so no one notices.

Don't mind them. You are the bravest person I know.

Ross x

"How are you?" Tess whispers as we spill out of the class for lunch.

"Sooooo embarrassed," I answer.

"Don't worry, still not as embarrassing as the time I called her 'Mummy'. Remember that?"

I smile and she smiles back. I really wish in that moment that I can tell Tess my secret. But I don't dare.

Because even though the magic is exciting and fun and thrilling, it's also scary and mysterious and daunting and I can't explain everything that's happening right now. And the truth is I don't think anyone would *really* understand other than Fred. Or Blue.

Tess thought she was magic once. Because when she left all her dirty clothes on the floor in her bedroom, they disappeared and then all somehow magically reappeared back in her drawers washed and folded a few days later. Unbelievable! She then discovered it had actually been her mum and dad and she should really say thank you more often.

But this is different.

"Hey," she says, and I think she sounds a bit shy, which is weird because Tess is never shy. She once sang in front of a whole room of people. On purpose. "Sit together at lunch?"

For a moment I'm so tempted.

Then I shake my head. "I'm going to do some homework," I say and I turn and walk away.

That night in bed I look out of my window in the still of the night and stare up at the sky, wishing like I always do on a thousand stars. The moon shines back at me, offering nothing.

"I promised I'd love you to the moon and back. That I would mind you," I whisper. "I will. And I will get you back."

I sit cross-legged on the bed in my pyjamas and close my eyes. Here I go — through the eyeball, turn right at the skull, down to the left past a pile of mushy brain stuff and then it's the second door on the right. Gold, with a shiny doorknob.

"Fred," I call through the door. "FRED?"

I knock twice, do three burps and—

The doorbell rings. I open my eyes with a start.

The Thoughtopolis door doesn't have a doorbell.

The Real World door does.

I hear Dad walk from the kitchen, down the hall and open the front door.

And then a gust of wind blows through the house.

It smells of potatoes.

"Is she here?" I hear a voice say from the front door.

IT'S GRANNY DORIS!!!!!

HOW i IMAGINE GRANNY DORIS TO LOOK AT THE DOOR

CHAPTER FORTY-TWO

MEMORY LANE

"GRANNY DORIS! WELCOME!" I hear dad yell, and I slap my hands over my ears and scrunch my eyes to try and focus.

"Flo, look," says mum. "It's Granny. Granny Doris is here." And of course Flo is squealing her banshee-like-squeal, which everyone pretends is delightful, even though their eardrums **MUST** be close to bursting point. **I AM CLOSE TO BURSTING POINT!**

I need to get back to Thoughtopolis. Now!

"Where's Frankie?" Granny Doris asks. Now they're all whispering, and I'm panicked as I run back to the Thoughtopolis door.

"Frankie?" Dad calls.

"Frankie?" I hear Granny Doris say, ready to bundle me into a sack of spuds, lob me over her shoulder and head off a billion miles away from my home.

"Frankie?" Mum pleads, worry in her voice.

"Here! I'm in here! Don't worry!" I lie. I'm trying

357

to get the door to Thoughtopolis open. I can hear their voices and I want to get as far away from them as I possibly can.

And I really, *really* don't want them to worry. "I've got Fred, it's OK!"

But I don't have Fred.

I DO NOT HAVE FRED!

And with that I push with all my might at the golden door. I run at it. I pummel my fists at it.

I kick it.

Until finally, I'm in.

Back to Thoughtopolis.

AT LAST.

But everything here is **DIFFERENT**.

There are no blue skies. No singing birds. No noises of joviality from the funfair, the park, the playground. It isn't dark like before either, but it's grey.

The ferris wheel in the Fantastical Fairground creaks in the wind. Tufts of discarded candyfloss blow across the ground like tumbleweed. I see a squidgenflidge scurry down the path and dive for cover in a burrow.

An eerie quiet greyness lies all around. Like nothing is

working. And there are no engineers trying to fix things.

And, most importantly, there's no Fred.

Only an all-consuming loneliness that creeps into my bones like rising damp.

I shiver and the skies darken further, threatening rain. The wind picks up and circles Blue and I, like it wants to swallow us.

Blue whimpers. "Sorry," he says. "I don't know how to say this feeling in actual words."

You and me both, Blue, I think to myself.

Where are Bundlenugg and Pickle? Are they OK? I walk around, lifting up discarded posters scattered by the wind; I look around corners of swings and at overturned slides lying on their sides. Is there anybody here at all?

"HERE, FRANKIE! OVER HERE!"

It's Bundlenugg and Pickle. I feel sick with relief. "Do you have Fred?" I will my eyes to find something, anything in the greyness.

"We don't have Fred," Bundlenugg says.

"Well, do you know where he is?" I cry frantically. "Please, he might be here somewhere, lost without me! I couldn't ... get back in!"

Bundlenugg shakes his head. He looks tired, his fur

grubby and worn. "They changed the password. There was a complete system shutdown. I … I don't think Thoughtopolis can take much more…"

What does that mean?

"Frankie, you are running out of time."

I shut my eyes tight.

"No! **NO!!** I have **NOW. I HAVE TIME NOW!!**"

I take out my Journey Journal and magnifying glass. I have three stamps: Lost, Scared and Exhausted. I need two more and then I'm there! I'm getting close!

"I think," Pickle says in a gentle growl, like her deep voice is shaky and unsure, "you should get back on the Train of Thought."

The greyness dissipates a little and I see that we are standing by a platform.

"The train will take you to the fourth destination," says Bundlenugg. "We will come with you this time. Sometimes you can do this on your own. Other times … well…"

I follow them on to the train, feeling grateful for their company, but missing Fred all the more. I'm used to having all my adventures with him.

The seats on the train are ripped and dusty, the floor

scuffed. There are splintered cracks in the glass windows. The trolley stands empty and abandoned in the galley, and the dinner lady is nowhere to be seen. There are no other passengers.

Everything is quiet and the large door clunks closed.

Where are you, Fred?

Where are you?

I stare out of the window, holding Blue tightly on my lap, as Thoughtopolis begins to flash past. A blurry mix of things zipping by. A myriad of different shades of grey.

I grip the seat with one hand as the train loops in dizzying circles, dips with no warning, climbs uphill, chugging, coughing, spluttering plumes of steam as it wills itself further ... inches itself higher...

I *have* to be getting closer. Even though it feels almost impossible to keep holding on.

The train comes to a shuddering, creaking halt. It lets out a scream of steam from its colossal chimney as it comes to rest in the train station.

We step on to the platform and I look around to get my bearings.

And I look for Fred. Always. It's as though I look for him in everything.

I haven't been to this part of Thoughtopolis before, yet it feels strangely familiar. I'm standing on cobbles; my feet look far away in the twilight. It isn't misty like the Land of Exhaustion. It's foggy in a different way.

And a heaviness hangs in the air. Like the calm before a storm.

"Where are we?" I ask.

"This is Memory Lane, Frankie," Bundlenugg says, giving my leg a sudden hug. I bend down to him. "Oh, wimble bottoms, Frankie," he says. "I knew it would be a difficult journey, but even I didn't think it would be as difficult as this. I guess one never does. Until you're in it."

He has been so kind to us, and I try to ignore the worry in his eyes.

"I'm OK, Bundlenugg," I say, feeling a little ray of bravery flash from somewhere on the inside.

"Fred?" I turn suddenly.

But there's nothing.

I turn back to Bundlenugg.

"You are braver than you know, Frankie," Bundlenugg says, as if reading my thoughts. "This might be hard. It's a place where your memories live. Some will be good and some will be … not so good."

"Will I find Fred here?" I ask pleadingly.

There's a pause. "You will," he answers finally.

"Let's go, Frankie," Pickle says gently.

I check my Journey Journal and magnifying glass are safely in my pocket and we head off down Memory Lane.

CHAPTER FORTY-THREE

THE FOG AND THE PUDDLES

Memory Lane is a pretty, twisting narrow street lined with shopfront windows, all emitting a golden glow that warms the cobbles underfoot as we walk. Small cottage-style shops stand in terraces on either side of the lane, some have thatched roofs, others slate tile ones.

Sprigs of ivy grow up the walls and stretch along the rooftops the length of the entire lane.

Blue, Bundlenugg, Pickle and I walk in silence as we steal curious glances inside the windows. As I look in each one, a street lamp lights up, helping to reveal what's inside.

Under the soft amber light, I see the shop windows are filled with mirage images of great adventures Fred and I have been on in the Real World. It's like a line of Christmas windows with moving images of our very best, very happiest memories.

Fred coming home from hospital as a baby in a funny bonnet Gr-Annie knitted him. Mum only pretended to like it and she would rush to put it on him whenever Gr-Annie called to say she was dropping by. Even worse was that Gr-Annie had also knitted *me* an even more ludicrous one. Mum knotted it under my chin. I was three and looked ridiculous. Fred was only a tiny baby but I could have sworn it was the first time he smiled.

Another memory of Fred and I selling cookies, raising money for local snails with broken shells. Fred making me a clay frog in school for my birthday. Fred blowing up a bag of balloons, even though his cheeks went purple and he almost passed out. Fred and I making up a dance show and charging Mum and Dad and Gr-Annie and Granddad two euro each for front row seats. We were saving money to go on a trip to Antigua, we told them. When Mum asked us if we knew where that was, we said we were pretty sure it was just past Wexford. She said, "Close enough," and she laughed and Dad kissed her.

Dad wrestling Fred and I on the couch, tickling us until we could barely breathe. Mum playing tag with us in the garden, all of us exploding in giddy shrieks as the summer sun shone down. Fred and I dressing Blue in

Fred's baby bonnet. Fred and I making dens, squirrelling away to make our plans. For a million more adventures.

40% OFF ALL MEMORY REVISITS THIS WEEK ONLY! a massive sign reads beside one of the windows.

"I love a good bargain," Blue sighs and I agree with him.

This is such a beautiful part of Thoughtopolis; a warm happy place. A welcome change from all the worry of late.

Even though it sort of also gives me a lump in my throat that I can't explain. I guess it's like sometimes when you're really happy you can also start crying. Which is really confusing when you have to try to tell someone that you're really, really happy about going on a surprise visit to Santa while at the same time bawling in their face. If they have already invented crying for being sad, could they not have invented glitter flying out of your nose or something for being happy, instead of your eyeballs leaking all over your face for both?

That is just lazy inventing.

Emotions are weird.

Bundlenugg reaches up and takes my hand. I smile down at him. My lovely furry friend.

"Look, Frankie! Fred's first day at school!" Blue squeaks in delight, seeing the particular memory light up a shop window to our left.

AWWWW, he looked **SOOOOOOO** cute with his knobbly knees knobbling out in his shorts as Mum knotted his tie and buttoned up his blazer. Blue playing tug-of-war with Fred's tie as I helped him with his laces. I was so proud that day, I remember, bringing him to school with me for the first time.

And I sat on the bench with Tess all yard time, just close enough to keep an eye on him. Just far enough to give him space to make new friends.

"Gosh," says Blue. "Sorry about the tie. I was so immature as a kid."

OOOOH, another good memory! Our family holiday to France where we snuck seven snails into Mum's suitcase and brought them all the way home with us! Mum wasn't pleased when she opened her case and there was snail snot all over her clothes. But we were delighted we had such a multicultural garden when we released them and we promised the Irish snails we would perhaps organize an exchange programme for them the next time.

Another window, another memory – Dad building

370

the tree house in the garden! Also known as the **COMIC-READING, HOT-CHOCOLATE-DRINKING, WHAT-SUPERPOWERS-WOULD-YOU-HAVE-IF-YOU-HAD-A-CHOICE FIGURING-OUT HEADQUARTERS**. Invisible shield for me, with the possibility of magicking fizzy jellies from nowhere. Turning spiders into gerbils for Fred. And woodlice into koalas. He really loves koalas.

We were so happy, I think, watching Mum and Dad climb the ladder to come and join us.

Mum said she'd choose to be able to teleport anywhere in the world, most likely a beach in Fiji. Dad wanted to be able to get through paperwork with lightning speed and run along rooftops to beat the traffic. Perhaps in all of this, I've forgotten that adults can have flashes of not being boring.

I still like Fred's turning spiders into gerbils the best.

"Dad," Fred asked, "you know when you swallow something, it comes out the other end?"

"Yes?"

"Well, if someone accidentally swallowed a bee, would it sting their bum on the way back out?"

"I'm not sure, Fred, but please don't try it, OK?"

He looked like he wasn't going to commit to a yes or no either way.

I watch my life from the outside as we all giggle together. I want to smash the glass and crawl back in there.

Why did Flo have to come along and ruin everything?

"Blue! It's Vinny!" I smile, pointing at another moving window.

I watch younger me feeding Vinny flakes of fish food as he swims happily around his tank. It's so weird, I had no front teeth and two side fangs which made me look like a bat with pigtails. *How* do adults think kids are cute? I'm lifting Fred up so he can reach the bowl to feed Vinny.

And there's a memory of Granny Doris and I painting rocks! We're laughing! We're having fun! I had forgotten all about those times. Perhaps she was painting rocks because they reminded her of potatoes, but either way we look like we are enjoying ourselves.

"When you put them all together like this, Frankie," she had said, placing the rocks in a group on the ground, "you get a rock concert!"

Granny Doris hadn't always been obsessed with potatoes and weather reports, but maybe she had to start liking other things now Grampa Pinky is gone and she has all this spare "liking energy". Because she had put so much of her energy into liking him.

Which wasn't difficult.

Because everyone liked Grampa Pinky. He was kind and generous and he had a laugh that made you feel like you were really special and talented, even if you had just done a fairly average handstand against the wall, not managed to colour inside the lines, or only got half of your spellings right. He always said that half of something is better than a whole of nothing, and I like to think that he was right.

He also gave the best hugs as well as the best fivers, and I miss him a lot.

I feel bad now that I've been so harsh on Granny Doris, but I still do not want to go there to stay with her. I guess, if I'm being honest, any time I've been to her house it makes me miss him more. I find it easier just not to go.

It's like the armchair he sat on is now extra empty. And the silences in the house without his laugh are doubly more silency. And the hugs without him there are extra less warm and huggy.

But here on Memory Lane, I can see him, remember him, and be *happy*!

It's like he isn't gone at all!

"Hi, Grampa Pinky!" I call out.

He doesn't answer.

As I watch, Fred and I burst through the door of the sitting room of their cottage.

"OH, HELLO, FRANKIE! HELLO, FRED!" Grampa chuckles warmly, putting his paper down and looking over the round-lensed glasses sitting on the end of his nose. "Where are you two off to?"

"We are off on an adventure, Grampa! We are going to make a rocket to the moon," I tell him.

"Well, I know you'll help her, Fred. And you know where I am if you ever need me, Frankie. Don't be afraid to ask for help. Careful when you fly, you hear? It's stormy out there!" he says, adjusting his glasses and picking his paper back up again.

The storm, I think now as I feel the first drops of rain.

I swallow back a rising wurp in my tummy as a blue cloud puffs out of Blue's bottom.

"Sorry," he says. "Brain fart. But it matches my name, so it's cute." I'm glad they're only visible for dogs here.

They really have no privacy at all anywhere when it comes to bathroom issues.

I look along the curb of Memory Lane and see the leaves on the ground dancing as though being picked up and spun around by the wind.

The dance is getting faster. The leaves are losing control now as the wind cuts through them, sending them in frenzied scatters.

I turn back to the window. The glass has fogged over a little. I rub it with my hand, desperate to see a little clearer. To see more.

"HEY, FRANKIE!" I hear Grampa call out. I come closer, pushing back the dark thoughts creeping into the corner of my mind. I can see them in the form of grey clouds sliding in across the sky at the end of Memory Lane. He passes a crisp new five dollar sense Thoughtopolis note out to me and holds my hand in his briefly. It feels rough and soothing and warm. It feels familiar. His pinky finger is jutting out.

Wow. How can he talk to me? When I'm outside all of the other memories looking in.

"I told you I'd look out for you, didn't I?"

"You did." I nod. Maybe that's how. A how I can't

explain. But I do know I need him now.

"Buy something silly," he says conspiratorially, before settling back into his chair.

He always said this: "A surprise fiver should never be spent on anything sensible." That's why I always bought bouncy balls with pretend eyeballs in them, slinkies or fake teeth.

"I love you, Grampa."

"And I love you, Frankie. I don't need to remind you what kind of love it is, do I?"

"AN ALWAYS LOVE," Grampa and I chorus in unison. Grampa smiles.

"That love goes on for ever. It's always around you. Even when you think you can't see it, it's there. And here," he says, tapping his chest with his hand. I assume he is gesturing to his heart and not the hankie in his top pocket. I love Grampa, but that doesn't mean I have to love his snotty tissues. That's going too far for *anyone*.

"Until next time, Frankie. I love you," he says, his big kind eyes crinkling as he smiles.

"ALWAYS," I reply on the other side of the glass, feeling the happy tears squeeze out of my eyes. And then glitter sprinkles right out of my nose!

FINALLY!

Thank you, Thoughtopolis!

Before I turn to go, Grampa lifts his pinky finger like he always used to, like he's able to pick up the weather signals.

"Mind yourself out there, Frankie. Some tricky weather coming."

I look around, through the rain; a thicker fog seems to be settling around us.

We walk further along the shop windows. The memories are getting harder to see now.

CHAPTER FORTY-FOUR

THE PUDDLES AND THE MUDDLES

"I can't see these memories so well," I say uneasily.

"That's normal," Bundlenugg assures me. "Certain memories get foggy sometimes."

Like the particular memory I'm looking at next. The one of me and Fred dressed as superheroes at Halloween, skipping down the road, flashing our powers on all the other trick-or-treaters and jumping out at people from behind walls. It was the only time I've ever heard Margery Lonergan do a **"WART"**. This was different to a wart on, say, a witch's face, and different to a "wurp" in that it is a worry fart and escapes from your... Well, I guess you know where it escapes from. It was so hard not to laugh. And I think behind Mum's cross face she was dressing up a teeny tiny smile.

Haha! I love that memory so much! Fred and I adore

Halloween. I watch us, swapping and trading our candy collections, munching, laughing, telling each other ghost stories, until we eventually fall asleep on the couch in a tangle of happy, worn-out fun.

It was such a busy night the memory is foggy in places. Fred had eaten so many fizzer sticks his face was green even when we washed off his green face paint. Dad eventually carried us both to bed. "You'll feel better in the morning," he'd said to Fred.

The clouds leak further into the sky overhead, like sprawls of navy ink bleeding into black.

More rain starts to fall.

My chest is aching in a way I can't explain. These memories … what use are they? Are they leading me to Fred? Why is he only in the memories in Memory Lane and not out here? With me? Where is he? Am I any closer to finding the buried secret? To getting my spark back?

The rains are coming even heavier and faster.

"Come on, Frankie," I hear Blue whisper as we follow Bundlenugg and Pickle further down Memory Lane.

Puddles form in front of us, so big I think I might get lost in them.

Another memory catches my eye in a passing window.

This one is foggy too, but I press my nose right up against the glass. Fred and I are chasing each other in the park, dancing and sploshing at puddles in our wellies.

More memories in window fronts blur past. Happy, joyful, funny memories. Sadness fills my eyes and I feel tears mixing with the rain as they spill down my cheeks.

Fred and I selling Mum's make-up outside our house and donating the money to Save the Donkeys. We were so thrilled! Far more thrilled than Mum was, it turns out, but we reminded her how adorable donkeys are.

Sleepovers in our cousins' houses.

Putting on a concert for our neighbours and charging everyone a fiver. It had possibly been overpriced – we only sang half of one song – but it had been a very fun song about raisins so we hoped they'd felt like they'd got their money's worth.

Scratching our names in the wet concrete near our house, wondering if we might get into trouble but thinking how interesting it was that they would still be written there in a billion years when aliens ruled the earth.

Did the Martins see it? I wonder now.

Everything is getting foggier.

I see a light flicker in one of the windows.

I walk over cautiously. It's completely misted over and I rub my sleeve along the glass and press my face to see. More fog creeps in as quickly as I rub it away.

I squeak my fingers across the shopfront glass, seeing only shapes and colours before it fogs back over again.

I will my eyes to see. I pray to all the carrots I have ever eaten in my life to help me in this very moment.

The rain continues to run in rivers down my face and I blink through the rainwater, trying to refocus.

I can see something.

Is that … Fred? In bed?

Sick … in bed?

He looks pale and sleepy, too still for a boy with so much energy.

I am curled beside him. With Blue curled beside me.

"Frankie," Mum is whispering. "You need to get some sleep."

"I'M NOT LEAVING HIM," I say, holding on tighter.

"FRED!" I cry out in the rain from the other side of my memory. **"WHEN WERE YOU SICK?"** I ask, struggling to find my words, struggling to sort my fears from my actual memories as the rain continues.

Fred closes his eyes in the bed.

"No, Fred, please wake up. Please don't leave me," the memory-me says.

"NO, NO, NO!" I yell, the rain and wind now howling around me. I turn to Blue. "What do you know, Blue? What do you remember?"

He stands beside me, his ginormous eyes glistening like the giant puddles.

I turn back and I see Mum and Dad again now, dressed in black, holding on to each other in a tight embrace. I see myself, watching them from the landing through the crack in their bedroom door.

And I can no longer see Fred.

I run to another window, panicked. I rub the foggy glass, but no matter how hard I try, I can see nothing clearly.

Where is he?

Where is Fred?

"WE HAVE TO FIX THIS. I CAN FIX THIS! I KNOW I CAN! IF I JUST TRY HARDER!"

I turn to Bundlenugg, Pickle and Blue.

"What does all of this mean?"

None of them answer, their eyes swollen with worry.

"Frankie," Bundlenugg says gently. "The storm is about to break. You need to get to the buried secret before it does. You need to get to it before the storm gets to you first and all of Thoughtopolis is ripped in two."

I shake my head. I can fix this, I know I can – I just have to try harder. "I need to find Fred," I say firmly. "What if the storm breaks and I haven't found him?"

I try to run, but ahead of me is a puddle the size of a lake.

"I–I CAN'T FACE IT..." I shake my head. "I can fix this. I can! **I CAN!** I just have to try harder."

"Don't be afraid to go through it," Bundlenugg encourages softly.

And just then I spot something. I reach for my magnifying glass and stare really closely, seeing faint traces of small footsteps. They're Fred's, I'm sure of it! Stretching out before me, leading to nowhere.

But they *have* be leading to somewhere!

"FRED????" I call out.

And then I follow the footsteps, right into the eye of the storm.

CHAPTER FORTY-FIVE

THE WORRISOME WOODS AND SOLVING THE CASE OF THE BURIED SECRET

For the first time, I get the next stamp in my Journey Journal and do not leave Thoughtopolis to go back to the Real World.

Once I've figured out how helpless I feel, how overwhelmed, I'm able to move forward.

Which means I just have to get one more stamp.

I must be so close.

And I am still here too. I cannot find the golden door to leave even if I want to. I know I have come too far this time. I'm trapped here for now one way or another.

I'm not leaving until I find the buried secret. Until I find my missing spark.

And I'm not leaving until I find Fred.

"Down this way," Bundlenugg and Pickle encourage as we go, Blue never straying far from my heels.

"You OK, Blue?" I ask.

Another little brain fart escapes and gets whipped away by the wind. I take that as, "Just about managing really." His gums are flapping again against the force of the gale.

I need to stay strong, even though I feel like I'm about to break. The storm is getting fiercer; it's harder to see, or to know which way I'm going.

I need to fix all this, I think again as we search for the train, looking around to scan for the familiar parts of Thoughtopolis I've grown to know so well.

We pass the **HOINKY TOINKY DINKY WINKY TWENTY-FOUR-HOUR TOYSHOP**, and I skip to see Mr McGranger, so tempted to run back to everything I've come to know. Everywhere I've come to find refuge.

"Mr McGranger?" I call. "Are you in here?"

I look around, taking in the wonder of this toyshop once more. This time I'm too distracted to notice the new dolls in their life-size houses, the magical wallpaper with even more miniature scenes that come to life, and their fairy-themed bed sheets. I'm too worried to bounce on the giant trampolines lined along the floor like springy tiles.

I'm too scared to even look at the robot toys to my left. They suddenly look like an army. An army ready to attack.

None of it feels the same any more.

"Mr McGranger!" I call. "**MR MCGRANGER!!!!!** Where are you? **WE NEED YOU!**" I call so loudly, I surprise even myself.

The dolls rattle in their houses, their faces looking more shocked than happy now.

"FRANKIE? FRANKIE, IS THAT YOU?"

It's Mr McGranger's voice. I turn around. Where is he?

"Where are you?" I shout impatiently. I can't see much, just rows and rows of toys lying about in the dark.

"Frankie. Frankie, I am right here."

I turn to see him, sitting right beside me at his desk. Has he been there all along?

He has his work apron on and a torch strapped on his head to help him see the small detail of the thing he's trying to mend.

There's something big and red and shiny lying broken in two on his desk.

What is that? I wonder.

"I need you to fix ... Fred! I saw that he was sick, but I don't know what's happened," I blurt, suddenly realizing how ludicrous that sounds. **"I CANNOT FIND HIM."**

Mr McGranger removes the monocle from his left eye and places it softly on his table.

"Frankie … I'm so sorry… I can't fix this for you…"

"But you have to! Of course you can! You can fix **EVERYTHING**," I babble, feeling a familiar panic rise through me.

"Oh, Frankie," he says, standing up from his bench and moving towards me, resting a hand on my shoulder. "Sometimes when things are broken into a million pieces, they can never really be fixed in the same way. They can never be exactly as they were. They can mend, but there will always be those cracks. And that, Frankie, can be OK. That is often how other love breaks through. How the light gets in."

I shake my head, unable to absorb his words properly.

I see his hands move slowly to the toy on his table. A mish mash of things, so jumbled and split it's hard to even make out.

"What is that?" I ask, watching him hold it gently.

"This is yours, Frankie. Your spirit; it's … broken."

What does he mean? I think, staring at this damaged "thing".

"Wait … that's not my spark?" I ask, confused.

"No, but they are linked…"

No. No, he's wrong. *Nothing is broken.* Everything is getting muddled up, surely!! **I'M FINE!!!**

Yes, my spark is missing, but other than that I'm OK!

"NO!!!!!" I scream, before feeling the ground underfoot shake and tremble. I look down, eyes wide in terror as the ground starts to crack and rip apart; a glow of molten red lava flows beneath.

"We need to find the train, fast!" Bundlenugg urges, pulling at my ankles. "We have to get out of here. Thoughtopolis is crumbling!"

"FRANKIIIIIIEEEEEEEE," I hear Mr McGranger call after me, before the noise is drowned out by the wind and the rain and the sound of my own cries.

We run and run until we reach the very edge of somewhere I've never dared to go. The place in Thoughtopolis I know of but always avoid.

The Worrisome Woods.

The trees creak and the winds howl as they rip in and out of the trunks of wood stretching up and clambering from the ground like they are trying to save themselves from something.

Just before the Worrisome Woods are the familiar

trees of the Teeny Tiny Forest, a place Fred and I always love to visit, though we have never dared to step outside of it into the foreboding woods beyond.

I hear a stomping behind me as the ground shakes again. I turn slowly, my heart beating in my chest. It's Harold, the teeny tiny hedgehog from the Teeny Tiny Woods. Except he isn't so teeny tiny any more.

Harold is as tall as a building! And Bundlenugg, Pickle and I are utterly dwarfed, like ants standing in front of an elephant.

I look around: all of our tiny friends, the squirrels, the mice, the other hedgehogs, are **HUGE!** Their giant nostrils blowing gusts of wind in our faces as they breathe.

Everything is muddled. And not in the way I've known before, not like it is in the ConfooZ Zoo.

I feel so small.

So, so tiny in the face of everything.

How am I going to fix this when everything else is so big?!

"Harold," I start.

"Harry, please," he interrupts. "We have been friends for a long time now, Frankie."

"HARRY, WHY AM I SO SMALL?" I cry, feeling tears

running down my cheeks. Even my voice is small, so quiet it feels like no one might ever be able to hear me from down here.

"Frankie, you are not. You are exactly the same size. You are strong. You are stronger than you know. It's your feelings. Your feelings are making you feel small."

A leaf the size of a boat flies past my face.

"But … what can I do?" I whimper.

"See them. Feel them, Frankie."

I stand there, bewildered by the weight of everything I have ever felt. And everything I've tried so hard not to feel.

We run from the Teeny Tiny Forest then, trudging through weeds and tripping over broken sticks, racing towards the one place I've always run from.

Finding the Train of Thought on the other side of the Teeny Tiny Forest, we board for one last terrifying loop of Thoughtopolis before it spits us out at the far edge of the Worrisome Woods. The train station is abandoned. The old station house looks eerie and creepy, its front door banging in the wind. The tracks look haphazard, unfinished.

"We cannot go with you to your final destination, Frankie," Bundlenugg says sadly, Pickle at his side. "It is your own secret to uncover. But know you can do this. This is the very last part of your journey and you must complete it yourself."

"You got this," Pickle roars, and I take strength from her.

"I'm proud of you, Frankie," Blue says, whimpering by my side and then scrunching his ginormous eyeballs and squeezing as hard as he can, before opening his eyes again. "Nope. I can talk, sure, but I still can't cry."

I turn back to look at my friends one last time.

I could not have done any of this without them. I wave, and they wave back sadly.

Blue whimpers again.

"I'll be OK," I mouth and then I turn towards the woods.

My breath catches in my throat. I feel my heart banging on my chest, warning me, pleading with me not to enter.

Gnarled knotted trees twist around me, their bark looking like contorted faces: ones of worry, of shock, of sadness. The branches reach out, as if pleading for help, trying to claw at me, to swallow me whole into their worry. Heavy thoughts howl through the wind in the trees.

This is the scariest place I've ever been.

I will myself to be brave. To be strong. I have to be to

find Fred. To find my secret.

Somehow I know that this secret is going to be bad. Worse than all my worries put together.

Worse than Monica, Veronica and Nell firing their lunch grapes at me from the end of their rulers and saying **HAHAHAHAHAHAHHAHAAA** *and* **PSHHHHWWSHHHHHHSSHH**.

Worse than my usual worry about Mum and Dad.

About villainous Flo.

Or school tests on a Friday.

Or Blue doing a poo in a slipper.

Or Margery Lonergan reporting me to *The Spy Monthly* for not listening.

What is ahead of me is worse than all of those worries.

I feel so heavy. But all on the inside, as though my heart is made of rocks. Like it's made of the heaviest secrets in the whole world. I quicken my pace, fighting as best I can against the wind. The storm screams into my face.

"Fred?" I call. **"WHERE ARE YOU?"**

I hear a flock of heronders overhead, cawing with screeches that knife the air. They dive and swoop at me and I cover my head with my hands for protection.

The wind whips at me.

The rain pelts me.

The ground splinters and rips under me.

"PLEASE, FRED! I NEED YOU TO HELP ME!!!!"

And then I can't do it any more. I can't keep going.

I drop to my knees as the storm rages on. I feel myself crying again as I reach my hands out to steady myself on the shaking forest floor of the darkest part of the Worrisome Woods.

My hands feel something cold and hard. I squint, trying to see what they have collided with.

A spade.

A large spade sits, speared in the ground at an angle.

Dig, Frankie, dig. It's buried here.

I know, then, that this is where the secret is buried; here, in the deepest furthest part of the Worrisome Woods.

I pick up the spade and dig. And dig and dig and dig and dig.

It's all familiar too. This spade, this mud, this place.

As though I've been here before. As though it was me who came here and buried it in the first place.

I hear a loud clunk as the spade meets with something flat and hard. I toss the spade aside and scrape away mud with my hands.

A golden box reveals itself.

I lift it out of the hole and place it on the earth beside me. It's beautiful. Even in the dark it glows like soft golden moonlight. I go to lift the lid, but it's stuck firm. Locked. I rattle it. Shake it. Try to prise it open.

Nothing.

I reach for my magnifying glass and in doing that, my Journey Journal falls on the ground and I see my four collected stamps – Lost, Scared, Exhausted and Angry – along with a new, peculiar-shaped stamp that I haven't seen before. I pick it up to examine it. Sadness. A lump catches in my throat and I swallow it down hard, and as I do my eyes start to prickle with tears at the corner, and my stomach feels like it's dropping in a falling elevator. I *am* sad. I am so, so sad. And it gets me thinking about the biology of sadness. It's everywhere. In my brain, my eyes, my throat, my stomach. The sadness is everywhere.

Looking at them all together, I realize they look like pieces of a jigsaw. All of the separate oddly shaped stamps make sense now sitting next to one another. Carefully I line them up and they form ... the shape of a key.

I lay my magnifying glass down, knowing that this is the end of the investigation, and I place the outline of the key next to the box. I close my eyes and allow a rush of emotions to race through me, every single thing I have felt in Thoughtopolis: happiness and escape, and everything along the journey to get me here. I am lost, scared, exhausted, angry and sad.

I think of everywhere the Train of Thought has taken me. The Tick Tock Grandfather Clock ride, where images of Fred disappeared after the age of eight. Loving Fred to the moon and back, but being unable to reach him, feeling untethered. The Land of Exhaustion, where I was drowning in tiredness. A tiredness so deep in my bones from trying to carry on like I'm OK. I am not OK. I am broken. Broken and lost without him.

And then to Memory Lane, the slow realization of what I've tried so hard to pretend hasn't happened. And where I went to bury it.

HERE.

Right here, in the eye of the storm. A storm that will destroy Thoughtopolis.

The storm of my own grief.

In that moment, just before it hits me, the force of the storm is almost unbearable. I think it's going to rip me in two. It howls and it rages and it ravages, threatening to break me from the inside out.

And then…

EVERYTHING STOPS.

EVERYTHING.

There's a calm I haven't felt before.

The feeling when a secret buried so deep gets revealed and you know it can't threaten you any more.

And in that moment I know.

I know what's staring back at me. My own heart that I had locked away and buried deep with the secret I never wanted to believe was true.

The secret that I know now.

I know Fred is gone.

I think of Mum and Dad dressed in black. How worried and upset they are all the time. I know that it isn't because of Flo or because they don't love me any more.

I know why all the adults stare at me like I'm about to break.

Because I already have.

I know that Fred has died.

That he has been gone from the Real World for some time now even though I haven't wanted to believe it.

But the Sixthwisp is now all around me and I know

what my Sixthwisp has been trying to show me all along.

I know that Fred only still exists here in Thoughtopolis.

That's why I keep escaping here – to be with him. The only place I can keep him alive. Where I can be with his memory, in all of mine.

But is that it?

Am I never going to see him again?

I reach into the box as the tears race down my cheeks, lifting out my heart. It is heavy and solid like metal, and it glows. And as soon as I hold it again, a sudden bolt so strong and so bright sparks in my hands and courses through my whole body like fizzing liquid gold, lifting me right out of the Worrisome Woods.

Taking me somewhere else entirely.

CHAPTER FORTY-SIX

THE HEART AND THE MISSING SPARK

I don't know quite how I got here, or where I am exactly, but I am here.

And in my heart I know.

Because, well, that's where I am.

The wind has stopped, the rain has stopped and the dawn has broken. I look around and drink in the warm sunshine.

There are no ominous trees. No wind. No howling rain.

I pat the ground and feel a warm comforting rhythmic beat.

I have made it out of the woods.

"HEY, BIG SIS."

I turn to see Fred.

"HEY, LITTLE BROTHER," I say, relief flooding me as I wrap him in a hug. "Where are we? Where have you been all this time?" I mumble, his familiar curls mushed against my face, my eyelashes brushing off his freckles

"Where have I been?" he answers gently. "In your heart, Frankie!"

He takes my hand and we sit together, looking at the warm golden and vermillion plains stretched out before us.

"Sometimes Grampa Pinky comes to visit too... But I think he's gone for a nap. I never thought I'd manage – there's so much blood pumping around." Fred laughs. "Remember the time Mum pulled your tooth out accidentally when it was really wobbly and I fainted?"

We both laugh.

"But..." he continues, "I like it here."

"I like it here too, Fred. I like it here with you."

"I know, Frankie." He pauses. "But it's time."

I can't look at him. I can't bear to hear it.

"You've been here too long, Frankie. You weren't ready before now. But you need to go back..."

"But—" I stop, unable to find the words. He takes my hand, something I've always done to him.

"I don't know what I'll do, Fred. Without coming to Thoughtopolis. Escaping to be with you."

I sit with one hand in his, the other on the beating

ground beneath us.

"The place where no one judges me for just wanting to be back with you."

"You know they've only been worried about you," he says softly. "Wanting to help."

I swallow. I think of the adults. All their eyes on me. Wondering what's going on inside that spaghetti brain.

Where do you go, Frankie?

And now I know.

I've been coming here to find Fred. To be with him. After he'd gone.

A lump grows in my throat again.

"Will I ever not miss you, Fred?"

"Probably not. Actually, **YOU'D BETTER NOT!**"

He punches me playfully on my arm and we both laugh.

"But you won't always feel this sad, Frankie. I promise you that. You have a whole life waiting for you," Fred whispers. "You deserve to be happy again, Frankie." He takes a deep breath. "I have a very important thing I need to ask you. I've needed to ask you for a long time now."

"What is it?" I say. "Anything! Anything for you."

"I need you to go back and live for the *both of us*."

401

My heart contracts with a fresh ache and I can feel it run along the scar of him. The scar of Fred.

"Do you think you can do that?" he asks softly.

I can't speak.

The words won't come.

I'll try, I promise. *I will try.*

He stands up. We are at the bottom of a large, red hill.

"What are you doing?" I ask, smiling now.

"COME ON! ONE LAST ADVENTURE!"

One last adventure.

I can feel fresh cracks splinter along my heart.

I can't.

I CAN.

Fred turns and offers me his hand, helping me to my feet. "Come on, Frankie!!! When you feel sad! When you don't think you can make it over another bump, the one thing that will carry you through, Frankie, is *hope.*"

I look at the mound before us as Fred starts to climb it. "This is Hope Hill, it keeps your heart strong! And sometimes the only way over it to the other side is to tell it your hopes!" he calls back.

"Like what, Fred?" I ask.

"All the things you are looking forward to, Frankie! Hope! Hope is what keeps us going, keeps us strong just when we feel we cannot go any further."

I wrack my brains. All I can think of is Fred.

"You're cheating, Frankie."

Ugh. I keep forgetting Fred knows all my thoughts already.

"OK, OK!" I laugh. "You are a tough taskmaster!"

I think again.

"I'm looking forward to making a snail hotel with Tess, if she still wants to."

"Great!" Fred calls, making our pathway further up the hill a little clearer. "I want you to have fun doing it!"

"I'm looking forward to Mum's birthday. And Dad said he'd teach me to rollerblade backwards."

"WAHOOOOO!" Fred cheers. "Dad is really good at that."

"I'm looking forward to Christmas and my last molars falling out and sticking glow stars on my ceiling."

"That's it, Frankie!" Fred encourages until we are both standing on the top of Hope Hill. "Keep going, Frankie," he instructs, hunkering down on the ground.

Haha! What is he doing?

"More things you are looking forward to! We need momentum! You need **HOOOOOOOOPE!**"

And he's off, barrelling down the side of the hill.

I get down on the ground and roll. Roll and spin as the fresh grass, blue skies, bright sunshine wheels in circles in front of my eyes.

I feel the heat on my skin, thankful for the warmth.

"Teaching Blue how to high-five! Learning to dive in the deep end! Making new friends at hockey!"

"YAHOOOOOOOOOOO! KEEP GOING, FRANKIEEEEEEEEEE!"

"Going to Kerry on the train with Mum! Raising the green flag at school! Learning French!"

"BONJOURRRRRRR, FRANKIE!"

We laugh. We laugh and laugh and laugh together until our giggles and screeches are all I can feel in my heart.

Worn out and happy, we finally reach the bottom of the other side of Hope Hill.

"Where to now?" I swallow uncertainly.

"Come on, Frankie. I want to show you something."

He leads me to a crack on the ground and we both place our hands over it. I feel all the cracks that have formed, broken away and fused back together again. The deep scars letting tiny fractures of golden glowing light peek through in ever so tiny little golden sparks.

"You hid it when you buried your heart away," Fred whispers. "But you've found it now. You've found your spark."

I stop and look up at him.

"But that's only because you are here and I am with you."

"This is where I will always be, Frankie," he answers.

He comes and sits beside me, tucking himself under my arm where he's sat before a thousand times.

"I'm proud of you," he says. "That was not an easy journey. But it will get easier. And I will always be here, helping you on it."

We sit together for a very long time; I hold his hand tighter, so afraid of letting go.

I want time to stand still, to sit with him with no goodbyes.

"You need to go back, Frankie," he says. "You need to leave me here now."

Red hot tears spill out of my eyes. As brave as I feel I have been, I can't stop them.

Being Fred's big sister is the best thing that I've ever been. Who is Frankie Finkleton if I have to be Frankie Finkleton without him?

"You won't be without me, Frankie," he says.

"I can't, Fred... I can't do it... I want to stay in Thoughtopolis where I can keep you alive in my head. I don't want to go back without you. I cannot say goodbye to you."

It's then that my voice cracks and overflows with a million sobs, a billion tears.

We cling to each other. A hug I have needed for ever.

"You don't have to say goodbye, Frankie. I will always

407

be here. In everything that you do. I just won't be in Thoughtopolis any more. The next adventure, and all the ones after that, are just for you. And Blue."

His big round eyes smile up at me, his gap-toothed grin widening. "Whenever you need strength or courage, I'll be here. You have your own. That's what's making your heart spark. And that's where mine will be too."

I feel my very own heart break and crack and I see it as it fuses together again in healing scars.

"It's so unfair you didn't get to live long, Fred."

"Some people don't get to be as lucky in their whole long lives as I've been in my little one."

I watch him scratch his name into my heart, just like we did on that fresh concrete together in the Real World.

And I scratch mine beside his.

"We're a good team." He smiles. "And you see? It's there for ever. Go back now, Frankie. To Mum and Dad. And Flo. You need to tell her she can hide bubblegum in her belly button when she's older and the adults will never know! I need you to be the best big sister to her. And I can't wait to feel all the adventures you will have in here with her."

He touches my heart; a spark lights up.

"Take this home. It's from me. Take it back and share it. I'm safe here, Frankie. And, Frankie?"

"Yes?"

"I love you," he says.

"I love you, Fred," I say, doing my best to stand up and let him go.

Knowing where he will be for ever.

CHAPTER FORTY-SEVEN

THE NOT SO BORING REAL WORLD

The Real World looks different when I finally get back to it. I start noticing colours and sounds and all sorts of things that scared me before. Being back in the Real World is kind of cool. Now that I have a *different* magical power.

No, don't worry, I'm not disappearing into my own head all the time! This is even cooler.

My heart has a spark that no one else's does.

My heart has a Fred in it that makes me braver and stronger than anyone else I know.

I have the extra power you get from carrying a person you love in your heart.

School starts to be more fun.

Sometimes.

I *do* have to do extra lessons, but they aren't so bad.

Monica, Veronica and Nell are less scary. I know we will never be friends because you can't be friends with everyone. And they are still pretty mean. They are just less scary now I'm braver. Now I have a new magical power in my heart that helps me stand up to them.

Nell says to me that sometimes she isn't laughing *at* me, she's laughing *with* me, or rather trying to make me laugh because she knows I'm sad.

She says her gerbil died so she kind of understands, even though I think there is sort of a big difference between a gerbil and a brother.

And then she says there are other times she is definitely still laughing *at* me.

"Always be kind, Frankie," Gr-Annie says to me. "But some people are just not your people. And that's OK once you both respect it."

I'm not sure Monica, Veronica and Nell respect much to be honest, and I know for a fact it was them who wrote "BUMS!" on the back of the bathroom door.

I don't mind Ross being loud because it doesn't bother me so much when attention is drawn to me. And even though he is very loud, he is always kind with it and Mum says that is one of the most important things to be. I'm still NEVER EVER going to marry him, though. Even though we made each other Valentine's cards. (This is now one of my new top secret secrets, since some of my other secrets aren't so secret any more.)

Ms Hammerhead is less sharky now and she tells me that I don't have to be brave all the time. Especially when the class are doing things like family trees in school that make me feel sad. At first I think she is acting fishy about it, but then I remind myself that her great–great–great–great–great–great–grandfather may not actually have been a shark after all. Or was he?

Some private investigators' case files can stay open for YEARS.

And Mr McNogg is less boring and even cracked a joke about the photocopier. I mean, it wasn't in the slightest bit funny, but that's not the point! He says he often wants to make jokes but he's afraid no one will find him funny and will laugh at him in the wrong way. I can understand that.

He smiled at me too last week! And it wasn't even his birthday! Perhaps he smiles more than twice a year after all and I've just never noticed. Although he did then start telling me the difference between a 2B, a HB and a 2H pencil, which was fairly boring. So some things will never change, I guess.

"2B or not 2B, that is the pencil!" I giggle in my head, thinking Fred would have laughed at that.

What was it that one of the Martins said? *Everyone is exactly the same in different ways.* Or something.

And I remember what the Martins said about communicating emotions. That having felt something yourself makes you understand others far better. And there's a kindness in this that you only ever really understand when you understand.

Margery Lonergan told me she feels lonely and looks out from behind her curtains every morning just so she can see the world go by. Just so she doesn't feel like she's all by herself in the world. She still has a subscription to *The Spy Monthly*, however, so I know I need to be slightly on guard. I don't need any *Mortified Local Girl denies swapping Valentine's Day cards with Very Loud Ross P. Rossdale* headlines any time soon.

And I don't need to be in *The Spy Monthly* to know:

    a) I am a really good private investigator.

    b) Because I uncovered the buried secret and got a lot of my spark back.

    c) And I discovered WHY I could magic myself to Thoughtopolis.

    d) Because I wasn't quite ready to let Fred go.

    e) Because I miss him.

    f) Because I always felt I was the best version of me when I was with him.

    g) And Fred is.

    h) In my heart.

    i) For ever.

Mr Gordon and I make up new sweet combinations in his Olde Sweet Shoppe on Fridays after school; I've never thought of mixing sour apple with sweet fizzy raspberry, and I miss the watermelon cotton candy Lillian Longstring had in her funfair, and the rainbow gumdrop in

Mr Guzzleworth's Sweet Shop with one P and one E. But these are nice too.

And Dr Hilda Stitch seems to understand me more now. Or rather I understand her more. Especially when she lets me sit on the high stool and try out her stethoscope.

She lets me sit there and be with my own feelings for a while, the lead of the stethoscope going from my ears to my heart. And I feel Fred there.

I go for mashed potatoes with Granny Doris and they aren't as bad as I imagined. She even adds butter and cheese. And I know why Mum and Dad wanted to send me to hers for a while. Because she lost someone she loved very much too, and they hoped it might be a help for us to seek comfort in each other.

She had come to check on me that night. She had been really worried about me because she had been through her own sadness too. It wasn't quite a little brother, but a granddad is still definitely worse than losing a gerbil.

I realize that Granny Doris isn't boring after all. Sure, she loves spuds and wants to know the optimal time to dry her knickers on the line, but she was also a scientist when she was younger! And we did an experiment in the garden with pepper and water and soap. And I studied them closely with my magnifying glass.

Granny Doris says that some adventures are great and some are small and the key to it all is finding the magic and the fun in both.

And I understand that too as I watch a snail pop out of its shell and do nothing else other than that.

And I pick up a dandelion clock and blow the fluff. And I make new wishes. Ones to look forward to. And I watch them carry in the breeze like new tufts of hope.

I sit with Granny as she tells me stories about Grampa Pinky and I know she knows that I know what it is like to really miss someone. For your heart to break into a million pieces and slowly fuse back together again. Scarred and sore. Never the same, but with new cracks of light that can shine through.

We talk about Grampa Pinky. And we talk about Fred. And I imagine them there together in both of our hearts. Minding each other.

And I still sit on Gr-Annie's lap when I need to. When both of us just sit and *be* and don't need to say anything at all. And I teach Granddad how to do a French plait and we do one in Biscuit's hair. She looks lovely.

I still get muddled in my head at times, me and my good old spaghetti brain. But it doesn't feel quite so messy. Which makes me think of another joke Fred told me.

"Hey, Frankie, what does a piece of pasta say when he's on his own? Hey! I'm Cann-e-lloni! Kinda lonely? Get it?"

And I laugh instead of it instantly making me want to cry. Even though I accept I will always feel cann-e-lloni for him.

Tess and I have become best friends again, and I realize she hadn't gone off me at all. I had just shut her out when I had buried my heart and closed it off to anyone else.

I hadn't known how to be. And she said she hadn't known the right things to say, so we had drifted from each other in the confusion.

Dad says that people don't always know the right thing to say and that's OK, because sometimes there is no right thing to say.

And it turns out Mindy is really nice and has invited me around to her house too to shout "LETTUCE" at her tortoise with her.

We teach Blue how to high-five and we learn to rollerblade backwards in the park with my dad, and we make the first ever seven-star snail hotel in the garden. I'm pretty sure our concierge is French! And we even invite Gary, Larry and Barry to the grand opening.

And I enjoy it all, just like I promised Fred.

And I let Mum and Dad hug me like they used to. And I let them know I'm OK if they cry and they let me know it's OK if I do too.

And I crawl into their bed when I miss Fred most. With Mr B and Ms P, whose full names are Mr Bundlenugget and Ms Pickle – just like Bundlenugget and Pickle, our Thoughtopolis mentors.

When I need to feel close to them all, I don't hide them under my bed and pretend I don't need them any more. I don't try to hide much, because I know sometimes it's braver not to.

"You know we were never trying to replace Fred, don't you, Frankie?" Mum says softly to me, brushing her fingers through my hair.

I know that accepting Flo is here feels like accepting that Fred isn't, and I just wasn't ready yet.

"Flo came along, I think, just when we all needed *hope*," Dad adds, and I can't help thinking of Fred and how he wanted us all to have that in our hearts.

"Fred would want you to have your spark back, Frankie," Mum adds. Her words layered with relief as she kisses the top of my head.

"I know," I reply. And I really do know.

We cry. And we also laugh. We laugh so much together. Watching Flo learning to walk, trying to say our names, chasing through the hall on her walker.

I let her fall asleep nestled in beside me on the couch. In worn-out tired hugs, her hot sticky little hand curls into mine. And I feel my heart spark against hers, and I know it's him. I know he is helping me.

I make a promise to Flo as she sleeps in the spot I had always reserved for him, that we will have so many adventures together.

And that I will be the best big sister I already know how to be.

EPILOGUE

(FROM MY WORD OF THE DAY BOOK. IT MEANS "A FINAL NOTE ON WHAT HAS HAPPENED")

Hi, my name is Frankie Finkleton, aged exactly twelve years and two hours old. I can now do seven cartwheels in a row without feeling dizzy and I have an enquiry pending with the *Guinness Book of World Records* if this is enough to get me in. I am still of average height for my age group, but I did have a growth spurt recently and now some of my trousers look like three-quarter length leggings and I'm mortified about it but I'm not entirely sure why.

I get mortified about a lot of things recently. It's my latest feeling I'm trying to figure out.

I have a scar on my eyebrow from when I was playing a game of chase with my brother Fred and I didn't realize there was an entire wall in the way.

And I have a scar on my heart from when he died.

I might still be a private investigator when I'm older, but I also might just have it as a side hustle because I might be a cool scientist like my Granny Doris when I turn into an adult.

Which brings me to my Secret Book Of Secrets That I Never Got Around To Renaming Because I Went On A Secret Undercover Mission To Find My Spark.

I jump off my bed and poke my hand around for it underneath. It doesn't feel quite as scary in there any more.

I pull it out and open it up, letting the spine rest on my leg as the pages fall open.

I have quite a few updated secrets.

1. It's not really a secret but the cat is out of the bag (well, the dog is out of the ... oh, never mind) about the local golden retriever being blamed for eating that cake. Blue and Rufus Rutherford have made up and even play chase together in the park and I'm glad for him because he must have been in a bit of a pickle missing Pickle.

2. I will NOT admit it to their faces but ALL ADULTS ARE NOT BORING. Mum entered a singing competition and she's been selected to go on our local TV station! She wrote a song about hope and it is so good that even though I sort of get mortified whenever she sings,

I'm also really proud of her. Mum is so brave, and one of my heroes. But I also can't tell her that because it sort of makes me mortified.

3. I know I said that adults don't believe in magic, but actually sometimes they do. It's just in a different way (not as cool as kids, but I feel like they should get some credit at least). The very old adults definitely believe in magic and I think it's because when you've been around for hundreds of years and go through all sorts of life journeys it gives you a particular wisdom and appreciation for things that feel the closest thing to magic without, say, riding on a unicorn or going invisible. Granny Doris told me all about this and I agreed with her before feeling quite embarrassed about the whole thing. This is not really a secret, and it's definitely not a secret that old people don't like to feel invisible. We should remember that they were kids once too with lives and loves and hopes and dreams, but I have written it in for now and sometimes I still go on tangents so I think I'll just leave it here for now anyway.

4. I get mortified about EVERYTHING. Dad tells me it's all a part of growing up, which is super embarrassing.

5. I still fart in the bath, but I have someone else to blame now. Flo! And she's only really starting to talk so I reckon I still have some time before she can properly defend herself.

6. I really like Flo. She is very, very funny. She is a good hugger too. I'm sure this isn't a huge secret as I like spending so much time with her, but still. We have come a long way, Flo and I.

7. I accidentally ate a mushroom and ... liked it? This can never get out. It would ruin my reputation.

8. Sometimes I still sneak into Fred's room. I lie on his bed and look out at the stars and think of him. It's not that it needs to be a secret, but some things are OK just to keep for yourself. He will always be my *anam cara*.

9. It is OK to feel sad, and there will be bad days. This is my not-secret secret when I talk to others about how I'm feeling.

10. Tess kissed Gary from Barry, Gary and Larry fame.

11. I went back to Thoughtopolis a couple of times after everything that happened, but it just didn't sparkle the same without Fred. And after the second visit, I realized there was so much of Fred in the Real World for me to enjoy: in Mum and Dad, and Flo, and in all the places we spent time together. And I know he's always in my heart. So now I don't go to Thoughtopolis really any more. But that doesn't mean I don't still have lots of magic on the inside!

12. That's it. For now.

THE END

NAME:

AMY HUBERMAN

AGE:

ONE OF THOSE ADULTY TYPES

FROM:

DUBLIN, Ireland, the World, the Universe, the Galaxy

OCCUPATION:

FULL-TIME ADULT

ACTRESS (although she hasn't done one of those Christmas plays where everyone shouts "IT'S BEHIND YOU!" so I'm not sure she's really made it yet)

SCREEN-WRITER (think that means she writes on screens, which if you ask me should be considered vandalism)

AUTHOR

MUM

BEST KNOWN FOR:

Creating me, Fred, Blue and Thoughtopolis

LIKES:

FANCY CHEESES with funny names like "Halloumi"

MATCHING HER SUNGLASSES TO THE COLOUR OF HER DRINKS (odd!)

STRESSING OVER THE FLOWERS IN HER GARDEN (these adults!)

SHEEP (see below)

DISLIKES:

FOODS THAT BEGIN WITH THE LETTER Q

SHARKS (particularly hammerhead sharks)

BULLIES

FUN FACT:

If you type Amy's name into the Internet, it says she's a shepherd. So I have taken the initiative and added "SHEEP" to her Likes.

NAME:
KATIE KEAR
AGE:
ANOTHER ADULTY TYPE
FROM:
ENGLAND, the World, the Universe, the Galaxy
OCCUPATION:
FULL-TIME ADULT

ILLUSTRATOR (This means she
draws fun stuff for a living! Maybe I should do that instead of being a part-time vet?)

BEST KNOWN FOR:
Drawing me, Fred, Blue and Thoughtopolis

LIKES:
BOOKS (That's quite a commitment because not all books are interesting like this one)

ADVENTURES IN NATURE

CHOCOLATE (who doesn't!?)

THE SMELL OF CHERRIES (I'll add it to my To-Do List and report back)

DISLIKES:
WHEN SHE'S NOT DRAWING

SNEEZING MORE THAN FOUR TIMES IN A ROW

BRAIN FREEZE when your ice-cream is too cold

FUN FACT:
Katie has a Corgi dog called TOASTIE, but as of yet, hasn't tried to turn him into a hot sandwich!

TALKING HELPS...

Being in Thoughtopolis was fun, but at times it was scary and lonely. Talking to someone in the Real World about my feelings around losing Fred would also have helped, and there are people you can talk to as well if you miss a loved one.

If you live in Ireland, visit one of these websites for resources and information:

- **WWW.CHILDHOODBEREAVEMENT.IE**
- **WWW.CHILDRENSGRIEFCENTRE.IE**
- **WWW.RAINBOWSIRELAND.IE**
- **WWW.BARNARDOS.IE/OUR-SERVICES/ WORK-WITH-FAMILIES/BEREAVEMENT-SERVICES**
- **WWW.ANAMCARA.IE** (this one is for your parents)

If you live in the UK, visit one of these websites for resources and information:

- **WWW.CHILDBEREAVEMENTUK.ORG**
- **WWW.CHILDHOODBEREAVEMENTNETWORK.ORG.UK**
- **WWW.GRIEFENCOUNTER.ORG.UK**
- **WWW.BARNARDOS.ORG.UK/WHAT-WE-DO/SERVICES/ CHILD-BEREAVEMENT-SERVICE-GENERAL**
- **WWW.TCF.ORG.UK** (this one is for your parents)

We all have **MAGIC** inside of us, but sometimes the best thing is just to tell someone else how we're feeling.

ACKNOWLEDGEMENTS

Firstly, a big, massive thank you to **YOU** for reading this book and coming along on this adventure! I shall take a leaf out of Frankie's book – literally – and make a list of who it is I need to thank. I would name check you guys for reading, but, you know, it could be a GDPR nightmare!

First and foremost (well I guess it's second after all you lot, but that might make Yasmin sound less special and I assure you she is **VERY FABULOUS AND SPECIAL**), I would like to thank my editor Yasmin Morrissey at Scholastic for being the best editor a writer – who had written books before, but it had been a while ago and she was unsure if she would write another and would it be a children's book?!? – could ask for!

I had written books for those adulty types but had never thought to write a children's book. Yasmin, thank you for backing me into a corner and making me do this (only joking, I was so happy you asked me/backed me into a corner). Thank you so, so much for reaching out to me and inviting me on this incredibly-fulfilling, fun, educational and brilliantly-exciting journey. For all of your encouragement, cheer-leading, guidance, sensible problem-solving, enthusiasm, humour, super-braininess and insight. You have made it a joy and I could

NOT have done it without you!

To our **FABULOUS** illustrator Katie Kear: thank you so much for your vision and talent, and helping lift Frankie's world off the page and sprinkling it with your magic.

Thank you to everyone at Scholastic for being so supportive and adding me to your books, again literally. It is an honour to be amongst such wonderful authors. To Sarah Dutton, Aimee Stewart, Arub Ahmed, Cathy Liney, Georgina Russell, Emily Burns, Lauren Fortune and Catherine Bell, thank you all so much for your hard work.

To Genevieve Herr and Jenny Glencross for combing through all the knots of the first few drafts. I have learnt so much! I am very grateful for all your input and hard work.

To my agent Faith O'Grady at The Lisa Richards Agency. When I wrote my first book, it felt like we were almost as young as Flo! We are both out of nappies now, thankfully, and I've loved the journey of writing these books – where it all started and where it has come to. I'm very much looking forward to where it leads next.

I feel incredibly fortunate to get to write; it is a job that doesn't feel like a job and I truly love it. That doesn't mean at times it doesn't feel difficult or frustrating or I don't get wobbles of self-doubt or imposter-syndrome, but in ways, I am grateful for all of it as it is invariably part of the process; or my process at least! And I feel very lucky to do it.

Thank you also to Eavan Kenny at the Lisa Richards Agency who has helped so much with juggling my writing commitments with my other-job-acting-and-things commitments too. You are a very good juggler, and I know you would join a circus if you weren't too busy being an agent. **BEING AN ADULT REALLY IS A FULL-TIME JOB!**

To my own friends and family, you are a constant flow of support and fun and advice and encouragement and inspiration. I feel so very grateful for you all. To my husband Brian, thank you for your constant support, loyalty, fun, love and friendship. I would be lost without you.

And to my children Sadie, Billy and Ted: thank you for being the magic-makers in my world, my inspiration, and making my heart so full. I love you all so much. (And I am very much looking forward to you reading this down the line and saying **"OMG, MUM, CRINGE!"**)

To my own siblings, Mark and Paul, for filling my childhood with so much fun, love and good humoured banter. It gave me the foundations I could only hope for, for my own children. Yasmin had said that this book was a "love letter to siblings", and that feels very true.

To all the siblings out there who become our first friends, our first confidants, our first life adventure partners (with plenty of the inevitable squabbles along the way, and the fiercely competitive **"THAT'S MINE! I'M TELLING! GET OFF! GET OUT! GET MUM!"** shouting competitions).

To my Mum and Dad and brothers, I am so grateful for you all – so grateful to have grown up in a house of fun and laughter and encouragement and to being told **"TRY IT", "GO FOR IT!"**

A big thank you also to Senior Clinical Psychologist Dr Claire Barrett for your time and insight while researching the themes of this book.

To anyone who has lost someone they love, I am sending you love. Grief is a personal journey that is so different for so many. But I hope the love that was and is there helps as a comfort and balm for the very hard days.

To my own Dad, I'm so happy you knew all about this book before you left us. *I miss you so much, but I know where you will be. Forever* x